P9-AZW-915

continued . . .

Sweetheart, INDIANA

Suzanne Simmons

B

BERKLEY SENSATION, NEW YORK

This is a work of fiction. Names, characters, places, and incidents either are the product of the author's imagination or are used fictitiously, and any resemblance to actual persons, living or dead, business establishments, events, or locales is entirely coincidental.

SWEETHEART, INDIANA

A Berkley Sensation Book / published by arrangement with the author

PRINTING HISTORY
Berkley Sensation edition / August 2004

Copyright © 2004 by Suzanne Simmons Guntrum.
Excerpt from *Goodnight, Sweetheart* copyright © 2004 by Suzanne Simmons Guntrum.
Cover illustration by Hiroko.
Interior text design by Julie Rogers.

For information address: The Berkley Publishing Group, a division of Penguin Group (USA) Inc., 375 Hudson Street, New York, New York 10014.

ISBN: 0-425-19779-4

BERKLEY SENSATION™
Berkley Sensation Books are published by The Berkley Publishing Group, a division of Penguin Group (USA) Inc., 375 Hudson Street, New York, New York 10014.
BERKLEY SENSATION and the "B" design are trademarks belonging to Penguin Group (USA) Inc.

PRINTED IN THE UNITED STATES OF AMERICA

10 9 8 7 6 5 4 3 2 1

For Ray,

because you inspire me,
because you make me laugh,
because I will love you always.

Sweetheart,
INDIANA

WELCOME TO SWEETHEART, INDIANA
WHERE EVERYONE IS YOUR FRIEND
POPULATION: 11,238

Chapter
one

 "Jacob, you crazy old son of a bitch, what are you up to this time?" Samuel Law scanned the letter attached to the front of the legal document. The names at the top of the watermarked stationery were familiar to him: it was the letterhead of the New York law firm of Dutton, Dutton, McQuade & Martin.

Of course, Sam had known something strange was coming his way. His old law school buddy, Trace Ballinger, had tipped him off via a telephone call several months ago.

"We're sending you a client," Trace had informed him without preamble.

Sam had swiveled in his office chair, propped his feet up on the windowsill—telltale scuff marks on the wood's dark patina indicated this wasn't the first time he'd used the edge of the floor-to-ceiling window as a footrest—and cradled the receiver between his ear and his shoulder. "Exactly who is we?"

"The firm."

"Why?"

Trace had snorted softly on the other end of the line. "You don't mince words, do you, Sam?"

"Nope." He never had. He never intended to. Not if he could help it. "Saves time," he'd said.

"But not always trouble," Trace had reminded him.

They both knew trouble was Sam's middle name. Trouble of the how-*not*-to-win-friends-and-influence-people kind had been behind his decision to call it quits and hightail it out of New York a few years ago, despite a once-promising career as a public defender.

Sam had always insisted it was a matter of living by the principles he believed in. One of those principles was the absolute conviction that a man was either ethical or he wasn't. There was no middle ground.

At the time his so-called friends, including a half-hearted fiancée, had labeled him pigheaded and a misguided fool. Colleagues on both sides of the bench had been more circumspect, but the writing was on the wall: His unwillingness to compromise was a ball buster and a career destroyer.

Since Sam refused to go along with the politics of the D.A.'s office, he'd decided to say adios to the Big Apple and head back home to Indiana. He did so with the blessings of one man: Trace Ballinger.

Trace had returned to the reason he'd called. "Like I said, counselor, we're sending you a client."

Sam had discovered he was more skeptical than curious at that point. "Should I thank you?"

There was a pause. "Hard to say."

Curiosity had gotten the better of him. "Why?"

"It just is."

There had been a hint of indulgence in his voice as he'd gone along with whatever game Trace was playing. "Okay, I'll bite, Ballinger. Who is it?"

After ten, maybe fifteen, seconds of silence the answer had finally been forthcoming. "Gillian Charles."

Sam's feet had hit the floor. "Any relation to Jacob Charles?"

"She's his granddaughter."

He remembered thinking: *This is getting interesting.* "Why would a granddaughter of Jacob's become my client?"

"She's got no choice."

Sam had snickered softly into the telephone. "What's the real reason?"

"I'm not joking," his old friend had said very deliberately. "Jacob Charles made it clear that after his death he wanted you to handle the whole business."

Sam had sat up straighter in his high-backed "gen-u-ine Corinthian leather" office chair. At least that had been the sales pitch when he'd bought the chair for five bucks at a local furniture store. The hand-printed signs plastered across the front window of Weaver's Emporium had declared:

MIDNIGHT MADNESS SALE!
EVERYTHING MUST GO!
NO OFFER REFUSED!
NAME YOUR OWN PRICE!

So he had.

Sam wasn't sure who had made out on the deal in the end: Mr. Weaver or him.

"You're not kidding about Jacob's granddaughter becoming my client, are you?"

"No, I'm not."

He'd waited for the other shoe to drop. When it didn't, he'd finally said, "Okay, tell me more."

So Trace had. "Gillian Charles is a native New Yorker. She was born and raised somewhere in the region of Central Park West. Growing up, she attended only the best private schools, including the Hewitt School right here in Manhattan and a fancy Swiss finishing school. There were riding lessons. Tennis lessons. Ballet lessons. Piano lessons. Even origami lessons." Paper rustled. A moment later, "Summers were spent in Newport, of course."

"Of course."

"She had what society pages described at the time as the most elegant coming-out party of the year, maybe of the decade. It was rumored to cost more than a quarter of a mil."

"Jesus, Mary, and Joseph," Sam had said.

"She graduated from Sarah Lawrence. I think she majored in art history, but I'm not one hundred percent sure of that." There had been a brief pause on the other end. Trace must have been scanning some kind of fact sheet on his soon-to-be client. "She spent time in England."

"Riding to the hounds?"

"Not unless the hunt has been added to the curriculum at Oxford," Trace said. "She also studied at the Sorbonne for a year. Even did a stint at Cordon Bleu."

"She can cook."

"I don't think so," had come the slowly spoken, evenly spaced words. "She speaks several languages fluently. Besides English."

"That must come in handy along Central Park West." Sam had shifted in his chair. "What else?"

"Well, she's unique."

Warning bells had sounded. "What's wrong with her?" he had demanded to know.

"Nothing's wrong with her," Trace had reassured him. "Ms. Charles is simply *upper* upper class."

Sam had felt himself growing impatient. He'd picked up a pen and tapped it rhythmically against the base of the telephone. "What does that mean exactly?"

Trace's voice had taken on a definite edginess as he spelled it out. "It means that she's a socialite who has spent her life living in the lap of luxury, Sam. It means that when she's not in residence at the family's Manhattan brownstone, you'd probably find her in London or Venice or Rome, or traveling the world, staying at five-star hotels. It means that she's used to the best of everything."

"It means that she's a royal pain in the—"

Trace had intercepted him. "Tush? Caboose? Back bumper? Derriere?"

Sam had laughed heartily. "Yeah, if you say so, Ballinger."

"You'll have a chance to find out what she's like for yourself." Trace had gone on to explain. "Gillian Charles is due to arrive in Sweetheart in a couple of months."

"She's coming here?"

"You've got it in one."

"I was hoping"—Sam had been hoping and praying and everything else he could think of—"Jacob would take care of this mess during his lifetime."

"Well, he didn't. He wouldn't even discuss it with Thaddeus Martin or with me. Now he's left it all up to his granddaughter."

"And to me."

"And to you."

He'd taken a wild guess. "Ms. Charles doesn't exactly sound like the Sweetheart type."

Trace had confirmed his suspicions. "I doubt if she's

ever been in a small Midwestern town before, Sam. Certainly not a town like Sweetheart, Indiana."

"Christ almighty," he'd muttered under his breath. Just what he *didn't* need: a high-maintenance client who would demand his undivided attention; a spoiled, pampered, rich young woman who would expect to be entertained and who would think "roughing it" meant staying at the local Holiday Inn.

Well, it would if Sweetheart had a Holiday Inn.

Which it didn't.

Visitors had their choice between the Sweetheart Bed & Breakfast, a large Victorian monstrosity that had once qualified as the town's one and only mansion, and a flea bag motel at the edge of the city limits. Most people wisely chose the B and B.

"High-society types," Sam had complained.

"High-society types," Trace had commiserated.

"Wait a minute." At that juncture in their conversation Sam had tossed the ballpoint pen down on his desk and bounced to his feet. He'd punctuated his words by jabbing his index finger into the air. "Aren't you marrying one of these high-society types yourself?"

"Schuyler's different," Trace had claimed.

Sam wasn't convinced. "Different how?"

"Different good. The trappings of wealth and privilege are unimportant to Schuyler."

Sam had groaned. That implied the trappings of wealth and privilege were important to his new client.

"What was Jacob thinking?" he'd griped, not realizing he had spoken out loud until Trace answered him.

"Beats me. He seemed to think he was doing his granddaughter a favor. Even called it his last gift to her."

"Some gift."

"Well, that's how Jacob put it to Thaddeus Martin."

Then his old friend had tacked on as an afterthought, "The rich really are different, you know."

Sam had given a short, humorless laugh. "Thanks for the words of wisdom."

"You're welcome."

He'd quickly added with genuine appreciation, "And thanks for the warning."

Even if the phone call from Trace hadn't been enough to raise a red flag, the arrival of a special-delivery "package" ten days ago certainly had been.

After all, how many people shipped themselves a Steinway grand piano?

"Well, crap." Sam tossed the letter and the accompanying legal document onto his desk.

He'd read and reread the document a dozen times or more since it had arrived via FedEx a few weeks ago. The result never changed. Not only was Ms. Gillian Charles going to be a royal pain in the ass, she was going to ruin what was left of his spring.

In fact, his entire spring, summer, and fall.

Chapter
two

He looked like trouble.

    Maybe it was the ridiculously broad shoulders. Or maybe it was the too-handsome masculine features, although he wasn't pretty in the least. Maybe it was the straight black hair, one strand falling at a rakish angle across his forehead. Or maybe it was the uncompromising posture of the lean, athletic body or the muscular arms or the chiseled jawline. Whatever it was, the man seemed to be daring the world to wipe the smirk off his face.

    Gillian Charles leaned back against the leather upholstery. Frigid air blasting from the vents of the limousine made the seat icy cold to the touch except where her body had warmed it during the long drive from the Indianapolis airport. She ignored the chill and focused instead on the photograph in her lap.

After studying the snapshot for a minute or two, she decided the various and assorted parts did not equal the sum of the whole. As a matter of fact, when carefully scrutinized, the stranger's features appeared to be commonplace, even rather ordinary. But when they were taken together, they created a man who was gorgeous. Devastatingly so. A virtual knockout.

This was the type of charismatic male who would still be attracting women when he was seventy or eighty or even older. There was clear evidence of strength about him, of confidence, of arrogance.

Was it his broad shoulders that gave him away? Or the cocky angle of his head? Or was it the way he stood there, one hand casually stuffed into the pocket of his jeans, the other one strong, tanned, fingers splayed against rough tree bark?

The photo was a candid shot. The subject in question was leaning against the trunk of a huge sprawling tree that was weighed down with golden yellow blossoms; blossoms that appeared to be brushing against his head and shoulders.

In the background there was a house (a small white bungalow with green shutters, a matching green front door, and matching green ivy that vined its way along the old-fashioned wraparound porch), a white picket fence that ran the perimeter of the yard, and a dog sitting on its haunches at the man's side.

The man's hair was dark, blue-black in the bright sunlight. It was sleek and straight and for the most part cut close to his head. His chin was square. His mouth was unsmiling. His nose was emphatic without dominating his face.

Although the snapshot was in full color, the color of his eyes was a mystery. He stared straight at the camera as if he were defying the photographer, and the world in general, to make him anything but what he was.

And what the man was, Gillian decided with a degree of certainty, was Trouble with a capital T.

If there was one thing she didn't need in her life right now, it was any more trouble. She'd had enough in the past three months to last her a lifetime.

It was one of the senior partners at Dutton, Dutton, McQuade & Martin who had sat across the conference table from her on that dreary day in February, the Manhattan skyline behind him charcoal gray against a gray winter sky, and said, "It was your grandfather's wish, Ms. Charles."

"His wish?"

The gentleman in the elegant, tailored business suit had not shuffled the papers in front of him. He had not squirmed in his chair. He had not avoided eye contact. In fact, he'd been straightforward with her, even blunt. "All right, your grandfather's ironclad instructions, at least in the legal sense."

Gillian had taken in and let out a deep breath. "You'd known my grandfather for a long time."

"Yes, I had."

She'd moistened her lips. "You were his personal attorney for twenty years."

"That's right."

Gillian had looked unflinchingly at the senior law partner. "Why did he insist upon attaching such"—she thought about using the word "crazy" and decided on a slightly more diplomatic approach—"unusual conditions to a trust?"

Thaddeus Martin, great-grandson of *the* Martin in Dutton, Dutton, McQuade & Martin, had admitted, "The most I could ever get out of Jacob was: 'It's my last gift to Gillian.'"

"Gift?" She'd nearly choked on the word. Her grandfather had referred to this insane situation as his last gift to her?

"Those were Jacob's exact words." There was a moment

or two of silence in the conference room. "Our hands are tied," he had gone on to tell her, making no excuses or apologies for the legal quagmire in which she found herself. "We're required to hand this entire affair over to a local attorney."

"Anyone in particular?"

"As a matter of fact, Jacob did specify an attorney at law at the other end." Thaddeus Martin (Taddy to his oldest and dearest friends) had settled deeper into his chair and had turned to the other man in the conference room.

She knew Trace Ballinger was the youngest partner in the long and illustrious history of the firm. At that point he'd spoken up. "Jacob knew an honest man and a brilliant lawyer when he saw one."

She'd kept a firm grip on her emotions. "My grandfather did have a gift for seeing the best in people."

"He knew you'd be in good hands, the best of hands with Samuel Law," Trace had assured her.

Gillian didn't know Trace well, but she was aware that he'd represented Cora Grant up until her death last year, and that he had recently handled some business for an old friend of hers, Schuyler Grant. She also knew he was now engaged to Schuyler and the two of them were soon to be married.

"So Samuel Law is my new lawyer?"

"Yes," he'd confirmed.

It was at that juncture in the meeting that the senior partner had handed over the snapshot. "This is the only photograph of Mr. Law we have on file."

She had taken the five-by-seven photo from him and given it a cursory glance. Without specifically addressing either lawyer, she'd asked, "Do you know the man?"

"I've met him once or twice. But I mostly know Samuel Law by his reputation." The prominent attorney at law, even by the standards of a city with thousands of prominent attorneys at law, had leaned back again in his ergonomically correct executive chair and slowly stroked his chin as if he were tugging on an invisible beard. "I believe Trace is personally acquainted with him."

Trace had adjusted his tie—it was a discreet blue on blue stripe—rested his elbows on the edge of the conference table, steepled his fingers, and cleared his throat before telling her, "As a matter of fact, I know Sam well. Or at least I used to. We went to law school together."

"Harvard, wasn't it?"

He'd nodded. "Sam also worked here in Manhattan for a few years after graduation and after passing the bar."

Gillian had taken a moment to consider the implications. "So the small-town boy came east to the big city."

"Something like that."

"Evidently he decided to return home."

Trace Ballinger had nodded his head a second time. "About three years ago."

The hotshot attorney was wearing his courtroom face. Gillian couldn't tell much from his expression. "Despite conventional wisdom to the contrary, perhaps you *can* go back home."

"Perhaps you can," he'd finally allowed.

Yet in her heart of hearts Gillian had always believed that going home again was like trying to change the past: It was a colossal waste of time, energy, and emotion.

Gillian had looked from one man to the other. "I have no choice, do I?"

Thaddeus Martin had responded. "You have no choice, Ms. Charles, unless . . ."

The unless was left unspoken. Unless she refused. Unless she was determined to go against her grandfather's wishes. Unless she was ready to give up everything.

Everything included the only home she had known since that fateful summer when she was eleven, the summer she had gone to live with her grandparents in their New York brownstone. The four-story residence had been in the Charles family for generations, and consisted of room after room of museum-quality paintings, heirloom furniture, and valuable antiques, as well as one of the largest and most photographed private gardens in the city.

Even if it hadn't meant sacrificing her inheritance or forfeiting her home, Gillian would have done as Jacob Armand Charles had asked because she had loved him utterly and completely. That's all it would have taken: a simple request.

She wasn't sure why he had felt it was necessary to go to such extremes, to give her an ultimatum in writing. Had he distrusted her in the end? Or had her grandfather, at the age of eighty-five and somehow without her noticing, become a bit senile?

Gillian had kept her doubts to herself and slid the photo back across the table.

"Why don't you keep it?" Thaddeus Martin had suggested in a magnanimous tone. "At least that way you'll know what one person in town looks like."

"All right." She'd taken the photograph and paperclipped it to the file in front of her.

"Do you have any other questions?"

Only one, and it wasn't really a question. She was just double-checking. "I understand there's a time limit."

"There is a time limit," the senior partner had said to her. "You'll need to reach your destination by the first week of May."

Gillian had heard herself sigh as she'd turned to look out the window of the office building.

Now she turned her head and gazed out the window of the hired limousine. The tinted glass gave the landscape an overcast hue, yet she knew it was a beautiful spring day. She took off her sunglasses and pressed the button at her fingertips. The window quietly retracted into the door.

That was better, she thought. Now the world was as it should be: blue skies, white clouds, gently rolling green hills, and splashes of color here and there where wildflowers had sprung up.

The air was drenched with the scent of lilacs in full bloom and newly mown grass and something she couldn't quite put her finger on, something heavy and sweet and cloying.

There was a tumbledown barn set back from the road. A faded Mail Pouch Tobacco sign appeared to have been painted on its side decades before. The once brick red color was now weathered to a dingy brown. In places the paint on the building had been stripped down to the bare wood. There was a hole in the roof of the barn the size of the dilapidated tractor, weeds sprouting up past its rusted seat, that was permanently parked nearby.

As they drove along the country road, Gillian caught a glimpse of a well-kept farm: house, barn, assorted outbuildings, a pond with a flock of geese in residence, a herd of cattle in a nearby field, and a covered pen. A wrought iron weathervane, forged in the likeness of a flying pig, was perched atop the roof of the structure. The whimsical winged creature fluttered back and forth in the breeze.

"We're coming into town now, Miss Charles," the driver politely informed her.

"Thank you, James."

James took his foot off the accelerator and threw over his shoulder, "Speed trap."

"Speed trap?"

The limo driver bobbed his head up and down. He seemed only too happy to expound on his personal conspiracy theory.

"The local law enforcement just sit and wait for the unsuspecting tourist."

Did a small town in the middle of nowhere get many tourists? Gillian wondered as they slowed to a snail's pace.

James seemed to be well acquainted with the pitfalls and perils of driving in rural Indiana. "The speed limit drops sharply right at the edge of town. By the time your brain registers the change, sirens are wailing, lights are flashing, and you find yourself slapped with a hundred-dollar speeding ticket. Two hundred if you're real unlucky."

"Is that legal?"

"Sure it's legal." James glanced at her in the rearview mirror. "As a matter of fact, it's how a lot of these burgs get the money to balance their municipal budgets."

"I see." Gillian realized she had just learned something new about small towns.

Apparently none of the money from speeding tickets had been spent on local highways. It was an ancient, pot-holed, and bumpy two-lane asphalt road into town.

There was a sign posted at the outskirts of the city limits. It read:

WELCOME TO SWEETHEART, INDIANA,
WHERE EVERYONE IS YOUR FRIEND.
POPULATION: 11,238.

Someone had scratched out the current population and spray-painted graffiti underneath: *Bubba drove drunk. Now Bubba's in heaven. Population: 11,237.*

There was a run-down motel with crabgrass growing up between the cracks in the sidewalk on one side of the road and a hamburger joint on the other. An orange neon light hung precariously in the front window of the restaurant. Clearly visible, even through dirty windows and in the light of early evening, the sign flashed between two messages: EATS and OPEN. The center of the E was broken off and the O was burned out so the message repeated as CATS . . . PEN . . . CATS . . . PEN . . . CATS . . . PEN.

Just beyond the eatery was a trailer park. Laundry flapped in the breeze. Kids and dogs seemed to run wild in equal numbers. A young woman, leaning over a chainlink fence, was chatting with her neighbor. Behind her a young man sat on the cement-block stoop at the front of a trailer drinking from a bottle of beer.

There was a gang of boys playing kick the can in the middle of the unpaved street. Loose gravel sprayed half a foot into the air each time one of them sent the dented coffee can flying. Nearby, an older couple, enthroned in flamingo pink plastic lawn chairs, were watching the evening's entertainment.

Goose bumps suddenly covered Gillian from head to toe. She closed the window of the limousine, replaced her sunglasses, pulled the fitted jacket of her Armani suit more closely around her, and sank back against the leather car seat.

Her heart tumbled to her feet. "What in the world have you done, Grandpa?" she whispered softly.

Chapter
three

 She was late.

Sam felt a spurt of irritation, then reminded himself to relax. There was no sense in making a federal case out of a little thing like a 3:00 appointment who still hadn't shown up at—he glanced at the clock on the wall—6:07.

He tugged at the designer tie he'd loosened the minute he had walked out of the courthouse this afternoon. Jerry Garcia neckwear was one of his few remaining concessions to the fashion gods, or so he told himself. The truth was he hadn't bothered to shop for any new ties since . . . hell, he couldn't remember since when.

Where did a man buy halfway fashionable neckties in Sweetheart, anyway?

He was still pondering that sartorial question when his

secretary knocked on the door between their offices, peered around the corner, and announced, as she did every evening at exactly 6:15, "Anything else tonight, Sam?"

He made a polite but dismissive gesture. "Nope. I've got it under control. Thanks, Carol."

Carolyn Hart took a good look around almost as if she suspected someone had managed to slip past her and into his office undetected. "I thought she'd be here by now."

They both knew who *she* was.

Sam gave his tie another tug. "So did I."

"You'll wait a little longer."

He nodded.

"You won't work half the night again, will you?" Carol said in a maternal tone.

Carolyn Hart was his secretary, his paralegal, his Gal Friday, and his self-appointed *in loco parentis* since his mother and father had set off in their RV last winter at the first sign of snow. His parents were still wandering around the USA. In fact, just last week he'd received a panoramic photo postcard from them of Mount Rushmore.

"I'll try not to work half the night," Sam said.

He didn't promise, however. There was no sense in making a promise unless he intended to keep it. A man's word still meant something in Sweetheart.

Carol glanced at the clock on his office wall. Some called it an antique; he thought it was just plain old. "It's nearly Max's dinnertime. You won't forget to feed him."

"I won't forget."

"If push comes to shove, Ms. Charles will simply have to be the one who waits."

"Don't worry. I won't let Max go hungry." He changed the subject. "Where does Truman buy his neckties?"

"He doesn't."

Sam arched a quizzical brow.

Carol explained. "He gave up wearing ties when he retired." She waited. "Is there anything else, Sam?"

"Nope."

"I'm off then," she told him.

He gave a wave with his hand. "Have a good evening and give my best to Tru."

Truman Hart, Carol's husband of more than forty years, was a former math teacher and an animal lover. He had been known to take in any type of injured creature, domesticated or otherwise.

As a matter of fact, the man who had taught the art of logarithms to three generations of Sweetheart high school students, including Sam, was currently nursing a pair of barn owls back to health after some stupid fool had used them for target practice.

Sam blew out his breath and rubbed the back of his neck. The trouble with the world (at least according to Bertrand Russell, and Sam had to agree with him) was that the stupid were cocksure and the intelligent were full of doubt.

He wasn't certain if he was the former or the latter, but he knew one thing for damned sure: It didn't take a Philadelphia lawyer—or for that matter, a Sweetheart, Indiana, lawyer—to figure out that Gillian Charles wouldn't be pleased if she were the one kept waiting this evening.

An hour later Sam pushed away from his desk, stood, and stretched. He paced the hardwood floor of his office, then went to stand at the row of windows that overlooked the courthouse square. He allowed his mind to wander for a minute.

It was warm for early May. And humid. There had been plenty of rain this spring; too much rain, according to area farmers, who were struggling to get their crops planted.

Still, thanks to the almost daily "Irish mist" that had fallen, the courthouse lawn was a carpet of emerald green. The local horticulture society had planted tulip bulbs by the hundreds last fall and now each of the four corners of the town square was patriotically awash in red, white, and blue.

Sam leaned a forearm against the window frame. He took in a deep breath, held it for a count of ten, and then slowly exhaled.

Sometimes he loved this town and sometimes he hated it, but Sweetheart was in his blood. It was a part of him. It was where he'd been born and raised. It was where he'd attended K through 12. It was where he'd kissed his first girl: Mary Lou with the blond curls, age eight, in the coatroom just before recess.

It was also where he'd gotten into trouble for smoking on school grounds. The first and last time he'd been dumb enough to make that mistake. It was where he'd played varsity football and led his team to a state championship his senior year. It was where he'd been introduced by his English teacher to Harper Lee's Atticus Finch, who had pretty much singlehandedly inspired Sam to become a lawyer. And it was where he'd broken a few hearts and where he'd had his heart trampled on once or twice.

In the end, Sweetheart was where he'd run away from and where he'd come back to. It was where he intended to spend the rest of his life. And it was where he intended to die. Not anytime soon, of course.

How old had Jacob Charles been when he'd succumbed to pneumonia this past winter? Mid-eighties, anyway.

The news of Jacob's fatal illness hadn't taken Sam completely by surprise. He'd heard that the man appeared older, frailer, and definitely more fragile since his wife's death two years ago. Jacob and Emily Charles had been inseparable for more than sixty years. Little wonder Jacob hadn't wanted to go on without her.

That was love.

That was commitment.

That was the way marriage was supposed to be.

His own parents had been happily married for thirty-six years. He'd been born exactly nine months later to the day of their wedding, followed in quick succession by his twin sisters, Allie and Serena, and then two years later, the youngest, his brother, Eric.

They were all married now. Or had been. All except him. He'd thought about marriage during the year he'd been engaged, but Nora wasn't the only one who had been halfhearted about their relationship. He didn't blame her for breaking it off when he had decided to leave New York. After all, Sweetheart hadn't been part of the bargain.

Besides, a good relationship meant an investment of time. Time he didn't have. Time he never seemed to find any extra of. Time he wasn't willing to give to anything but his work. Hell, most days he had to scrounge for enough time to take Max for a walk.

Sam's reverie was interrupted by the sound of a car door slamming shut somewhere below him on Main Street. He glanced out his office window. A big, shiny black limousine was parked lengthwise at the curb; it seemed to stretch halfway down the city block.

A man in a plain dark suit and a plain dark tie—the tie definitely wasn't one of Jerry Garcia's—opened the rear passenger door and then stood waiting at attention.

The young woman who stepped out of the vehicle was dressed all in black—the kind of monochrome look favored by chic women from New York to Milan: black head scarf, black designer sunglasses, black jacket, sleek black skirt—*nice legs*—black leather handbag, and black sling-back shoes—no doubt expensive *and* Italian.

She pushed her sunglasses onto the top of her head and took a moment to glance around the town square. Then she turned and stared up at the modest two-story turn-of-the-century brick building that housed his office.

"Ms. Charles, I presume," Sam said under his breath.

Chapter
four

 He *definitely* looked like trouble.

Samuel P. Law, Attorney at Law, according to the discreet sign stenciled on the glass door downstairs, was standing behind an oversize antique desk, his back to a row of floor-to-ceiling windows. Behind him, framed as a backdrop, was the town square and the county courthouse.

He wasn't wearing casual blue jeans or a denim shirt as in the photograph she'd studied during the drive from the airport. He was dressed in a gray pinstripe suit, slightly wrinkled, a white dress shirt, also slightly wrinkled, and what Gillian recognized as a Jerry Garcia tie—the design was bright red and green chili peppers.

Surely this small-town midwestern lawyer wasn't a Deadhead, she thought as she paused in the doorway of the office.

Not that stranger things hadn't happened. She'd once been the houseguest of an eccentric Italian aristocrat who had insisted upon going barefoot year round, wearing wildly colored floral shirts, drinking margaritas, and listening exclusively to the music of Jimmy Buffet. His friends and foes alike had referred to him as Prince Parrothead.

"Excuse me . . ." She waited until she was certain she had his attention. "Are you Samuel Law?"

Gillian already knew the answer to her question. There was no mistaking that face, those shoulders—the breath backed up into her lungs—that body.

Samuel Law didn't crack a smile. He didn't even bother straightening his tie. "I am."

She took another step toward him and tried not to appear tentative. "I'm Gillian Charles."

He came around the desk and extended his hand. "I've been expecting you, Ms. Charles."

His handshake was strong, firm, resolute, absolutely no-nonsense. Gillian had a feeling that her newly appointed attorney didn't suffer fools—or anyone else, for that matter—gladly.

Behind him dusk was descending on Sweetheart. The evening sky was awash with vivid pinks, deep purples, and stratified blues from robin's egg to royal to navy.

One by one, spotlights flickered on, illuminating the front of the limestone courthouse and the marble statue of Lady Justice mounted above its portico. The figure was carved in the classic pose: blindfolded, a two-edged sword held in one hand and the scales of justice balanced in the other.

Gillian said the first semicoherent thing that popped into her head. "You have a nice view."

"Yes, I do," Sam said, without turning around.

"It's appropriate, as well."

"So they tell me."

"I assume it's not an accident."

His head moved; it wasn't a definite yes or no. "This building has always housed a law firm."

"It's tradition, then."

"Actually I think it's more the convenient location. The courthouse and the Bagley Building were built in tandem back in 1903."

"This, I take it, is the Bagley Building."

He nodded. "Originally it was Lyle Bagley's office. Eventually it became his son's and then his grandson's."

The provenance meant nothing to her.

"Lyle Bagley was an attorney in Sweetheart when the courthouse was first constructed. His son practiced law in the years before the Second World War. Bert was the grandson. He took over when his father retired. Bert Bagley was the leading attorney in this community for fifty, maybe closer to sixty, years. He was also a lifelong family friend. Anyway, he dropped dead of a heart attack a couple of months before I moved back to town."

Gillian didn't know what to say besides, "I'm sorry."

Samuel Law's voice altered slightly. His resonant baritone went from authoritative to something that sounded like crushed velvet rubbing against her skin. "Bert was ninety-four. He loved his family. He loved this town. He loved his work. And he loved his garden. He never had a sick day in his life until the morning he died."

"He lived a long and happy life."

"Yes, he did."

Gillian gave him a sidelong glance. "Then this office has a leading attorney tradition about it."

He didn't really agree or disagree with her. "I suppose you could say so."

She made small talk. "I understand you once practiced law in New York."

"I did. It was a while ago. I've been back in Sweetheart for a few years."

"You're one of only a handful of people I know who have returned to their hometown."

"A lot of people never leave their hometown in the first place," he pointed out.

"I'm one of them," she said, then almost immediately relented. "Except for the time I spent at a boarding school in Switzerland. Then there was a semester at Oxford and a year of study at the Sorbonne. But I never really left New York."

"Well, at this point in my life I can't imagine living anyplace other than Sweetheart, Indiana, warts and all."

She was genuinely curious. "So, you don't have any regrets about your decision."

"None."

She indulged her curiosity a little longer. "You must have come back with your eyes wide open."

"Had to." Samuel Law shrugged those broad shoulders of his. "If there's one thing I've learned the hard way, it's that perfection doesn't exist."

"There is no perfect place, i.e., there is no perfect hometown," she said, drawing her own conclusions.

"Exactly. For me, Sweetheart is as close as it'll ever get. Besides, people around here will tell you that the Laws have always been the law in these parts."

She didn't pretend to understand.

"My grandfather was sheriff of Sweetheart County for three decades," he explained. "My father retired just this past September from the same job. In my family it was pretty much a given: I was going to end up in law enforcement like my father and grandfather. As it turned out, my twin sisters, my younger brother, and I all decided to study law."

"Sounds to me," she said, only half in jest, "like the Laws are a law unto themselves."

Samuel Law shook his head; that one untamed strand of blue-black hair Gillian had noticed in the snapshot suddenly materialized on his forehead. It gave him a slightly "bad boy" appearance. "No man or woman is above the law."

She couldn't resist. "But weren't laws supposedly made to be broken?"

" 'If the law suppose that, the law is an ass, an idiot.' " He cleared his throat. "At least according to Charles Dickens."

"What about the law of the jungle?"

"Kipling wrote about that particular one while he was actually in the jungles of India."

She pressed her lips together. " 'The first thing we do is kill all the lawyers.' "

His response was instantaneous. "Shakespeare. *King Henry the Sixth,* if I'm not mistaken."

He wasn't.

"I seem to remember reading a newspaper article about a defendant in a capital murder case. His lawyer napped through most of the courtroom proceedings. His conviction was appealed, but he was still found guilty because a panel of judges ruled it wasn't an absolute constitutional right to have an attorney who stays awake during the trial."

The man standing in front of her related another story. "Then there's the one about the attorney who'd represented himself and lost. He claimed on appeal that he'd failed to adequately inform himself that acting as his own lawyer was foolish."

She had one more. "How many lawyers does it take to change a light bulb?"

"How many can you afford?" he said, supplying the punch line to the joke.

She was convinced. "Maybe you have heard them all."

Sam chuckled, but there was a hint of irritation in his voice. "Believe me, I've heard them all."

"You probably got a lot of it when you first moved back to town," she said, speculating.

"Every person I ran into on the street, in the courthouse, even between the snack aisle and the frozen food section of the grocery store, stopped to tell me the joke or the story I hadn't heard."

"But you always had."

"Always." Samuel Law leaned back against the corner of his desk, folded his arms across his chest, and changed the subject. "We have a few things we need to discuss, Ms. Charles." He freed one hand and motioned toward the nearest empty chair. "Would you like to take a seat?"

"If you don't mind, I'd prefer to stand for a while. I've been sitting all day on planes and in limos. And the name is Gillian."

"Welcome to Sweetheart, Gillian. I'm Sam."

Then he smiled. The impact was immediate and unexpected. There was a flash of perfect white teeth. Well, nearly perfect. There was a small gap between the two middle teeth on the bottom. The masculine lips were full, yet not too full. There was a dimple in the chiseled facial contours, but only the merest suggestion of one. Nothing overt. Nothing cute.

As a matter of fact, Gillian thought, the last word she would use to describe Samuel Law was cute.

There was heavy five-o'clock shadow on his jawline and intelligence, along with a hint of weariness, in his eyes. The color of those eyes was still a mystery. At first glance she'd thought they were silvery gray, a little like his gray pinstriped suit. Now she wasn't so sure.

Gillian sighed and straightened her shoulders, wishing she could reach back and massage the knotted muscles below the base of her skull. "I owe you an apology."

One dark eyebrow arched. "For what?"

"I'm late." She was hours behind schedule; not that it was entirely her fault. Her plane had been delayed leaving La Guardia.

He didn't glance up at the clock on the wall or down at his watch. "I suppose you are."

She was determined to be polite. Shifting her weight from one high-heeled sandal to the other, she said, "I hope it hasn't caused you any inconvenience."

Sam neatly sidestepped the issue of blame. "I'm usually in my office at this time of the evening." He pushed off from the edge of the desk, walked around to the other side, shrugged off his suit jacket, and draped it over the back of his chair. After a short while he offered his condolences. "I was sorry to hear about your grandfather."

"Thank you."

He looked up from under naturally well-shaped black eyebrows. "I had a lot of respect for Jacob."

Gillian released the breath she'd been holding. "Apparently he felt the same way about you."

He looked at her squarely. "There were times when we butted heads, but we genuinely liked each other."

Gillian stood a little straighter; not that she had ever been one to slouch. A lady never slouched, according to her late grandmother. "What did you butt heads about?"

Sam seemed disinclined to discuss specifics. "Let's just say Jacob and I had our differences of opinion."

She'd loved her grandfather, but she hadn't been blind to his faults. "He could be stubborn."

"So could I."

Gillian knew what was going through the man's mind: *So could I. So am I.*

She was curious. "How did you and my grandfather meet?"

"It was a few years before I left New York. I was asked

to sit in on a meeting with Jacob at Dutton, Dutton, Mc-
Quade and Martin. I was familiar with Sweetheart, of
course, and I knew the lawyers on both sides."

"I see."

Apparently the social niceties had been observed.
Samuel Law cleared his throat again and suggested, "What
do you say we get down to business?"

"Certainly." Gillian decided she was ready to accept his
earlier offer. She took a seat in the nearest chair and tugged
on the scarf wrapped around her head; it fell into folds
around her shoulders. She stuffed her sunglasses into her
handbag, smoothed out the solitary wrinkle in the skirt of
her black suit, crossed her legs, and waited.

A short silence ensued before Samuel Law began. "I assume that Thaddeus Martin and Trace Ballinger have re-
viewed with you the terms of your trust."

She nodded.

"Do you understand what's required?"

Gillian was suddenly tired. No. Not tired. She was exhausted. "I think so."

He was all business and absolutely no nonsense. "You
need to know so."

Gillian clasped her hands very tightly around her handbag; the leather was buttery smooth and cool to the touch.
"I'm sure you'll explain it to me, Mr. Law."

"Sam," he reminded her. Then, without skipping a beat,
he picked up where he'd left off. "You had to arrive in
Sweetheart no later than the first week of May. You made
it"—he glanced up at the clock—"with four hours to spare."

She bit her tongue. *Nitpicker*.

"The second requirement is that you reside in Sweetheart for a period of six consecutive months."

Six months in Sweetheart, Indiana. Gillian sighed. It
would seem like an eternity.

He sat down opposite her and shuffled through several manila folders in front of him until he apparently found what he was looking for. He studied handwritten notes. "You're not to disclose or discuss these terms with anyone."

"Except you, of course," she piped up.

"Except me," he said, very deliberately.

She wouldn't have said anything to anyone, anyway. It wouldn't be very polite to whine to the local townspeople about being forced to live in Sweetheart.

Sam glanced down at quickly scribbled notations. "Since I know the local real estate market and you don't, I've taken the liberty of securing a house for you."

"A house?"

"Trust me, you don't want to spend the next six months living at the Sweetheart Bed and Breakfast."

She opened her mouth. Before she could utter a word he added, "Mary Kay can talk the ears off a field of corn."

"Mary Kay?"

"Mary Kay Weaver. She used to be married to Doodles Weaver. Now she runs the B and B."

Gillian wondered if being married to Doodles Weaver and running the B and B were mutually exclusive in Sweetheart.

She opened her mouth again.

Again he interjected, "There's no Holiday Inn in town. And the only available rental is the size of a rabbit hutch. I knew you would need more space than a twelve-by-fourteen efficiency apartment that barely had room for your piano, let alone any other belongings."

He was presumptuous, but he was right. "Thank you for finding me a house."

"You're welcome. I've also arranged for a young woman who's willing to clean, do laundry, that kind of thing."

He seemed to have thought of everything.

"By the way, the piano tuner showed up last Monday. Said he was from company headquarters."

"Mr. Biaggi?"

"Yeah, that was the name."

"I wouldn't exactly refer to Mr. Biaggi as a piano tuner, but he is the best in the business."

"What business is that?"

"Mr. Biaggi is a genius. He's highly intuitive and he has a special relationship—almost a spiritual connection, if you will—with fine keyboard instruments. He's also an accomplished pianist."

The look on Samuel Law's face clearly said: *Well, hey, thanks for putting me straight on the subject of Mr. Biaggi.*

"I was going to arrange for transportation as well, but I thought you might like to pick out a car for yourself."

Gillian avoided looking him straight in the eye. "That won't be necessary. I don't drive."

He more or less echoed her words. "You don't drive."

"I don't have a driver's license."

He sat there and stared at her.

"I've never learned how to drive an automobile." Anticipating his next line of inquiry, she explained. "I live in Manhattan. As you know, most of us don't drive cars. We ride the subway. We take trains and buses and taxi cabs."

Gillian saw no reason to mention that for her sixteenth birthday her grandparents had presented her with a Rolls-Royce. It had come with one string attached: She was to leave the driving to a chauffeur.

Sam whistled tunelessly. He turned his head and appeared to be studying the stack of publications piled on top of the barrister's bookcase to his right. They were weighty tomes with titles like *Indiana Criminal Law, Indiana Law and Property, Jurisprudence and You, Torts and Taxes,* and *Divorce: It's Not for Amateurs Anymore.*

"In that case," he said at last, "I guess you've got one of three choices." Gillian knew he was going to tell her what those choices were without any prompting on her part. "One"—he held up a finger on his left hand; *no wedding ring,* she noticed—"you keep the car and driver you've already hired."

She shook her head. "James lives in Indianapolis. He's married and the father of four children, all under the age of twelve. He's not going to want to be away from home."

"Two"—he held up another finger alongside the first—"you could get Doodles to take you wherever you want to go."

"Doodles Weaver, ex-husband of Mary Kay who can talk the ears off a field of corn."

"The very one."

"Is Doodles a taxi cab driver?"

"He would be if Sweetheart had a taxi cab."

"Is he for hire?"

"Yes and no." Sam stroked his chin. "It's more accurate to say Doodles is willing to drive anyone just about anywhere. He likes to think of himself as being neighborly. But there's a tip jar on the dashboard if anyone wants to show their appreciation."

"What's my third choice?"

"You could learn how to drive."

Gillian gave herself a moment to consider the third option. "Who would teach me?"

Sam paused before answering. Then he seemed to make up his mind about something. "I would." He gave her another quick glimpse of those nearly perfect white teeth. "Think of me as a full-service attorney."

"But are you a good driver?"

"Yes, I am," he said, with no unnecessary modesty.

"In that case, I accept your offer."

"That settles it, then. We'll go with a combination of the second and third. Doodles will drive you around town until I can teach you how to fend for yourself."

"It's a deal." She leaned forward and stuck out her hand. He took it in his and held it for a moment.

"Do you have any questions?"

Of course she had questions. Lots of them. But she'd start with the obvious one. "Do you know why my grandfather wanted me to live in Sweetheart for six months?"

He exhaled on what sounded like a frustrated sigh. "Honestly, I don't."

The muscles in her neck tightened again. "There must be some reason," she said, mostly to herself.

Sam shot her a glance. "When it came to his family, did Jacob ever do anything without a damned good reason?"

Gillian felt her throat constrict. Tears burned at the back of her eyes. The self-possession she had maintained in public since the funeral suddenly threatened to shatter. She managed a barely distinguishable, "No."

"There was always a method to your grandfather's madness," Sam said in a voice that lifted the hair on her nape.

She swallowed with difficulty. "So, it's up to me to find out what it was."

"In my opinion, you're the only one who can." Sam paused and then said, "Jacob wanted you to personally see to things. The paperwork involved could have been handled by lawyers and real estate agents without you ever setting foot in Sweetheart." He slowly moved his head from side to side, thinking out loud. "It must have something to do with the properties he owned."

It took a minute for his words to sink in. "Properties? Yes, I remember now. Thaddeus Martin did mention my grandfather owned something here in town."

"Is that all he said to you?"

Gillian resisted the urge to rub her eyes. "It was at the end of a long day and an even longer list of assets," she told him. An endless list of assets that she hadn't cared a fig about at the time. She still didn't.

Sam visibly stiffened. "You may have the luxury of being disinterested in those so-called assets, but I guarantee you they're of the utmost importance to the people living in those houses or earning their livelihoods from those Mom-and-Pop businesses."

He was angry with her. Gillian could see it in his expression, read it in his body language, hear it in his voice.

She hadn't meant to sound uncaring. She was simply too tired to deal with this right now.

Sam set his jaw; it resembled the stone on the front of the courthouse behind him. "You really don't have a clue, do you?"

Gillian flinched at the question, and realized right then and there that she might not like this man very much, after all. He was too bloody handsome for his own good and too bloody arrogant for hers.

He spelled it out. "You, Ms. Charles, own this town."

She didn't believe him. "Nobody owns a town."

Samuel Law leaned forward, intent on pressing his point. His eyes were suddenly very dark, nearly black, and disapproving. They narrowed to slits. "You do," he said.

Chapter
five

She was a damned debutante. She had no idea how the other 99.99 percent lived. As a matter of fact, Sam wondered if the young woman sitting opposite him had ever concerned herself with anything more pressing than making sure that her designer shoes matched her designer outfit before she left the house.

Gillian Charles certainly had no experience with paying two mortgages while trying to put kids through college, or supporting a family on minimum wage, or living from paycheck to paycheck, hoping, praying the money would stretch to the end of the week. Talk about being out of touch with reality!

She is who she is, Sam, he reminded himself. He didn't have to like her. He didn't have to respect her. He certainly didn't have to marry her. All he had to do was make sure that she was legally represented to the best of his abilities.

Looking on the bright side, at least he wouldn't have to deal with the perennial problem that drove most lawyers nuts: feuding heirs. There wouldn't be any unpleasantries or unseemly squabbles—certainly no murder or mayhem— over who got their hands on Aunt Minnie's prized Majolica or the antique pie safe that had been handed down from grandmother to granddaughter since pre–Civil War times.

His newest client was going to inherit the whole shebang as long as she met the conditions set down by Jacob Charles.

Sam blew out his breath and leaned back in his chair. Interlocking his fingers behind his head, he alternately tensed and relaxed the muscles between his shoulder blades.

Maybe he was too hard on her. She couldn't help being what she was any more than she could help being a cool— make that *ice-cold*—slender blonde with unusual blue-green eyes.

Some men might find her pale, patrician features attractive, he supposed. But Ms. Charles definitely wasn't his type. Not that it mattered. She was his client. He never mixed business with anything even remotely resembling pleasure; it was one of the cardinal rules he lived by. Which no doubt explained why his social life was nonexistent.

Oh, he'd tried to casually date a couple of women when he'd first moved back to town. It turned out that casual dating and being an eligible bachelor was an oxymoron in Sweetheart. Matchmaking was a local obsession. So was gossiping. The wise man quickly learned to walk softly, carry a big stick, and watch his back at all times.

As it was, the gossips were going to have a field day, Sam thought, leaning back even farther in his office chair.

Gillian Charles was the biggest news to hit Sweetheart since the killer F3 tornado that had wiped out nearly half the trailer park, and a few unlucky souls, back a couple of summers ago.

He glanced up at the clock on his office wall, then brought the palm of his hand down flat on his desk. "Aw, shit." He immediately apologized. "Pardon my French."

"I believe you mean *merde,* then."

Ms. Charles had a sense of humor. He was surprised. He hadn't expected that.

"Is anything wrong?" she inquired.

"I forgot about Max," he confessed.

Porcelain skin on a not-too-high and yet not-too-low forehead momentarily wrinkled. "Max?"

Sam sprang to his feet, grabbed his suit coat off the back of his chair, and stuffed his arms into the sleeves. "I've got to go feed him right now or Carol will have my hide."

His client seemed vaguely bemused. "Who's Carol?"

"My secretary."

"And Max is . . . ?"

"A Belgian sheepdog."

Gillian Charles followed his lead and stood, quickly gathering up her belongings. "Well, we wouldn't want the SPCA after you, now would we?"

"No, we wouldn't. My secretary's husband is head of the local chapter. She's second-in-command. They take their responsibilities toward our four-footed friends very seriously."

The elegant woman in black waited in the doorway of the outer office while he fished around for his keys. "How would they know if you were late feeding Max?"

"Goldie would tell them." He wondered if he should explain about Mrs. Goldman. "Goldie lives across the street from me. She's all alone and a little lonely now that her husband has passed away. Anyway, she likes to keep an eye on the neighborhood. It gives her something to do." He didn't think he'd mention the binoculars. Not yet, anyway.

"Goldie also enjoys talking to anyone who will listen, which is everybody in town since she's always got the latest scuttlebutt."

His gaze settled on her face. For the first time Sam noticed there were dark smudges under her eyes as if the woman hadn't slept well in quite a while.

"Don't you have any privacy?" she said.

"Not much. Not in Sweetheart," he told her, flicking off the lights and indicating she should precede him down the flight of stairs to the ground level of the Bagley Building.

The hired limousine and its driver were still waiting patiently at the curb.

"Is this all of your luggage?" Sam asked once the trunk had been opened to reveal two modest-sized Louis Vuitton suitcases inside.

"The rest of my things are being shipped," she said.

He should have guessed. Gillian Charles didn't strike him as someone who believed in traveling light.

"My SUV is parked around the corner," he volunteered. "Why don't you let James be on his way back to Indianapolis and I'll make sure you and your suitcases get home safely?"

Gillian agreed to the plan. James was slipped a tip that looked like a hundred-dollar bill. At least the woman knew how to be generous. Sam had met plenty of rich people who held on to every dollar as if it were their first *and* last one.

Oddly enough, his elegant passenger didn't look out of place in his mud-splattered, five-year-old, one-hundred-and-twenty-thousand-miles-on-the-odometer used Ford Explorer. In fact, she looked right at home. He wondered if Gillian Charles's adjustment to Sweetheart would go half as well.

"If you don't mind, I'd like to stop at my parents' house long enough to feed Max."

"I don't mind." A moment later she posed a question. "Do you live with your parents?"

He shook his head. "They're out of town on a trip." He didn't have the time, the energy, or the inclination to try to explain about his parents living out their dream by traveling around the country with a motorboat and a pair of fishing rods hitched to the back of their RV. "Max and I are housesitting."

"I see."

Maybe she did. Anyway, he decided to give her the benefit of the doubt *and* the nickel tour. "Across from the courthouse is the city park and the bandstand."

She turned to look.

"The First Presbyterian Church is on the right. Kitty-corner and on the left is Saint Mary's Catholic Church." He made a gesture with the hand he wasn't gripping the steering wheel with. "There's Jayne's Epicurean Delights. Best vegetarian restaurant in three counties." *Only vegetarian restaurant in three counties.* "Stella's Nails is next. Just down the block is Ann's Art Gallery and Scrapbook Supplies. Weaver's Emporium coming up on your side. Used to be a furniture store. Now it's an antique mall. You own the building, by the way." He thought to add, "Actually, you own the whole city block."

She didn't say anything to that.

Sam took the scenic route home. Tree-lined streets. Picturesque bungalows with painted shutters at the windows. Immaculate lawns and neatly trimmed beds of flowers: yellow daffodils, pink tulips, purple dwarf lilacs, late crocuses.

His passenger stared out the window.

What would he be thinking if he were seeing Sweetheart for the first time and through Gillian Charles's eyes?

She finally turned to him and said, "This is actually a very pretty town."

Sam breathed easier. "Yes, it is. Looks even better in the daylight." He pulled into his parents' driveway, killed the headlights, and opened the door of the Explorer. Before he could make it around to the passenger side, Gillian had extricated herself and was standing on the front sidewalk, waiting for him. He leaned over and rooted around in a pot of fake geraniums for the spare house key. "You like dogs?"

"Yes."

"They like you?"

"Usually."

"Well, don't be offended if Max doesn't take to you. It's nothing personal."

"What is it, then?"

"Max isn't partial to women." Sam supposed it had a lot to do with the absolute bitch who'd owned Max before him.

He slipped the key into the lock, turned the doorknob, and reached around the corner to flip on the front hall light. From long-established habit—he'd spent his growing-up years living in this house—Sam took a step back and replaced the key.

As he stood to one side to let Gillian enter, he got a whiff of something faintly floral and slightly exotic. He didn't think it was the fake geraniums. It must be the perfume she was wearing. Probably custom-blended and undoubtedly very expensive.

Sam turned on lamps as he made his way toward the back of the modest two-story house. By the time they walked into the kitchen, Max was poking his head through the opening that had been the doggie door for a steady stream of family pets over the years. The other side led to the fenced-in backyard.

"Have a good day, Max?" Sam said, going down on his haunches and ruffing the fur around the dog's neck and behind his ears.

Max did his dance of delight.

Sam let him work off some of his excitement before making the proper introductions. "Max, this is a new friend, Gillian." He glanced back over his shoulder at the fashionable woman standing in the middle of his mother's kitchen. "Gillian, this is Max."

To his surprise, Gillian Charles came down beside him and held out her hand in a nonthreatening manner, palm-up. "Hi, Max," she said softly.

Max sniffed her skin. He licked her fingertips several times and nuzzled her hand. Then he rolled over and presented his underside to her. She reached out and rubbed his belly, then scratched him in his very favorite place to be scratched.

Eyes rolled back into his head, the persnickety sheepdog—the one who usually despised all females, young or old—was practically purring like a damned cat.

Make a liar of me, Max.

"Dinnertime, pal." Sam picked up the dog's water dish and refilled it from the kitchen tap. He dug around in the cupboard and brought out Max's favorite Kibbles 'n Bits.

Max took his food seriously. He ignored the human beings and dug into his dinner. For the next few minutes the only sound in the kitchen was the clinking of his dog tags hitting against the side of his dish.

At first it had felt odd—even intrusive—following Samuel Law into someone else's house, even if that house did belong to his parents. There were the family photographs proudly displayed on the bookshelves in the living room, the homemade afghan casually thrown over the back of a sofa, a dried and dusty floral arrangement in a cut-glass vase in the center of the dining room table, a handwritten note fixed to the front of the refrigerator with a magnet: *Sam, don't forget to water the ficus in the front hallway. Love, Mom.*

A house is not a home.

Wasn't that the title of a song?

Well, this was definitely someone's home, Gillian thought as she leaned back against the kitchen counter. It was cozy. It was comfortable. It looked lived-in. The air smelled faintly of furniture polish and disinfectant and something kind of lemony. There were dishes in the drain rack by the sink, a pile of mail on the kitchen table, and a stack of old newspapers by the back door.

She'd expected to feel like a stranger in a strange land, or at the very least like a fish out of water. Instead, she felt welcomed. Maybe it was Max. He'd made no bones about it: He liked her.

That was one of the reasons she'd always wanted a dog. Dogs didn't judge you by appearances. Dogs didn't care if you were rich or poor. Dogs didn't pretend. They didn't know how to. A dog didn't hide his feelings for you. He had no ulterior motives for his unconditional love and devotion beyond getting an extra doggie treat. And a dog was always—*always*—happy to see you.

At the age of eleven she'd wanted a dog more than anything else in the world. She had been given piano lessons, instead. Her grandmother had carefully explained that their house wasn't suitable for a pet. They couldn't take any chances that a dog might pee—of course, her grandmother had used the far more genteel phrase "relieve itself"—on the Louis XVI Savonnerie rugs.

Gillian was grateful for the music lessons. She'd become a very accomplished pianist over the years. But she still regretted not having a dog when she was growing up.

Samuel Law opened the back door. He whistled, then coaxed, "C'mon, Max. Let's take care of business so we can get Ms. Charles home sometime tonight."

She wanted to tell Sam she was in no hurry. She could stay in his mother's kitchen, fix herself a cup of hot tea, sit at the table slowly sipping it, and be perfectly content for who knew how long.

Instead, within minutes she found herself being escorted back to his vehicle. Max jumped into the rear and stuck his nose out between the front seats. She could feel the dog's warm breath on her skin. Without thinking, she bent over and nuzzled him. Max immediately dropped his head onto her shoulder.

"Well, I'll be doggoned," Sam said as he backed out of the driveway. "You've got the magic touch, lady."

Gillian went on rubbing the sheepdog behind his ears. "What makes you say that?"

"Like I told you, Max usually doesn't take to women. As a matter of fact, until tonight I would have labeled him a woman hater."

"What happened to him? A dog doesn't just suddenly decide to hate all females."

"What happened to Max was a vicious and vindictive woman named . . . we'll call her Sheila." Sam smiled a smile without a trace of humor in it. "The names have been changed to protect the *not* so innocent," he said in a voice laced with sarcasm.

Gillian wondered who the vicious and vindictive "Sheila" was and what she had been to Samuel Law.

Apparently Sam read her mind. "Sheila was my first and, I hasten to add, my last divorce case."

"Nasty business?"

"The nastiest." He concentrated on his driving; both hands on the steering wheel. "Unfortunately I'd agreed to represent her before I realized she was wacko. Anyway, her husband had left her for another woman, an older woman at that. Sheila was convinced she'd never live down the humiliation. She became obsessed with the idea of punishing her soon-to-be ex in any way and every way she could think of."

"Max got caught in the middle."

"That's about the size of it."

Gillian was curious. "Go on."

Sam put on the brakes and the vehicle rolled to a stop. "Long story short: I worked out a deal with the so-called Sheila."

"What kind of deal?"

"I wouldn't tell anyone all the dirt I had dug up on her if she'd allow me to take Max in lieu of my fee."

Gillian was riveted. "You blackmailed her."

"Blackmail is an ugly word." Not that Sam denied it, or seemed in the least remorseful about it.

It was ten seconds, maybe more, before she asked, "What was the so-called Sheila going to do to Max?"

A heartbeat or two later the answer came. "She was going to punish her ex by having Max put down."

Gillian leaned closer to the black, sleek-coated, beautiful animal and whispered in his ear, "I would have bitten the bitch."

Sam laughed out loud. "He did." He shifted into park and announced, "We're here."

She looked around. "We're just down the street from your parents' house."

"More or less."

"We're right next door."

"Not *right* next door," he begged to differ. "These lots are easily an acre or two each. Lots of trees in between, too."

In the rapidly fading light of evening, Gillian peered at the white bungalow with green shutters at the windows, the

matching green front door, and matching green ivy that
wended its way along the old-fashioned wraparound porch.

There was a white picket fence that ran the perimeter of
the yard and a huge sprawling tree that she distinctly remembered from the snapshot. Apparently later in the summer the tree would be weighed down with golden yellow
blossoms.

"But . . ."

"What?"

Gillian looked up at him. "Isn't this your house?"

He'd had every intention of telling her the truth, the whole truth, and nothing but the truth. Just not the second she hit town.

"I can't take your house," Gillian said, sitting beside him, her back ramrod straight, one hand motionless on Max's neck.

"You aren't taking my house." Impatience, mixed with irritation—aimed primarily at himself, not at her—rose in Sam's chest; it left an acrid taste in the back of his throat. He swallowed, and adjusted his tone of voice to sound conciliatory. "Like I told you, I'm housesitting while my parents are gone."

"I doubt if you were actually living there. I'll bet you were only running over to check on things and water your mother's ficus and take in the newspaper and mail."

She was observant, dammit. And smart. Actually, she'd make a good witness.

"Look, Gillian," he said, turning her to face him. "Expediency is going to rule the day here. I've got to keep an eye on my mom and dad's place. You need somewhere to live. This arrangement is the best I could do on short notice."

He wasn't about to tell her that the original arrangements he'd made had become obsolete the morning her concert grand piano had been delivered.

Her posture was uncompromising.

Sam went on. "The bungalow is comfortable. It's convenient. It's reasonably clean. And the owner was very understanding about the necessity of knocking out a couple of porch posts and the front window so your piano could be moved in."

Her gaze was unwavering. "You're the owner, aren't you?"

Ms. Charles didn't miss much. "I'm part owner along with the First National Bank of Sweetheart, which, for your information, is one of the businesses you inherited from your grandfather." He reached down and turned off the ignition. "So, in a funny kind of way, I guess that makes us co-owners."

She didn't say a word. Sam wondered if she had any idea how pale and vulnerable she appeared, sitting there beside him, her chic black—or funereal black depending on your point of view—wrapped around her like a protective cloak. She looked tired, pretty much at the end of her rope, and very alone.

Damned if he wasn't feeling sorry for the woman.

Finally she stirred. She moved her mouth as if it were an effort to form the words. "For the sake of expediency."

"It's only common sense," he said.

"Common sense," she repeated.

Sam didn't waste any time. Before she could change her mind or come up with any further objections, he'd carried her suitcases up the porch steps, unlocked the front door, and handed her the keys. "Welcome to your new home."

Gillian stepped inside. Max followed at her heels.

"I should warn you I had to leave some of my stuff behind. Primarily furniture." Sam set her suitcases down in the middle of the foyer and flicked on the lights. "I don't have a dining room table; I do have a pool table, so—"

"There's a pool table in the dining room," Gillian said, finishing his sentence. She looked to her right and into what should have been the formal dining area. Suddenly she smiled; it transformed her face. "I must say it's a unique decorating scheme. I've heard of early attic and post-college bachelor digs and even bargain basement, but what do you call this?"

Sam hit the switch for the antique crystal chandelier. "Midnight madness."

She laughed out loud; the sound was pure and sweet, joyous, unexpected, something Sam realized instantly he wanted to hear again. It was ironic. Sometimes the littlest thing could change your mind about someone. He hadn't expected to like Gillian Charles's laugh. He hadn't expected to like her. He thought he might have to reconsider on both counts.

"What's midnight madness?" she inquired.

"A sale."

"A sale, I assume, which starts at midnight."

He shook his head. "Nine P.M. In Sweetheart we roll up the streets long before midnight." He continued, "As luck would have it, shortly after I moved back to town, Weaver's Emporium was having a going-out-of-business sale. Their prices were rock bottom. I was able to make a deal with old Mr. Weaver. And *voilà*"—Sam made a sweeping gesture with his hand—"I instantly became the owner of a billiard table, a pair of barrister bookcases for my office, several desk chairs, a leather sofa, an area rug or two, you get the picture."

She was amused. "It's nice to know that my attorney is such a shrewd negotiator."

Sam cleared his throat and did a one-eighty. "Anyway, Mr. Biaggi selected the location for your piano." He indicated a large alcove off the living room, which was situated on the opposite side of the foyer. "The gentleman seemed distressed there wasn't an actual music room in the house. He kept muttering something about drafts."

"That's because drafts are a piano's natural enemy." Gillian walked over to the beautiful instrument and ran her fingers along the keys in a graceful movement. "Perfect pitch." She glanced up at him. "Mr. Biaggi worries too much."

"Apparently so. He spent two full days tuning your piano. He was still fretting about it when he left the message that he'd be back again within a month. Sooner if you need him."

"Thank you for taking care of moving my piano into your house, Sam." She touched his arm as she brushed past him. "It means more to me than you know."

He cleared his throat and followed her into the adjoining room. "This is the study. At least that's what I used it for. Considering the age of the house is turn-of-the-last-century, I suppose it was originally an informal parlor adjacent to a formal parlor. I had to leave my books. There just wasn't any place for them at my mom and dad's." Sam realized he was rambling. Something he never did. In fact, he was known for being succinct, for getting right to the point, in *and* out of court. "If they're in your way, I can pack them in boxes and store them in the attic."

"That won't be necessary." Gillian picked up a volume at random and glanced at its spine. He read the title over her shoulder; it was one of his favorite novels by David Baldacci. She returned the book to its place on the shelf. *"Mi casa, su casa."*

"Well, I promise I won't take unfair advantage of your hospitality," he assured her.

"The kitchen has been remodeled," Gillian observed as they continued their tour.

"By the previous owners," Sam said from the doorway. "I can't say I care much for the color."

Gillian stopped between the kitchen and the dining room/pool table room. "Then you wouldn't mind if I had the walls painted?"

"Suit yourself." He thought to add, "By the way, the laundry room is the same shade of pink."

"Not for long," his houseguest said.

He opened the door of the refrigerator. "I wasn't sure what you liked to eat, so I had Sylvia lay in a few basic supplies: eggs, milk, bread, butter, Dunkin' Donuts."

"Who is Sylvia?"

"My neighbor one block over. Immaculate housekeeper. She's been working for me a couple of years. I mentioned her willingness to clean, do laundry, and the like back at my office. If you don't hit it off with Sylvia, I'll give you some other names."

Gillian ran her finger along the edge of the counter; there wasn't so much as a speck of dust to be found. "I'm sure Sylvia and I will get along famously."

"You can decide after you meet her. She comes every Friday." Sam had finished the grand tour of the first floor. They found themselves once more in the foyer. "I'll take your suitcases up for you."

Max was already waiting for them at the top of the

staircase, his tail wildly, happily swishing back and forth. He nudged at Gillian's hand with his nose until she reached down and gave him an affectionate pat.

"Those are two smaller guest rooms," Sam said, indicating the hallway on the left. "I haven't gotten around to doing much in the way of decorating. There's hardly any furniture in either one. You can do whatever you like to them."

Gillian murmured her agreement and then paused briefly in the doorway of the master bedroom.

He followed her into the room and put her bags down. "Same goes for in here."

Through her eyes Sam saw for the first time how spartan his bedroom appeared. There was the bed with a cedar chest at its foot, a single oversize bureau, a Mission-style chair, and a three-legged table by the window with a flowering azalea sitting on top. Sylvia must have brought in the plant; he'd never seen it before.

The walls were the identical nondescript beige as the rest of the upstairs. The curtains were hand-me-downs from his sister, Allie. He'd never taken the time to go shopping for drapes. The walls were bare of personal touches except for a pair of faded Cinzano prints from his first apartment and a piece of wire sculpture created by his younger brother, Eric, in tenth grade art class.

"This is a beautiful antique sleigh bed," Gillian commented as she ran her hand along the mahogany footboard. She gave him a sidelong glance, eyes suddenly serious and dark green in color. "I can't kick you out of your own bed, Sam."

He tried to make light of the circumstances. "Don't think of it as mine. Think of it as my grandparents'. I inherited a bunch of their furniture when they moved to

Florida a couple of years ago." He added for good measure, "My grandmother decided she wanted white wicker for their condo in Saint Petersburg."

"White wicker seems—"

"A drastic change from mahogany?"

Her mouth turned up a little at the corners. "I was going to say appropriate for Florida."

Sam followed his client as they made their way back down the flight of stairs. "I guess that's pretty much it except for the cellar. I doubt if you'll want to venture down there."

She crooked an eyebrow. "Mice?"

"On a good day." He cleared his throat. "There's a detached garage out back and a large fenced-in yard. A bunch of old sycamore trees. An overgrown vegetable garden. I'm not a gardener, but the odd cucumber or tomato still pops up during the growing season. Feel free to help yourself." He opened the screen door and stepped out onto the postage stamp–sized back porch.

Gillian came up and stood beside him. "What's beyond the fenced-in yard?"

"A small pond."

"And beyond that?"

"A cornfield. Then a soybean field. Then another cornfield. Then State Road 3."

Gillian peered into the darkness. She didn't say anything for a minute or two. "It's so . . ."

"Lonely."

She nodded. "And quiet."

"Yeah, it's real quiet." Sam could guess what was bothering her: it was entirely *too* quiet. "I had a hard time sleeping when I first moved back from New York. No traffic. No blaring horns. No city sounds. No nighttime noises at all except the wind in the sycamores and the hum of insects in the summer and the occasional frog song coming from the pond." His voice dropped to just above a whisper. "You'll get used to it."

He wondered if she would. Some people did. Some didn't.

"By the way," he said as they went back inside, "I'm going to give you my cell phone number. You can reach me any time of the day or night." Taking out one of his business cards, he quickly jotted down the information for her. "Call me if you have any questions. Or if you just want to talk. There doesn't have to be a reason. Sometimes being in a strange town and in a strange house and in a strange bed can feel downright—"

"Strange," supplied Gillian.

He smiled. "Yeah."

"Thank you, Sam," she said, slipping his business card into her handbag.

He was standing at the front door with his hand wrapped around the antique brass knob when the realization hit that he was reluctant to leave Gillian Charles on her own. He'd fully intended to say good night, walk straight out to his Ford Explorer, get in, and drive away. Instead, he turned back. "I know you must be tired." She looked exhausted.

"I am a little."

"But since it's your first night in Sweetheart and since there isn't much food in your refrigerator, would you like to grab a bite with me?" He supplied her with the specifics. "I'm just going down the street to the local pub for a sandwich. It's nothing fancy."

There was only the merest hesitation on her part. "I'd love to get a sandwich," she said.

Sam reached around and flicked on the porch light, then

issued a reminder. "Don't forget your house keys." He gave a soft whistle. "Want to go for a ride, Max?"

Max didn't have to be asked twice. He raced past them, out the front door of the bungalow, down the sidewalk, and straight through the open gate at the end of the white picket fence. He was the first one to reach Sam's SUV.

Chapter

seven

Mary Lou Preston had the hots for Samuel Law.

It had started in the third grade when she'd cornered him in the coatroom just before recess, demanded a kiss, and wouldn't take no for an answer. In those days she'd been both taller and stronger than Sam. That had changed sometime during the eighth grade when he'd gone through a growth spurt and shot right past her and everybody else in Mrs. Moore's social studies class.

Anyway, that day in the coatroom Mary Lou had insisted, so he'd obliged her. It had been more *and* less than she'd expected: Sam had kissed her as if she were a cross between one of his kid sisters and the pet bull frog she knew he kept in a glass terrarium on the windowsill in his bedroom.

Still, their brief encounter had left her curious about one

thing for the rest of her elementary, junior high, and high school days, until she'd dropped out in the tenth grade to marry Warren Preston: What would it be like to really be kissed by Samuel Law?

After that she'd caught an occasional glimpse of Sam whenever he was home on vacation from college, or during the summertime while he was working on road construction, shirtless, muscular arms and chest tanned a deep golden brown.

Anyway, a couple of years later she'd heard through the grapevine that he had won some kind of scholarship to Harvard Law School, and she knew their paths weren't likely to cross in the future.

No one had been more surprised than Mary Lou when Sam had suddenly up and moved back to Sweetheart. Not that their relationship had changed much during the intervening twenty-seven years since The Kiss. She still had the hots for Sam, and Sweetheart's most eligible bachelor still treated her like a kid sister.

The truth was Sam treated all the women in town like a kid sister, or a maiden aunt, or sometimes even a grandmother, depending on their age, which had led to the on-again, off-again speculation under the hair dryers at Blanche's Beauty Barn that he was gay or one of those "cellbaits" that could do it, but didn't by choice.

Sam's engagement—well, his broken engagement—to a New York socialite always entered the conversation at that point, along with the name of Patsy Hicks from neighboring Paradise County, whose sole claim to fame was she'd gone "all the way" with him in high school. Patsy had never stopped talking to this day about how the earth really *had* moved under her feet.

Finally someone would pipe up and say in Sam's defense, for not seducing the daughters and sisters of Sweetheart now that he was back in town: "Maybe he's so busy doing the right thing it never occurs to him to do the wrong thing."

And someone else would invariably add, "Leave the guy the hell alone."

And that was always that.

End of discussion.

Of course, Mary Lou still allowed herself to dream about spending one wildly exciting and erotic night in Sam's bed, even though she'd done the wrong thing more times than she cared to count in her own life. Which, she supposed, was the reason she was thirty-five years old, the thrice-divorced mother of two teenagers (she'd gone back to the Preston name after her last divorce, for their sakes), a part-time student going for her GED, and when Mike needed extra help serving up sandwiches and beer, an occasional waitress at McGinty's.

Tonight Samuel Law walked into McGinty's Pub with the kind of woman Mary Lou Preston knew she would never be: classy with a capital K.

It was Mike, himself, who drew everyone's attention to the front door of the pub when, in his Irish brogue, he called out, as he did with all of his regulars, "Sam, you old *sleeveen*."

A wave of his hand, a flash of perfect white teeth, and a killer smile from Sam were followed by, "Hey, Mike, how's it going?"

"I can't complain." Mike kept right on wiping the bar with the damp cloth in his hand. "Although I'm still looking for that pot of gold the leprechaun promised me." That elicited chuckles from several of his customers. Mike shrugged his burly shoulders. "And at least according to Hilda, I didn't make a total *gobdaw* of myself today." When he spotted the woman with Sam, Mike McGinty stopped in mid-swipe. "Do you want a booth?" They all knew Sam usually grabbed a sandwich right there at the bar.

"A booth would be fine," Sam said, his hand hovering at the woman's waist. He didn't actually touch her, but he still managed to steer her toward the one open table in the pub.

"Mary Lou'll be right with you," Mike called after them.

"Who's that with Sam?" came an insistent female voice at Mary Lou's elbow.

She tore her gaze away and poured coffee all around. "I don't know, Mrs. Goldman. I don't think she's from around here." Mary Lou knew everybody in the county. She'd never laid eyes on the tall, slender blonde before.

Mrs. Goldman peered over her bifocals. "Black's not her color."

The woman across the table from her spoke up. "What makes you say that?"

Goldie raised the coffee mug to her mouth, blew across the surface of the scalding liquid, as if that were going to be enough to cool it down ten degrees to a drinkable temperature, and pronounced, "Black makes her appear kind of peaked."

Her dinner companion and lifelong friend, Minerva Bagley, took advantage of the opportunity and offered her two cents' worth. "She looks fashionably pale, Goldie."

"Pale smale," the woman muttered.

"Pale's the 'in' thing these days," Minerva informed her. "It's a lot healthier than tanning yourself to the color of cowhide. Didn't you read the article in *The Journal Gazette* last week about the ravages of the sun's UVA and UVB rays on the human skin?"

"I must have missed it, Minerva." Goldie took another sip of hot, unsweetened coffee. Her eyes followed the woman with Sam. "She looks expensive."

"She looks very expensive," was the consensus of opinion. "I wonder if she's a model."

Goldie shook her head. "She's not tall enough. Most of her height is in those black stilts she's wearing." She sniffed. "I'll bet they cost a pretty penny."

Minerva Bagley sighed a little wistfully. "I remember when I could wear high heels. Remember when we wore high heels, Goldie? Oh, I don't mean these chunky old-lady shoes like we've got on now, but real high heels. Skinny three- and four- and even five-inch high heels. The kind that made us feel tall and elegant and all dressed up, even if we were only going to the movies."

"They gave us bunions and ruined our feet," Goldie reminded her. Like a dog with a particularly juicy bone to gnaw, she wouldn't let go of it. "I wonder who she is." She didn't bother lowering her voice. Speaking her mind, to Goldie's way of thinking, was part of the compensation for growing older.

"She's very elegant," Minerva said with just the teeniest bit of envy in her voice.

"She looks like city folk. And she looks like she comes from money." Then Goldie's eyes widened. "I'll bet she's that fancy-smancy fiancée of Sam's."

"Ex-fiancée."

"Maybe not so ex, after all," Goldie speculated with barely contained curiosity. "She's here, isn't she?"

Minerva Bagley didn't argue with her friend's logic. "Yes, she is here." She dared to venture another opinion of her own. "I think they make a perfect couple."

Goldie held her cup out to Mary Lou for another shot of hot, pitch-black coffee. "Why, in heaven's name?"

Minerva went on, "It's the old saying about opposites being attracted to each other."

"And they're opposites, in your opinion?"

"Yes. You don't have to look very far to see that she's very chic and cosmopolitan. Sam is small town for all the years he spent out East. She looks like she's got money to burn. We all know Sam is as poor as a church mouse. She's pretty in a soft, subtle, pale sort of way. And Sam is tall, dark, and drop-dead handsome."

"They do look well together." Eyes narrowed, lips pursed, Mrs. Goldman was apparently willing to concede that much. "You know what this means, don't you, Minerva?"

"What?"

"I was right all along." Goldie puffed out her chest. "I've been saying for years that the woman in his past had to be the reason Sam's ignored our local girls since he moved back."

"I suppose it does explain a lot," Minerva said, her eyes glued to the pair.

"Of course it does." Elvira Goldman smacked her lips. "Well, well, well, Minerva, maybe it's going to be an interesting spring in Sweetheart, after all."

Mary Lou Preston, for one, had heard quite enough. She taped her pencil a little impatiently against her order pad. "You ladies want strawberry or apple pie for dessert?"

Gillian's eyes went to the sign mounted over the bar at McGinty's: BEER IS PROOF THAT GOD LOVES US AND WANTS US TO BE HAPPY—*Benjamin Franklin.*

"What'll you have, miss?"

Gillian glanced up at the waitress hovering over their booth. There was a stub of a Number 2 pencil clasped in her right hand; it was poised to write on the recycled green paper order pad held in her left. Gillian almost blurted out that she hadn't had a chance to study the menu yet, but decided to go with, "I'll have whatever Sam's having."

Sam looked up at their waitress and gave her a friendly smile. "The usual for me, Mary Lou."

The woman smiled back at him, her whole face softening in the process. "Sure enough, Sam. Then that will be two corned beef on rye, extra cheese, light on the sauerkraut, dressing on the side, two stacks of home fries, and two beers."

Sam turned and focused his attention on Gillian. "Are you sure you want what I want?"

She hesitated, then swallowed with only minor difficulty. "Sure I'm sure."

"I'll be right back with your beers," said the woman Sam had called Mary Lou.

Once they were alone again, he leaned toward her and asked, "Do you even like beer?"

"As I always say: 'When in Rome . . .' " Gillian allowed the thought to trail off.

"You've been to Rome, of course."

"Yes." She didn't feel it was necessary to mention how many times. "I prefer Florence."

"Ah, Tuscany." Sam didn't say another word until their drinks had been served. Then, with a traditional beer glass held in one hand and a bottle of beer in the other, she watched as he poured the dark liquid down the side, creating the perfect head of foam. He looked at her. "Is it true what they say about Tuscany?"

"What do they say?" She attempted to emulate his skill, and discovered it was much harder to manage the bottle of beer and the glass than it had first appeared.

"The light in Tuscany is supposed to be different than the light anywhere else on earth."

"It's true," she said, taking a sip from her glass and trying not to grimace as the taste of bitter ale washed over her tongue. "Personally, I think it's the combination of crystal-clear air, an abundance of sunlight, and indescribable and yet subtle variations in the marble used for everything from reproductions of Michelangelo's *Pietà* to the grand cortiles of the countryside palazzi." She ran her tongue along her lips. "And all that Chianti, of course."

Sam was grinning at her from across the table. "That's a personal theory of yours, is it?"

Gillian nodded and took another sip of her beer. It wasn't quite so bitter the second time around.

Sam seemed amused about something. "Do you have a head for alcohol?"

She made a face and admitted, "Not much of one."

"Then you might want to go easy on the Guinness," he advised. "At least until our sandwiches arrive."

Gillian wondered if their sandwiches would even be edible. Twenty minutes later, much to her surprise, she was saying to Sam, "This is the best Reuben I've ever tasted."

"I'll be sure to pass the lovely compliment along to Hilda," came a lilting male voice. They glanced up and discovered the pub's proprietor standing by their booth.

"I understand now why every table in your restaurant is filled, Mr. McGinty," she said.

"Call me Mike."

"If you'll call me Gillian." She smiled up at him. "Your food is delicious, Mike."

The Irishman beamed. "The secret is in the kosher corned beef and the sauce. The recipes have been handed down from generation to generation through my wife's family. Hilda helped her parents, and before that her grandparents, in the family's delicatessen back in Hoboken before she married me." Mike sighed and tucked the damp bar cloth into the makeshift apron tied around his waist. "Not that they ever forgave her for marrying a McGinty."

"Hoboken's loss is Sweetheart's gain," Sam reminded him, evidently not for the first time.

"Now you sound like Hilda." Then Mike grinned at her. "I'll let you get back to your food, Gillian, before it goes all mungy. I just wanted to say welcome to McGinty's." He wagged a finger at Sam. "If you need anything, anything at all, Samuel, you or your *mot,* you just let Mary Lou know."

"Thanks, Mike."

The pub's owner slipped back behind the bar, but not before promising them, "I'll send out slices of Hilda's fresh-baked apple and strawberry pie to your table. And wait until rhubarb is in season and you taste her homemade rhubarb pie."

Gillian groaned in appreciation. "I can't manage another bite. Does Mike hand out doggie bags?"

"He does. But around here they're actually meant for the dogs." Apparently Sam relented when he saw the disappointment on her face. "I'm sure we can have the other half of your sandwich and your share of the pie wrapped up so you can take it home with you."

She instantly brightened. "Good. It would break my heart to leave it behind."

At that moment two women of indeterminate years—not old but far from young—walked past their booth headed in the direction of McGinty's front door. One of the pair paused, tapped Sam on the shoulder, clicked her tongue several times, and issued him a stern warning. "Don't let her break your heart again, Samuel Law."

Gillian nearly choked on her beer.

Sam was surprisingly quick to respond. "I won't, Goldie." He added, "Good evening, Minerva."

The second woman acknowledged his greeting with, "Good evening to you, Sam," but her gaze never strayed from Gillian's face.

"It's not polite to interrupt their dinner, Minerva," the first woman said abruptly. Before introductions could even be made, she'd turned and walked away.

The one called Minerva had no choice but to follow.

Using a paper napkin to wipe her mouth and then mop up the watery residue from the bottle of ale, Gillian put her glass back down on the table. "What was that all about?" she asked once the pair had gone.

Sam shrugged.

She shot him a meaningful glance. "Trust is essential to a successful lawyer-client relationship, don't you agree?"

"Yes, I do," he said.

"And truthfulness?"

"Absolutely."

"So, who do those women think I am, Sam?"

"I can't say for sure, but it's just possible," he said, arguing his case, "that one or two of the locals may have assumed, incorrectly, of course, that you're my fiancée."

"Fiancée?" came out half an octave higher than Gillian's normal voice. Seeking some semblance of privacy, she leaned across the table toward him. "You're engaged?"

"No."

Her head was beginning to pound. She pressed her palm against her temple. "I don't understand."

"I'll try to explain."

Gillian waited for him to do exactly that.

He seemed to pick and choose his words. "From her comment, as she walked past us on her way out of the pub, I think that Mrs. Goldman thinks you're my ex-fiancée."

Gillian cupped her chin in her right hand—her right elbow was already propped up on the laminated table top—and stared straight into his eyes. "Did she break your heart, Sam?"

He blinked and appeared confused for a moment. "Who? Mrs. Goldman?"

Gillian heard herself snicker and was astonished the sound had come from her own throat. "No. Not Mrs. Goldman. Your fiancée. Excuse me, your *ex*-fiancée."

It was obvious he wasn't pleased with the direction their conversation was taking. "That's a rather complicated story."

She didn't let him off the hook. "A simple yes or no will suffice, counselor."

Eyes the color of the moon on a dark and stormy night, starless eyes, silvery moon eyes, found and held her gaze. "Then, no, she did not break my heart."

"Did you break hers?"

Sam finished off his beer before responding. "I'm not sure Nora had a heart to be broken."

"That does sound like a complicated story."

"It's also a story for another time," he said, rising to his feet. "I think we'd better get back and check on Max."

As he was reaching into his pocket for his wallet, their waitress rushed up with a doggie bag in each hand. "Mike said to tell you that this one is the leftover sandwich and pie for Gillian. And this one is a lovely bone for Max."

"Thanks, Mary Lou."

"You're welcome, Sam," she said a little breathlessly.

"Appreciate it."

The woman reddened slightly. "Anytime."

Sam turned back to her. "Ready to go, Gillian?"

Chapter
eight

"Why would anyone in Sweetheart assume that I'm the ex-fiancée who supposedly broke your heart, but who, you assure me, did not?" Gillian asked him once they were outside McGinty's Pub and strolling toward his Ford Explorer.

She wasn't going to leave it alone, Sam realized. He might as well tell her the truth. "Because the whole town knows I was once engaged to someone like you."

She stopped dead in her tracks and looked up at him. "What does 'someone like you' mean exactly?"

"A New Yorker."

She resumed walking, her high heels making little staccato sounds on the sidewalk. "They can tell simply by looking at me that I'm from New York?"

This wasn't going to get any easier. "Of course not. But

they can tell you aren't from around here." They walked another ten paces and cut across the parking lot before Sam came right out and said what was on his mind. "As you're well aware, Gillian, you have a certain style, a certain big-city look about you."

"I'll take that as a compliment."

"It was meant as one."

They reached his SUV and greeted Max, who was beside himself with excitement when Sam opened the doggie bag and presented him with the bone from Mike's kitchen. The sheepdog immediately took his prize between his teeth, plopped down on the backseat, and proceeded to ignore them.

"Was your fiancée from New York?"

So, they were back to *that* topic of conversation. "By way of Darien, Connecticut."

"You broke it off?"

"It was a mutual decision." He decided to skip the details and go straight to the punch line. "I didn't want to stay in New York. She didn't want to leave."

Gillian slipped into the passenger seat and waited until he was settled on the driver's side. "You've been back in Sweetheart for what"—she made a casual gesture with her hand—"three years?"

Sam nodded and forced himself to relax the stranglehold he had on the steering wheel. He backed out of the parking lot behind McGinty's, turned onto Main Street, and pulled up to the stoplight just as it changed from yellow to red.

"That seems like an exceptionally long time for rumors of a former fiancée to persist."

She *really* wasn't going to leave it alone.

Sam cleared his throat. "It's difficult to return to your hometown, where some people have known you since you were a snotty-nosed little kid, and be taken seriously as a professional."

"I can understand that," she said.

He raked one hand through his hair. "When you add in the social problem, it becomes downright impossible."

A blond eyebrow arched quizzically. "Would you care to translate that for me?"

Why not? "I discovered I couldn't be the lawyer I wanted to be or needed to be, and date anyone from this area." He might as well tell her the whole story. The PG-rated version, anyway. He blew out his breath expressively. "Not only the single women, but some of the married ones, were hitting on me."

She was quick. "The unmarried women heard wedding bells and the married women saw you as a diversion, or as another notch on their bedpost."

The light turned green. Sam once again directed his attention to the stretch of black road in front of the Explorer's headlights. "That's it in a nutshell."

"Interesting problem."

He supposed that was one way of describing the awkward situation in which he'd found himself. "Anyway, I went out with an old girlfriend from high school for a short while, and then I tried dating a local librarian—a librarian, for God's sake—and both times it was pretty much a disaster."

Beside him, Gillian murmured, "Aaaah . . ."

He made a movement in the air with his right hand. "What does 'aaaah' mean?"

"You were considered prime meat."

Sam wasn't completely comfortable admitting to her, "Dammit, Gillian, it was the only problem I'd failed to anticipate before moving back to Sweetheart." He shook his head in dismay. "I know times have changed, but I'm not naive. And I'm sure as hell not a prude. It just didn't occur to me that a man would have to guard his reputation like it was gold in Fort Knox."

"So, in order to protect your good name, you made certain the story about your broken engagement *and* your broken heart got around town. In short, you put up a No Trespassing sign."

"Nice summation, Ms. Charles."

"Thank you, Mr. Law." Then she tacked on what seemed to be an inspired afterthought. "I'll bet you told Mrs. Goldman."

He turned onto their street. "Actually it was my mother who confided to Goldie that I'd been cut to the quick by a heartless New York socialite and had sworn off dating women." He laughed sheepishly. "Well, you can imagine the rumors that one started."

"First, on behalf of socialites everywhere, I object to being cast in the role of the villain."

"Wouldn't it be villainess?"

"Second, it's perfectly clear to anyone with an ounce of common sense that you're heterosexual."

"I think that's the whole point, Gillian. People with common sense aren't the ones who spread rumors."

"Well, it's not fair."

"No, it isn't fair."

"I do understand," she said after a short silence.

Maybe she did.

Gillian cast him a knowing glance out of the corner of her eye. "Try being a single woman of independent means." She took in a deep breath and slowly released it. Then she turned her head. "All right, try being an heiress with a reputation, however undeserved, for having more money than sense."

When she stopped there, he urged her, "Go on."

Still, she hesitated.

"Hey, I've bared my soul to you," he said. "The least you can do in return is not leave me out in the cold all by myself."

Gillian opened her mouth and the words poured out. "Ever since I was a teenager, rumors have dogged me. According to the press, I've slept with, been engaged to, or even secretly married to several dozen different men on three continents."

He flipped the turn signal on and made a right at the next corner. "North America, Europe, and . . .?"

"Australia," she said, supplying the missing continent. "Anyway, I've been reported to be anorexic, bulimic, a drug addict, a sex addict, even an opera addict."

While she threw up her hands in frustration, he mouthed the words, "Opera addict?"

"Any day now I expect to see a grainy black-and-white photograph of myself on the front page of a supermarket tabloid with a headline reading: HEIRESS PREGNANT WITH ALIEN'S BABY."

Sam had never thought of what it must be like for her. "Do the paparazzi hound you?"

"I never use the 'p' word, myself," she said. "But yes, in the past they sometimes have."

"What do you do to protect yourself?"

She took several deep breaths and seemed to calm down. "What I've always done or what I learned the hard way. Live quietly. Choose my friends wisely. Avoid the limelight. Develop a thick skin. Ignore the press. Live my life as I see fit. And be very careful who I date."

"I can sure relate to that."

She turned to check on Max in the backseat. "Is that why you haven't married, Sam?"

He stuck to the standard excuses. "No time. And I never found the right woman. Besides, I'm not easy to live with." He stared straight ahead. "What about you?"

Gillian didn't answer him right away. When she finally spoke, her voice was so soft Sam had to strain to hear her. "I don't want to settle for someone I can live with. I want someone I can't live without." Even in the dark he could tell she was a little embarrassed. "I suppose that sounds sophomoric and stupidly romantic."

"It's never stupid to hold out for what you really want. It's only stupid to settle for less." The vehicle rolled to a stop in front of his house. Well, in front of Gillian's house.

"Thank you, Sam, for dinner and for everything."

"You're welcome." He turned to Max. "C'mon, pal, let's walk the lady to her door." They were standing on the front porch—Gillian was rummaging in her handbag for the house keys he'd given her earlier—when Sam noticed an envelope wedged in the jamb. "Looks like someone was here while we were gone."

Gillian turned the key in the lock and cracked the front door open. Sam reached out and caught the white business-size envelope as it fluttered to the ground. "Who's it addressed to?"

He turned it over. "There is no name or address." He held the envelope out to her. "Do you want to do the honors?"

Gillian slit the flap with the edge of her house key and took out the single sheet of paper inside. She unfolded it, held it up to the porch light, and read aloud: " 'Go back where you come from. No one wants you here.' " She examined both sides of the paper and then handed him the note. "No signature."

He shook his head. "There never is in these cases."

A small furrow formed between her eyebrows. "I didn't think anyone knew I was here."

"Limousines are hard to miss."

He could tell she was trying to keep her voice light, conversational. "You don't get many in town?"

"Outside of prom night, or the occasional funeral procession, no, we don't see a lot of big black shiny stretch limos on the main street of Sweetheart."

She sighed and conceded, "I suppose a few people were aware of my arrival."

"More than a few." Sam decided to name names; he ticked them off on his fingers. "Mr. Biaggi. The truck driver. The piano movers. The carpenters who temporarily removed the porch posts and the front window. My secretary, although she's discretion itself. Sylvia, but if she said anything, it would be a purely innocent remark because there isn't a mean bone in her body. Anyone who happened to spot your limo when it was parked in front of my office or anyone who saw us at the pub tonight." He ran out of fingers. "And of course, anybody any of those people may have mentioned your existence to."

"In other words, the whole town."

"Pretty much. It's a small community. News travels fast. You're news, Gillian."

"It must be a slow news day in Sweetheart."

"It's always a slow news day in Sweetheart," he said.

"Whatever happened to: 'Welcome to Sweetheart, Indiana, where everyone is your friend'?" she asked, crumpling up the note.

"Some people are friendly; some aren't." He added, "It's not really personal."

"I know." She sighed again and, he was pretty sure without thinking about it, reached down to pat Max.

"Are you going to be all right?"

She gave him a quick smile. "Of course."

He wasn't one hundred percent convinced. "You've got my cell phone number. Don't hesitate to use it."

"I won't," she said as he turned to leave. "Thank you again for dinner."

"It was my pleasure." He gave a low whistle. "Let's go, Max. It's getting late." The sleek black sheepdog proceeded to ignore Sam and sat back on his haunches.

Gillian reached over and gave him a gentle nudge. "Go on, boy. It's time to say good night."

Sam watched as his dog, tail thumping against the wooden floorboards of the porch, licked Gillian's fingers, nuzzled her hand, and gazed up at her with adoring eyes.

"C'mon, Max," he called out.

The dog didn't budge.

Sam paused in the middle of the sidewalk and looked back at the pair, then stared down at the ground for a minute.

He heard Gillian urge, "Time for you to go home, Max."

Max was unmovable.

Finally Sam raised his head, blew out his breath, and said to her, "Trouble is, you see, he is home."

"Oh, no, Sam," she said, guilt suddenly written across her face. "I already feel as if I've kicked you out of your house and your bed. I can't take your dog, too."

"It isn't a matter of what you can or can't do, Gillian. It's what Max wants," he pointed out.

"He's just confused, that's all."

"Maybe. Under the circumstances, it wouldn't hurt for him to stay with you tonight, anyway."

She caved in without any further argument. "Are you sure you don't mind?"

"I'm sure." He turned, tossing back over his shoulder, "Good night, Gillian. Be sure to lock the door behind you."

"Good night, Sam."

He closed the gate after himself and then waited in the shadows beneath the sprawling tree at the edge of his property until he was sure she'd followed his instructions. He couldn't make out the individual words, but he could hear her inside his house talking to his dog, and he felt a small jab of jealousy.

"You're pathetic, Law," he muttered under his breath.

So what if his loyal and faithful companion—and supposedly a man's best friend—had deserted him for a woman who had been in town less than three hours.

He was reaching for the door handle of his Explorer when he heard someone run their fingers over the piano keys. It was safe to assume it was Gillian. Max had never shown any signs of musical talent.

Sam cocked his head and listened. Gillian began with a series of scales, playing slowly at first, then faster and faster. She moved on to a piece he vaguely recognized. He was certainly no expert when it came to classical music, but he thought it might be Mozart. There was something precise, something kind of prissy, even a little eighteenth-century about the music; it made him think of women in ball gowns and men in white powdered wigs and satin waistcoats.

Besides, Gillian Charles struck him as the type who might like Mozart: she was cool all the way through and a blue blood, besides. Yessiree, she was ice cold and *very* refined.

Well, until she'd had that bottle of beer tonight at McGinty's. Sam grinned. Then she'd acted almost human.

There was a momentary lull in the concert, then came a resounding crash of chords, followed by music that was like a whisper on the night air. The whisper gave way to a crescendo of sound that took the listener right to the breaking point.

This music was the opposite of Mozart. It was big. Thunderous. Emotional. Slavic. Maybe Russian.

Sam figured the music was too modern to be Tchaikovsky. The only other Russian composer he could name off the top of his head was Rachmaninoff.

It occurred to him, as he stood there in the dark and listened to Gillian play, that it took physical strength and emotional fortitude—not to mention one hell of a lot of talent—to perform the music he was hearing.

It also struck him that maybe ice water didn't run through her veins, after all. Maybe there was a red-blooded, feeling, sensual woman underneath all that polish and good breeding.

The music ended on a hushed note.

It was followed by silence.

Sam discovered he was holding his breath. He exhaled and watched as the living room went dark. But it wasn't until he saw the lights go on upstairs that he finally got in the Explorer and drove down the street to his parents' house.

Chapter

nine

"I know what you're up to, Jacob Charles," Anna Rogozinski muttered under her breath as she hung up the telephone.

Anna reached for her cane, steadied herself as she rose to her feet, and slowly walked outside to the front porch, letting the screen door slam shut behind her.

It was a fine May morning. Maybe as fine as she could remember in Sweetheart. The tulips in her meticulously tended beds were in full bloom. The air was drenched with the smell of lilacs and honeysuckle and the flowering Bartlett pears by her porch. The sun was high overhead; a bright yellow ball in a cloudless blue sky.

The world seemed so peaceful on a morning like this, yet here she was all roiling emotions and jumbled thoughts on the inside, and not feeling peaceful in the least.

She carefully lowered her arthritic body into a cushioned chair, set her cane to one side, still keeping it within easy reach, and settled herself. Picking up the teacup she'd abandoned in order to answer the telephone, she took a sip and pronounced it, "Cold."

Anna gave a sigh and put the delicate china cup back on the table at her elbow. There was nothing more unappetizing than tepid tea. Too bad it was Esther's day off. Well, perhaps now that she was feeling a bit calmer, she'd brew herself a fresh pot.

Lord, who did she thinking she was fooling? She wasn't calm. She was flustered.

Anna touched her face. Her cheeks were flushed. Her hands were trembling. *She* was trembling. Her heart was racing and she couldn't seem to catch her breath.

"It's ridiculous to get upset at your age," she scolded herself. She was too old, and she'd been through too much in her eighty-one years, to get butterflies in her stomach at this stage of the game.

Although, now that she thought about it, she'd routinely gotten a case of jitters before a concert.

In fact, it was during her first world tour—it had been right after the war—that she'd learned to skip dinner the night of a performance, allowing herself only half a cup of weak tea. Any more could result in disaster, or at the very least acute embarrassment. After all, one simply didn't jump up in the middle of a Mozart sonata, make a hurried curtsy to the audience, and excuse oneself with the announcement: "The *Andante* movement will be delayed five minutes while Miss Rogozinski pays an unscheduled visit to the WC."

The notion made Anna smile.

Then she gradually came back to the present and to thoughts of Jacob Charles.

"You always had to have your own way, didn't you, Jacob?" she said aloud since there was no one to hear her. "You always had to be the one in control." There was another long, drawn-out sigh. "Well, it's beyond even your control now."

With the morning sun bathing her in its warmth, Anna allowed her eyes to drift shut. A soft breeze caressed her skin and played with the wisps of white hair around her face. She could hear the familiar call of a male cardinal singing to its mate, the sound of the wind rustling through the treetops, even the distant whistle of a train. She let the sounds gently wash over her.

"Good morning, Anna," came a voice from nearby.

Anna realized she must have dozed off. She sat up, raised a hand to shade her eyes, and squinted into the sunlight. Someone was standing on the sidewalk in front of her house. "Good morning, Minerva. You're out and about bright and early."

As if it were her *raison d'être,* Minerva Bagley said, "I had a special rush order to get out to a customer, so I was at the post office when the doors opened."

"Is business going well?" Anna inquired politely. She didn't put any credence in the mumbo-jumbo concoctions or the assortment of trinkets that Minerva packaged and sold, but some people in town swore by them.

Minerva pressed a hand to her chest, somewhere in the region above her heart, and took a moment to catch her breath. "As a matter of fact, business is booming."

There was no accounting for taste, Anna supposed.

Apparently Minerva had something on her mind besides her mail-order potions. "Did Goldie call you this morning?"

Anna Rogozinski's stomach flipped over. She reached for her cane, although she wasn't sure why; the feel of it in her hand was somehow comforting. "Yes, she did."

Minerva's bottom lip curled in disappointment. "Then

she's already told you about the woman we saw last night at McGinty's."

"She mentioned a 'fancy-smancy blonde'—those are Goldie's words, not mine—who was having dinner with Samuel Law." Anna wished her heart would stop pounding in her ears. "She seemed to think the young woman was his ex-fiancée."

"Maybe not so *ex,* after all. We don't really know the current state of affairs between them." Minerva colored. "I don't mean sexual affairs literally, of course." Her cheeks turned an even deeper shade of pink. "After all, Sam's personal business is really none of our business." She finally sputtered to a stop.

"I know what you meant, Minerva," Anna reassured her with a too-cheerful smile. "Would you care to join me for a cup of tea? I was about to make a fresh pot."

Her visitor brightened. "Why don't I make it for us?"

Since the herbal concoctions Minerva marketed to the public—they had names like Raspberry Razzle Dazzle, Our Daily Doze, and Sweet Dreams—had presumably been sent off to eager customers at the crack of dawn, Anna didn't think there was any harm in accepting her offer. "That's very kind of you."

They each had a cup of traditional English breakfast tea in hand before the subject was raised again. "I found out her name," came the surprise announcement.

Anna was pleased with how normal her voice sounded when she said, "Whose?"

"The woman who had dinner with Sam last night." Minerva wiggled in her chair, apparently torn between the desire to blurt it all out and holding her audience in suspense a few moments longer. "She's none other than Jacob Charles's granddaughter. Her name is Gillian." There was a pause. "She's moved into Sam's house."

A frown formed between Anna's eyes. "That doesn't sound like Samuel Law."

Minerva quickly went on to explain. "Sam has moved back into his parents' place since Judy and Joe are still gallivanting around the countryside."

"I see."

Minerva seemed to select her words with care. "Gillian Charles is an enchanting creature. Very chic. Very elegant. Quite pretty." She added, "Lovely laugh."

Anna purposely waited awhile before she inquired, "Did you speak to her?"

"No, I didn't want to intrude on their dinner. And of course, Goldie was there and you know how Goldie can be."

"Yes, I know how Goldie can be."

They both cleared their throats a little self-consciously.

Apparently Minerva felt she was being disloyal if she didn't mention, "Goldie's intentions are good."

Anna Rogozinski knew there were times when she tended to be too blunt; this was going to be one of those times. " 'The road to Hell is paved with good intentions.' "

Her companion's head moved up and down in sync with the mantra, "How true. How true."

"I wonder if the young lady is planning to stay in town long," Anna said as if were of no consequence to her either way.

"Gordy Howell thinks she's here permanently."

The hand clasping Anna's teacup froze in midair. "Why would Gordy assume that?"

"Because Sam had him tear out the big window in the front of his house when they couldn't get her piano through the door. Gordy doesn't think they would go to all that trouble if she was only staying a week or two."

Anna's pulse picked up speed. "She's a pianist."

"It would seem so."

"And she has a lovely laugh," Anna said softly as she exhaled, forgetting for an instant that she wasn't alone.

Minerva Bagley reached across the small wicker table between them and patted the hand Anna Rogozinski had wrapped tightly around her cane. "Yes, she has a lovely laugh."

Chapter
ten

 She was filthy rich.

Stinking rich.

Obscenely rich.

She had so much. He had so little.

It wasn't that he was unable or unwilling to work hard. Hell, he'd busted his butt ever since dropping out of high school his junior year. He'd done everything from digging ditches to hauling garbage to working in a factory twelve hours a day.

Factory work—slaving away on an assembly line screwing nuts and bolts into a never-ending succession of transmissions—had been a dirty job, but at least it had paid well. In fact, when times had been good, real good, he'd made eighteen dollars an hour, plus incentives, plus overtime. He hadn't even minded that he could never seem to get the grease out from under his fingernails.

Then two years ago the local transmission plant had closed down and the assembly line—along with the high-paying jobs—had moved south of the border to Mexico. Screw NAFTA! Screw the union! And screw the company! Since then he'd had to make do with whatever odd jobs he could find.

One thing had always puzzled him. He couldn't seem to figure out what some people did that allowed them to get ahead, that made them richer and richer; while the rest of the world's poor suckers seemed to get farther and farther behind.

He worked harder and yet he got poorer day by day. That's what he was: the working poor.

Still, he wasn't stupid. He knew things. Things other people didn't know, or maybe had once known and had long since forgotten. He didn't forget anything. He remembered everything. And he was smart enough to connect the dots.

He'd always been one to keep his mouth shut, and his eyes and ears open. That's why he saw things, heard things, figured out things other people didn't.

One valuable lesson he'd learned a long time ago from watching his daddy sneak around behind his momma's back—his old man had kept his liquor stowed in a small shed out beyond the barn in dark brown bottles marked POISON—everybody had their secrets. Everybody had a skeleton or two tucked away in the back of their closet.

Even, it turned out, his momma.

A boy didn't tell on his momma, of course—and God knows, she'd had just cause for doing what she did; his daddy had been a mean sonofabitch when he was drunk—but ever since, he'd figured it was a good idea to keep an eagle eye out. You never knew when somebody might try to pull a fast one.

Not that he didn't believe in the Golden Rule: Do unto others and all that mumbo-jumbo. Because he did. As a matter of fact, he'd been doing his Christian duty, helping out one of those in need, when he'd first come across *her* secret.

He reckoned people shouldn't leave private things lying around if they didn't want someone else to see them. Maybe they were asking, begging, to be found out. Yeah, that was it. Maybe they actually wanted the cat to be let out of the bag.

A game of cat and mouse: that's what it was. And you were either the cat or the mouse; the hunter or the hunted.

He was a hunter. His daddy had given him his first rifle, a .22 caliber, when he was seven years old, right before Momma put real poison in one of those dark brown bottles and waited for the inevitable day when Daddy would sneak one drink too many.

Anyway, the .22 was the best birthday present he'd ever received. Turned out he was a natural with a rifle. In fact, he seemed to have a talent for killing things.

He'd kept up with his shooting over the years. He practiced on small quarry: mostly squirrels or rabbits or birds, or sometimes, late at night, barn owls.

He liked to make a game out of hunting. How close could he get to his target? Close enough to get a bead on the critter before it even knew he was there? Close enough to smell its fear in the split second when it realized it was going to die? Close enough to put a bullet straight through its heart?

He liked games. He'd always been good at them. Oh, maybe not ones like they'd played back in school. Those games seemed to take some kind of quickness he didn't understand. Other kids had laughed at him, had made fun of how slow he'd been to catch on. But if a game took patience, or plain old dogged persistence, then he was definitely your man.

Well, now they'd play the game his way and by his rules. He knew who the lady was and what she really was. He hadn't told anyone else. It was their secret for now.

He was good at keeping secrets.

Chapter
eleven

 "Good morning, Sweetheart!" came the radio announcer's voice.

"It's a beautiful day out there in Heart country. Unseasonably warm at eighty-one degrees. The humidity is a comfortable thirty percent. The barometric pressure is twenty-nine point nine-four and rising. The temperature will top out at a balmy eighty-seven by midafternoon. No precipitation expected through the weekend.

"Your morning forecast here at WHRT, The Heart, ninety-eight point nine on your FM dial, has been brought to you by Demolition. Remember, nothing works better to wipe out corn borers than Demolition Insecticide. Using Demolition ensures that you never have to face the disaster of an infested field or a ruined corn crop again.

"At ten minutes past the hour it's time for a 'blast from

the past.' What year is it? Nikita Khrushchev becomes premier of the Soviet Union. The United States launches Explorer One, its first earth satellite. American Express cards are introduced. The Hoola Hoop fad is sweeping the nation. Johnny Unitas and the Baltimore Colts claim the NFL championship in sudden death overtime. If you guessed 1958, Heartlanders, you're right on the money.

"This request is from Peggy Sue and is going out with her love to Buddy. It's a classic, folks. Here's the late, great Conway Twitty singing his 1958 hit, 'It's Only Make Believe.' "

Gillian hummed under her breath as she poured herself a second cup of coffee and dug into the piece of apple pie left over from last night's dinner at the pub.

Even the morning after, the pie was delicious. The crust was light without being flaky. The filling wasn't too sweet or too sour. The apples were tender without being mushy. She detected a touch of cinnamon, a pinch or two of nutmeg, perhaps a little brown sugar, and something she couldn't quite put her cook's finger on. No doubt it was Hilda McGinty's secret ingredient. Something unusual. Gillian smiled to herself. Maybe a shot or two of Guinness.

She was rinsing off her dishes in the kitchen sink when Max came bounding in through the pet door. *Did every house in town have one?* He'd been in the backyard burying his beloved bone. He immediately sat down at her feet and gazed up with beseeching eyes.

"Hungry, boy?"

The sleek black sheepdog made a kind of half-growl, half-whine sound in the back of his throat which she took to mean yes, as a matter of fact, he was.

Gillian decided to come clean. "I'd intended to share my apple pie with you, Max, until I found a bag of Kibbles 'n Bits on the front doorstep this morning, along with your dishes.

"Then Sam called while you were outside. I told him about the incident with the toaster, by the way. He gave me the name of a repair shop. (She would simply have bought a new one, but this was Sam's house, not hers.) He also issued very clear instructions when it comes to your diet. So, I'm afraid I ate the pie," she said, breaking the bad news to him, "and you're getting the same old, same old."

She put down a bowl of fresh water and filled up his food dish. The sheepdog dug in with apparent relish.

"I guess you don't mind the same old, same old," she said, watching him wolf down his breakfast.

Max chose to ignore her.

"By the way, Sam asked how we managed last night. I told him my head hit the pillow and that's the last thing I remember."

No one could have been more surprised than Gillian when she'd opened her eyes and discovered bright sunlight pouring in through a slit in the ancient beige curtains. The clock on the bedside table had read half past eight.

"Sam inquired after you, as well. I said you were out like a light as soon as you got settled at the foot of the bed." Max looked up at her. "That's when I was informed you usually prefer to curl up on the braided rug in front of the bureau." Gillian took a stance, her arms akimbo, and tapped her toe several times on the linoleum floor. "You might have warned me, you know."

Max ruffed softly and went back to eating.

"I didn't want to hurt the poor man's feelings, so I made up some cock-and-bull story about the bed seeming less crowded to you because I'm smaller than he is, but I don't think he bought it." She poured herself another cup of coffee. "I also told him I slept well because I felt safe with you in the house. At least that much was true."

Gillian picked up her coffee cup, leaned back against the

counter, and surveyed the room as she took a sip. "Do you like the color yellow?" Then she paused. "Wait a minute. Dogs are color-blind, aren't they? In that case you're lucky, Max. It means you don't have to look at these Pepto-Bismol pink walls."

A vision of what this kitchen might look like had come to her this morning as she was waiting for her coffee to brew. She could see bright yellow walls, pristine white cabinets with beveled glass doors, and interior lights to show off a collection of colorful Italian pottery, a butcher-block island with comfortable, upholstered stools on one side for informal eating, polished marble countertops, imported one-of-a-kind artisan tiles inlaid in the back splash, and an antique oak-plank floor.

The ancient avocado green appliances would be replaced with modern stainless steel, including a six-burner restaurant-style stove and a Sub-Zero refrigerator.

She could even imagine the tiny back porch transformed into a spacious solarium with a glass roof and windows on three sides to let in the morning sun, and perhaps a red-wood deck beyond that with a table and chairs for alfresco dining.

And the garden . . .

Well, the less said about the weed patch Sam had referred to as a garden, the better.

What this place needed was a complete makeover by someone with lots of time on their hands and with at least some decorating talent. Not to mention a modicum of good taste and plenty of money. Someone, Gillian thought, like her.

She'd been wondering what she was going to do with herself for the next six months. If she didn't keep busy, she'd go stir-crazy.

That hadn't been a problem back in New York. She'd volunteered as a music teacher two days a week and she was the driving force behind The Edward and Elise Charles Memorial Foundation, which provided music lessons and "gently used" musical instruments for kids who couldn't afford to buy them new.

Then there were her other "pet projects," which mostly had to do again with music or children or animals. In the end, she'd had to enlist the help and talents of half a dozen people to fill in for her.

Well, she couldn't spend her entire time in Sweetheart simply lolling around reading, or playing the piano, or talking on the telephone to her friends, or even dealing with the seemingly endless and tedious legalities of her trust. Fixing up Sam's house and planting a few flowers in his yard seemed the very least she could do in lieu of the rent he wasn't allowing her to pay him.

"This house needs me as much as I need it," Gillian said out loud. She glanced down at the faded pink and gray patterned linoleum floor. "On second thought, maybe more."

Max polished off his Kibbles 'n Bits, sat back on his haunches, and looked up at her.

"By the way, did I happen to mention who's coming to dinner?" she said to him.

Ears perked, Max was doing his impression of the strong, silent type.

Gillian shrugged her shoulders—she was wearing a *noire* silk T-shirt this morning, along with jeans by Celine and a pair of strappy sandals that she'd picked up in Milan last fall—and rephrased the question. "Well, did I tell you who's showing up on our doorstep this evening with a Papa Tony's Pizzeria pizza in one hand and a bunch of papers for me to sign in the other?"

Max just stared at her.

She answered the question herself. "None other than your lord and master."

Apparently Max wasn't impressed. He sought out the one sunny spot on the kitchen floor and plopped down.

Gillian washed out her coffee cup and turned it upside down in the drain rack. "Anyway, I told Sam I'd make a salad to go with the pizza. So, for your information, I'm off to the grocery store as soon as my ride shows up."

It was the unmistakable sounds of Aretha Franklin, the Queen of Soul, that heralded the arrival of Doodles Weaver a few minutes later. Gillian reached the front door just as a bubble gum pink convertible pulled up in front of the house.

A middle-aged man sporting a ponytail—there was more curly gray hair dangling from the back of his head than there was on the top of it—got out of the car.

He was dressed in frayed bell bottoms that looked like he'd been wearing them since the seventies, a too-small madras print sports shirt, Jesus sandals, and dark-tinted sunglasses.

He reached up and removed the sunglasses before saying, "Sam sent me, Miss Charles. I'm Davison Weaver."

Gillian opened the screen door and stepped out onto the porch. She shaded her eyes with one hand. "I've been expecting you. Good morning, Mr. Weaver."

An unabashedly friendly smile was followed by the suggestion, "Call me Doodles. Everybody in town does."

She shook his hand. "I'm Gillian."

He pumped her arm several times before releasing it. "I understand you need transportation, Gillian."

"I do."

"Well, I can take you just about anywhere your little ole heart desires," he claimed.

She nearly blurted out: *How about driving me back to Manhattan?* Instead, she asked, "What kind of car is that?"

Doodles Weaver glanced over his shoulder as if he were making sure she meant his car; although, to her knowledge, it was only the third vehicle to drive by the house this morning. "Cadillac."

"I don't think I've ever seen such big fins," she said. *Or such pink ones.*

Doodles's voice dropped to a caressing drawl. "She's a real beauty, isn't she?"

Beauty was obviously in the eye of the beholder. Still, Gillian managed to give the man a genuine compliment. "You've kept her in excellent condition."

The middle-aged hippie's tone was reverential. "It would be a crime not to maintain a classic like the 1959 Fleetwood."

"I don't know much about cars," she admitted. *Try zero. Zip. Nada. Rien.*

"What do you drive?"

"I'm between cars at the moment." She brightened. "Sam's going to take me shopping soon for a new one."

"Well, he won't steer you wrong. You're in good hands, the best of hands, with Samuel Law."

Gillian was pretty sure she'd heard that somewhere before.

"Where are we headed this morning?" Doodles inquired, burying one hand in a frayed denim pocket that looked like it was literally hanging on by a thread.

"A repair shop called Jack-of-All-Trades."

Recognition lit the man's pale blue eyes. "I know where that is. Over on Pine Street. I took Mary Kay there once."

"Mary Kay?"

Doodles took his hand out of his pocket and thumbed in the direction of the Cadillac. "I named the Fleetwood after my wife." He cleared his throat. "Ex-wife now."

Gillian formed a round, silent O with her mouth.

"Anyway, Greg—he's the proprietor of Jack-of-All-Trades—was certainly no expert with cars. He told me he couldn't repair Mary Kay's brakes, so he made the horn louder." Doodles made a disgruntled sound. "Not to worry, though. Before it was all said and done, I had a real mechanic work on her brakes."

That wasn't as reassuring as it should have been. "Well, I'm taking Greg a toaster that burns everything to a crisp."

Doodles nodded; the movement sent his ponytail swinging back and forth. "What do you have to lose, then?"

That's what she'd already concluded. "I'd also like to do a little grocery shopping."

"Kinney's Market is the best in town."

"Kinney's Market it is," she said, that issue settled. "And is there a paint store nearby?"

Doodles stroked his chin thoughtfully. That's when Gillian noticed what appeared to be ink stains under his fingernails. "Oils? Temperas? Watercolors?"

"House."

He snapped his fingers. "What you want is Wal-Mart. There's a brand new store on the south side of town."

That was good to know. "Just let me get my shopping list." Gillian turned and reentered the house.

Grabbing her house keys, her handbag, and the toaster, she said to Max, who was basking in the sunlight streaming in through the kitchen window, "I'm going to Wal-Mart. I'll be back later." She added as an afterthought, "If you behave yourself while I'm gone, I'll reward you with a doggy treat."

The sheepdog rolled over and started to snore.

"Mind if we leave the top down?" Doodles asked as they walked out to his car. He didn't wait for an answer; he went right on to the next question. "Or are you one of those women who's always fussing about her hair getting mussed when she rides in a convertible?"

"No and no," Gillian said with a laugh.

She handed over the toaster and her favorite well-worn Gucci handbag, then reached back, pulled the hair away from her face, wrapped several long strands around the rest, and swept the whole thing up into an impromptu ponytail.

Doodles watched in amazement. "That was slick."

"Years of practice," she said, retrieving her belongings and tucking them under her arm.

"I don't have as much hair as you do," he said with a rueful grin, "but maybe you could show me how to do that sometime."

"I'd be happy to."

Her escort went to open the passenger door for her and hesitated. "Do you prefer to ride in the front or back?"

"The front."

"In that case," he said, helping her into the car, "just toss my sketch pad on the floor."

"I don't mind holding on to it for you." Gillian picked up the artist's sketchbook and settled it on her lap, along with her handbag, her shopping list, and the broken toaster.

She noticed the pages of the sketchbook were filled with detailed pencil drawings, mostly of human features. There was a rendering of the same nose from three different angles: left, right, and center. Eyes of every type and description. Eyebrows. Chins. Cheekbones. Jawlines. Lips. Mouths. Moles. Even smiles and frowns. And a veritable collection of human ears.

Doodles explained his penchant for drawing ears. "I

read somewhere once that ears are as distinctive and as individual as fingerprints. In fact, scientists claim that one day they'll be able to predict who might become a violent criminal by the shape of the earlobe."

There were also drawings of hands. Lots of hands: men's, women's, and children's, opened, closed, gesturing, pointing, waving, holding a drinking glass, even clasping a drawing pencil. She wondered if the hand was a self-portrait.

There was a preliminary sketch of a young man's aquiline profile, and a detailed drawing of an old woman's face, deep furrows etched by time between eyes that looked out from the page with pride and wisdom and serenity.

"What a remarkable face," Gillian said thoughtfully.

Doodles gave her a sidelong glance. "Miss Rogozinski is a remarkable lady."

"Do you mind?" she asked, indicating she was interested in looking beyond the open pages.

"Nope."

Gillian slowly leafed through the sketchbook. "These are really very good."

"Thanks."

"Are you a trained artist?"

"Strictly self-taught. In fact, I call it doodling." A brief, self-conscious smile turned up on the corners of the man's mouth. "Hence, the origin of my nickname."

Gillian was genuinely interested. "And how long have you been doodling?"

"I can't remember a time when I didn't have a pencil in my hand," Doodles told her.

He turned on the ignition, shifted into gear, checked the rearview mirror, and took off down the street while Aretha Franklin was singing something about taking a ride in her pink Cadillac.

That's when Gillian noticed the hula dancer, complete with fake grass skirt, plastic flower *lei,* and the word *Aloha* etched into the "sand" at her feet.

The figurine was anchored to Mary Kay's dashboard with double-sided tape. The paint had mostly chipped off the costume, the face, and the hands. There was a slot on top of the old-fashioned souvenir piggy bank for depositing coins and such.

Doodles's tip jar, Gillian realized.

Each time the Cadillac hit a bump in the road, the hula dancer's hips swayed back and forth.

The repair shop was their last stop on the way back to Sam's house that afternoon.

By then the backseat of Doodles's car was crammed with bags of groceries, including vegetarian and nonvegetarian varieties of dog treats, several rather nice pieces of Roseville pottery Gillian had found at the antique mall, three gallons of "Good Morning, Sunshine" yellow paint, and all the necessary paraphernalia to redo the walls of Sam's kitchen. The people at Wal-Mart had been very helpful.

In the behemoth trunk of the Caddy were four flats of bedding plants: petunias, impatiens, sweet William, and common geraniums in red, white, pale pink, and a vivid fuchsia, along with an assortment of gardening tools, a brimmed sunhat, and a pair of sturdy work gloves. Gillian couldn't recall the last time she'd had so much fun shopping.

Jack-of-All-Trades was located in a double-wide garage behind Greg's house. Gillian approached the entrance with the broken toaster tucked under her arm and stopped to read the sign posted above the doorbell:

WE CAN REPAIR ANYTHING.
(PLEASE KNOCK HARD ON THE DOOR.
THE BELL DOESN'T WORK.)

Gillian knocked hard, heard a gravelly voice shout "Come on in," opened the door, and went inside.

Five minutes later one of the middle-aged women who'd stopped by their table while they were having dinner last night at McGinty's was going into the repair shop as Gillian was coming out.

The woman smiled, hesitated, and then said, "I'm Minerva Bagley. I would have introduced myself last night, but we didn't want to interrupt your dinner."

"I'm Gillian Charles."

"Yes, I know."

Gillian supposed most of the people in town did know by now if Sam was right about news spreading like wildfire in Sweetheart. "Bagley? Are you related to Bert Bagley?"

"He was my uncle." The woman went on to tell her, "He was also an old friend of your grandfather's." Minerva Bagley was one of those pleasant people: pleasant looking, pleasant speaking, pleasant manner, just plain pleasant. "I'm on my way home as soon as I drop this anniversary clock off with Greg." Brown eyes blinked several times in quick succession. "Won't you join me for a cup of tea?"

"Well, Doodles is waiting . . ."

Minerva waved to the man in the pink Cadillac. "Doodles is always waiting. Sometimes I think it's what he does best. He sits in his car. He waits. And he sketches."

"He's quite good."

"Yes, he is. But then good artists are a dime a dozen, aren't they? It's the genius with his singular vision of the world who speaks to our hearts and souls."

Apparently there was more to Minerva Bagley than first met the eye, Gillian thought.

The woman dangled a carrot in front of her. "I have something of your grandfather's that I'd like to give to you."

"Well . . ." She looked back and forth between the woman and Doodles.

"Doodles won't mind. It will only take a few minutes. I live just down the street in that gray house with the white trim."

Gillian took the bait. "In that case, I'd love to have a cup of tea with you, Miss Bagley."

Chapter
twelve

"Witch balls," came the answer before she could inquire about the row of glass spheres dangling by hair-thin wires in the front window of Minerva Bagley's home.

The blue, red, yellow, and amethyst glass balls caught the afternoon sunlight and reflected a rainbow of colors onto the walls and ceiling of the enclosed porch.

Gillian stopped and stared. "How beautiful and how unusual," she said to the woman beside her.

"In the eighteenth century, witch balls were considered more than unusual; people actually believed they were magical."

She was intrigued. "Magical in what way?"

"It was thought the web of glass strands inside the balls would catch and trap evil spells."

"You have so many interesting things," Gillian remarked as they walked into the large Victorian house.

Against the far wall of the living room were a pair of matching curio cabinets. One was filled with porcelain figurines; the other with Venetian glass. Another display case contained dozens of art nouveau silver pieces adorned with the classical female figure of the era with her long, flowing tresses. A fourth cabinet was crammed full of geodes of every size and color.

A quick glance into the adjoining library revealed floor-to-ceiling bookshelves and thousands of volumes—many of them leather-bound—in addition to objects of every type and description.

The formal dining room on the opposite side of the foyer boasted Chippendale buffets overflowing with china: Wedgwood from England, traditional blue and white Chinese porcelain, a gold-rimmed vintage table service, possibly European in origin.

"As you can see, I come from a long line of incurable collectors," her hostess said, chuckling. "In fact, I don't think anyone in my family has ever thrown anything away." Minerva's dark brown eyes twinkled with amusement. "The people of Sweetheart have been calling us pack rats for generations."

There were worse things—far worse things—to be called, thought Gillian.

"It can be a bit overwhelming to keep up with all of this," Minerva admitted. "I can't manage anymore on my own, so Sylvia comes in two days a week to dust."

"Is that the same Sylvia who works for Sam?" And who now worked for her.

The woman nodded; a strand of mousy brown hair streaked with gray sprang free from a hairdo that had been shedding bobby pins as fast as she could stick them back into various parts of her head. The process seemed to be random and of limited success. "I'm Mondays and Wednesdays. Sam is Fridays."

"Who's Tuesdays and Thursdays?"

Minerva tapped the index finger of her right hand against her lower lip in a silent rat-a-tat-tat. "Well, Tuesdays used to be Anna Rogozinski until her arthritis got so bad she had to get someone to come in full-time to cook and clean and look after her. I can't remember who's Thursdays." She gave her hair a reassuring pat, only to send another bobby pin hurling into space. "Maybe Thursday is Sylvia's day off."

Gillian paused beside a model of the human head; it appeared to be fashioned of ivory, and was covered with writing. Next to the head was a similarly inscribed hand. "These are quite old."

"They're English, mid-nineteenth century, which makes them more than one hundred and fifty years old. They were brought back as souvenirs, curiosities really, by my great-great-grandfather, Reginald Bagley, when he took his Grand Tour of the Continent in the 1870s. Victorians loved their curiosities, and of course, that was long before importing ivory into this country was illegal."

Gillian read aloud a sampling of the words etched onto the surface of the hand. "I see 'Jupiter' on the index finger and 'Saturn' on the one beside that and here's 'Mercury' and 'Apollo,' and the phrase 'Mount of Luna' down by the wrist."

"Those are the mounts and lines in the human hand that are analyzed in palmistry."

"I had my palm read once by an old woman who was sitting by the side of a winding country road near the base of the Pyrenees," Gillian recalled.

Minerva made an interested "hm" sound, so she went on with her story.

"The fortune-teller was selling jars of pickles, bottles of homemade wine, and linen handkerchiefs trimmed with intricate lace that she had crocheted herself.

"When I went to pay for the items I'd picked out, the woman took the coins from my hand and dropped them into a small drawstring purse she wore around her neck. Then she tugged my palm closer and began to study it intently. She must have been half-blind because she pulled my hand right up under her nose.

"When I asked what she was doing, she mumbled something in Catalan, which was the only language she spoke. Fortunately I had some Spanish and French, so we managed to communicate." Gillian hadn't thought about the incident or the old woman in some time. "Funny, I can still hear her voice. And I still remember the beautiful lace shawl she had draped around her shoulders."

"Where was this?"

"Andorra. On the border of Spain."

Minerva was paying close attention. "Did the old woman tell you anything of interest?"

Gillian searched her memory. "She said I would enjoy a long and happy life." She allowed her skepticism to show. "Isn't that the standard prediction every fortune-teller hands out?"

Minerva wasn't so quick to agree. "Not necessarily," she said cryptically.

"Well, this one did. She also claimed I would find my true love at an unexpected time and in an unexpected place. And she mentioned six or seven children."

Minerva gave her a speculative glance. "Did you believe the fortune-teller?"

"No." Gillian paused, then reconsidered. "I suppose I wanted to. Not the part about six or seven children. I've always thought two or three kids were the perfect number."

She laughed; it was part amusement and part chagrin. "Trust me, it isn't going to happen, Miss Bagley. I don't even have a dog."

Minerva was optimistic. "There's plenty of time. For children. And a dog. Maybe even a cat or two. You're young. You have your whole life ahead of you."

Personal information kept popping out of Gillian's mouth. "I'll be thirty-two on my next birthday."

"Like I said, you're still young."

She didn't feel young. Not since her grandfather's death. She'd always known she would be on her own one day. That was the reality she'd had to face as an only child being raised by aging grandparents and with no other close relatives. She just hadn't expected, when the time came, to feel quite so alone.

Gillian shook off her melancholy mood. "Before I start on that brood of children, don't I need a Mr. Right?"

"Women seem to be having families all the time now with or without Mr. Right."

"True, but not this woman," said Gillian.

"In that case, Mr. Right may live right next door," Minerva pointed out, apparently trying to be helpful.

Gillian couldn't resist reminding her hostess of the fact that, "Samuel Law lives next door."

A radiant smile transformed the woman's otherwise plain features, making her appear almost pretty for a moment. "Exactly." She abruptly changed the subject, reverting to their earlier conversation. "As I was saying, palm reading and what we now call psychic parlor games were very popular with the Victorians."

Gillian switched gears with her. She examined the antique ivory head. "What's this piece?"

"A phrenology head."

She read off some of the words inscribed on the surface: "'Kindness.' 'Intuition.' 'Patriotism.' 'Spirituality.' 'Intensity.' 'Ingenuity.' 'Desire for liquids.'"

Desire for liquids?

An explanation was offered by the resident expert. "Phrenology was another one of the popular pseudo-sciences. Like palmistry, it was supposed to reveal personality traits, diagnose ailments, and foretell the future, only in this instance by reading the contours—the bumps and hollows, if you will—of the human skull." Inquisitive eyes studied her intently from behind gold-framed bifocals. "Has anyone ever told you that your head has an intriguing shape, Miss Charles?"

"No, I must confess they haven't." She felt it was only polite to add, "Please call me Gillian."

Minerva Bagley made a soft, humming sound in the back of her throat. "It might be interesting, and most revealing, Gillian, to take a reading of your skull."

Somehow she managed to squelch the urge to laugh and carried on with their conversation. "How did you acquire such a large and eclectic collection?"

"Well, like I said, it started with my great-great-grandfather. But it was really my uncle who inspired me to appreciate and care for what he called the 'family jewels.'" She laughed in spite of herself. "Uncle Bert had a wicked sense of humor. Anyway, everyone and everything fascinated him. He had an insatiable curiosity about the world."

"That's a wonderful thing to have."

"He was a wonderful man." Gillian was escorted to the rear of the house and into a big, bright, cheerful kitchen. Her hostess continued talking as she went about the business of making a pot of tea. "Anyone in town will tell you that Bert Bagley was a man ahead of his time."

"I've always thought the same was true of my grandfather," she said. "Perhaps it was one of the reasons they were friends."

"Perhaps. Anyway, long before it became popular, my uncle was fascinated by all things Japanese. He studied the language, the culture, the history, the music and theater traditions. He read about various philosophies and religions. He even built a moon-watching platform in the backyard." Minerva raised her chin. "It's still there."

Gillian glanced out the window. Beside a row of greenhouses, there was a simple deck structure and several comfortable-looking chairs. She made an educated guess. "A moon-watching platform is where you sit and watch the moon."

A precise amount of loose tea was measured into an antique silver tea ball before there was a response. "Exactly."

"Without the distraction of city lights, it must be excellent viewing from here."

"It is."

"I see you also have greenhouses." It was part observation, part question on Gillian's part.

"That's where I grow the herbs I use in my business." The middle-aged woman paused with a silver teaspoon in one hand and a delicate china teacup in the other. "But then you probably don't know anything about my business, do you?"

"No, I don't," she admitted.

Minerva peered over the rim of her spectacles. "I've had a lifelong fascination with herbs. Their history and lore. The way they look; the way they smell. I even love the sound of their names: blessed thistle, eyebright, feverfew, skullcap, slippery elm, bilberry, boneset, butcher's broom, passionflower."

Gillian arched an eyebrow.

"Not the ornamental blue passionflower, naturally. That particular plant contains the poison cyanide." Minerva kept right on chattering while she arranged cookies, small cakes, English scones, and lemon squares on a four-tiered dessert platter. "I'm speaking of genus *Passiflora,* of the family *Passifloraceae,* which is the passionflower commonly used as a sedative. It's also good for headaches, nerves, and insomnia. It even kills mold and fungi."

Gillian managed to keep a straight face during her companion's soliloquy.

Minerva paused for a brief, but well-deserved breath. "Anyway, years ago—frankly, more years than I care to admit to—my uncle gave me a plot of ground in the backyard and I started planting. Today I have a thriving business selling herbal teas, sachets, potpourri, and restorative elixirs. I offer my products at a handful of outlets here in town, but I primarily market them through a mail-order business. I work with a talented PR specialist named Sara. I even have a website and a brilliant webmaster. Her name is Cissy, so I suppose that makes her officially a webmistress."

"What do you call your business?"

"Water from the Moon."

"Water from the Moon," Gillian repeated thoughtfully.

"It's a traditional Japanese saying: It means something one can never have."

"Was the name suggested by your uncle?"

Minerva nodded as she poked her head into a cupboard well below eye level. By some miracle, no more bobby pins were dislodged in the process, and she emerged victorious with a matching cream and sugar service in hand. "Uncle Bert told me he'd first heard the expression from a friend of his during the Second World War." She paused for emphasis. "That friend was Jacob Charles."

Gillian went dead still. For a moment the only sound in the kitchen was the teakettle whistling on the stove. "My grandfather?" she said, her tone conveying her surprise.

"Yes." Minerva was caught up in a flurry of activity for the next few minutes. "I've made red raspberry tea for us this afternoon. I hope that suits you."

"It does."

"Red raspberry is particularly good as a female tonic. It strengthens the uterine walls, prevents spotting, increases milk production after childbirth, and helps alleviate canker sores."

There were times, Gillian thought, when you could know too much about a good thing.

How much to tell her?

Where even to begin?

"Let's take our tea into the library," Minerva suggested when her guest offered to carry the tray. "That's where my uncle stored his special keepsakes, including the one I want to give to you."

"I like this room," the younger woman said.

Minerva settled into a comfortable chair, took a sip of tea, and sighed with contentment. "So do I. In fact, this is my favorite room in the house. I can still remember how proud I was when Uncle Bert gave me permission to sit here in the library with him for the first time and read." It was one of her fondest childhood memories. "The book was *Little Women.* I was eight years old."

"I felt the same way when my grandfather finally allowed me in his study."

"How old were you?"

"Ten. Nearly eleven." Gillian Charles took a drink of red raspberry tea. "This is delicious. Not at all sweet as one might expect raspberries to be. In fact, it's surprisingly tangy." She took another sip. "I like it very much, Ms. Bagley."

Minerva was pleased. "Thank you."

The young woman put the teacup down on the table between them, stared off into space for a brief time, and then turned to her. "When did my grandfather meet your uncle?"

Minerva knew the story by heart. "It was in 1942 when Jacob was bivouacked at a nearby army base."

Gillian nodded in confirmation. "I knew my grandfather had been stationed somewhere in the Midwest during his initial training as an infantry officer."

"There used to be a huge military complex about thirty miles from Sweetheart. It was closed down by the government decades ago." Minerva chose her words with care. "During the war, my uncle considered it his patriotic duty to invite a soldier home for Sunday dinner or for the weekend if the GI's leave was the usual twenty-four or forty-eight hours. For most soldiers that meant there wasn't enough time to travel to see their own families."

"So your uncle invited them here to share his family."

"Yes, my aunt and uncle, my parents, my cousins; in fact, the entire Bagley clan at the time. Eventually the idea caught on with the whole town."

"That was a kind thing to do."

"Those were kinder times, I've been told. From the way my uncle talked about it later, he realized those men were destined to face dangers he would never know." Minerva added in an aside, "Uncle Bert was 4F due to poor eyesight. He'd been turned down by every branch of the military on all three occasions when he'd tried to enlist. So, welcoming strangers into this house was his way of saying thank-you to those who could serve their country in uniform."

"I wish I'd asked my grandfather more about the war," Gillian said with regret. "He didn't talk about it."

"A lot of the men from that era didn't." Then Minerva casually mentioned, "I take it, your grandfather didn't say much about Sweetheart, either."

Gillian shook her head.

"Well, Sweetheart always remembered Jacob Charles. And I don't mean because of his later wheeling and dealing in local real estate." She took a sip of tea. "You know, you still might be able to find a few old-timers who knew him way back when."

The young woman's face lit up from the inside out. "I'd love to talk with them."

"Well, I expect now that you're settled in Sweetheart for a while, you'll get to meet a lot of its residents."

"I expect I will."

After consuming another cup of red raspberry tea and a cake or two, Minerva reached across and patted the perfectly manicured hand. "My dear, I'm so happy you came today. But it's time I got those things for you before Doodles becomes restless."

"Ohmigosh, I forgot all about Doodles," her visitor confessed, blushing a shade of pink that rivaled Mary Kay's paint job.

"Don't worry. We'll placate him with cookies and cakes. Doodles never could resist my baking." Minerva went straight to the desk drawer where she'd stowed the items. "First, I thought you might like to have this snapshot of Jacob."

"Thank you." Gillian took the vintage black-and-white photograph from her and studied it for a minute or two in silence. "He looks awfully young," she said at last, her tone pensive.

"He was."

She exhaled deeply. "I wonder how old he was."

Minerva summoned up the details she had garnered over the years from conversations with her uncle. "Nearly a decade younger than you are now."

Her guest went quite pale again. "So young."

Minerva felt her own expression soften like warm taffy. "They were all young in those days," she said, "with young men's dreams and young men's passions."

It didn't take long for Jacob's granddaughter to ask the question she'd been anticipating. "Who are the other two people in the photograph with my grandfather?"

Minerva leaned forward and made a production of examining the trio of smiling faces. "The man is my uncle Bert and the young woman standing between them is Anna Rogozinski."

A frown formed on the delicate features. "You mentioned her name earlier."

There was a short silence. "Yes. Sylvia used to clean house for Anna."

"Doodles was talking about Miss Rogozinski just this morning. I saw a sketch he'd made of her. Even as an older woman, she has an extraordinary quality and a beauty about her."

"Anna was always beautiful. Beautiful and talented." Minerva paused meaningfully.

"Are you speaking of Anna Rogozinski, the pianist?" Gillian asked.

"Yes. Of course, she's past eighty now."

Gillian contemplated that briefly. "Perhaps she's one of the people I can ask about my grandfather."

"They knew each other," was all she said. Then, taking out the presentation case, Minerva handed it over with reverence. "This was my uncle's most prized possession."

Gillian opened the box. "What is it?"

"Your grandfather's Distinguished Service Cross."

Eyes the color of a roiling, turbulent sea stared at her. "I don't understand."

Minerva Bagley was taken aback. "You did know that Jacob was highly decorated several times over for his courageous actions during the Battle of the Bulge?"

Gillian slowly shook her head from side to side. "He didn't like to talk about the war."

Minerva stated it plain and clear. "It was Christmas of 1944. Your grandfather singlehandedly saved the lives of more than a dozen of his men by leading them to safety through the fog and snow and enemy lines of the Ardennes forest."

At some point her guest started to breathe again. "He was a war hero."

"Yes."

She paused. "Do you mind if I ask why he decided to give his medal to your uncle?"

Minerva blinked several times and recalled her facts. "Apparently Jacob told Bert it was because they were friends and because he was so grateful to him for all he'd done. He said that my uncle had distinguished himself in service to his country as surely as any soldier decorated for valor on the battlefield."

" 'They also serve who only stand and wait,' " her visitor said in a very soft but firm voice.

"In a manner of speaking. Anyway, I believe Jacob would want you to have this now. And Uncle Bert would, too."

"Thank you." The young woman closed the case and pressed it to her breast, just above her heart.

A few minutes later Minerva walked her visitor to the front door. "The plastic container is filled with cookies and cakes for Doodles. Tell him it's his reward for being so patient," she said. "And I put some of my special chamomile tea blend in a small bag for you. It works wonders if you ever find yourself wide awake in the middle of the night." Discretion and good manners prevented her from mentioning the dark circles under Gillian's eyes. "One day you'll have to stop by and I'll take you on a tour of the greenhouses and the lab where I mix my potions, as the townspeople call them."

"I'd like that very much."

"One last thing," she called out as the slender blonde reached the sidewalk.

Gillian paused. "Yes?"

She tried to keep her own voice light. "It was Jacob's favorite saying."

"What was?"

"Water from the moon."

The young woman stood there with a slightly disconcerted expression on her face.

Minerva felt compelled to explain. "Jacob once told my uncle that the real battle in life was learning to accept that there were some things you could never have."

"He was right," said Gillian as she turned and walked toward the pink Cadillac parked at the curb.

Chapter
thirteen

He needed three hands.

Sam grabbed his briefcase, the bouquet of Shasta daisies, and the bottle of red wine; the clerk at the local liquor store had assured him that the Oregon Pinot was as close to vintage burgundy as Sam was going to find in Sweetheart.

He stared down at the oversize cardboard box still on the passenger seat beside him. It contained one extra-large Papa Tony's Pizzeria triple pepperoni pizza.

Well, half triple pepperoni, half plain cheese; he wasn't taking any chances.

"Okay, let's try this again."

He'd been talking to himself a lot more in the past twenty-four hours, Sam noticed. Ever since Max had deserted him for a pair of soft feminine hands, a soft feminine voice, and soft blue-green eyes that seemed to change color along with the lady's mood.

In a town where the walls had ears, where privacy was scarce and gossip was the local hobby, he realized belatedly that the Belgian sheepdog was his confidant.

Max never repeated confidential or sensitive information about a client. Max never contradicted Sam's opinion about how to handle a case. He never criticized his arguments before the judge. He never found fault with him and he was never indiscreet.

Max was trustworthy. Max was loyal. He was the perfect listener and the perfect companion.

At least he had been until *she* came along.

"It's your own fault, Law."

Well, technically it wasn't anybody's fault. Common sense had dictated that Max was better off at home and that Gillian needed a watchdog more than he did.

Of course, she'd probably ruin Max forever, spoil him rotten, lavish him with affection and attention, allow him to sleep in her bed every night, take him for long walks, buy him special treats, and feed him Hilda's homemade apple pie when Sam wasn't looking. It was a dog's life.

"Crying shame," he muttered.

Sam tried again, this time juggling his briefcase, the flowers, the wine, *and* the pizza. He still came up one hand short; he'd forgotten his car keys were in the ignition.

To hell with it! If anyone happened by and wanted to steal a five-year-old, one-hundred-thousand-plus-miles-on-the-odometer Ford Explorer that leaked oil, needed the front brakes realigned, and the engine overhauled, let them. They'd be doing him a favor.

Once he managed to get everything, including himself, outside the vehicle, Sam wrestled with the urge to kick the door on the driver's side shut behind him. He used his elbow instead, giving it a good nudge. He was pretty sure that meant dried mud was now streaked across the sleeve of his navy blue suit.

Curtains fluttered on an upstairs window a couple of houses down the road. Across the alley at 33 East Street, there was a man watering the petunias in his garden. Two women were chatting over their common side yard fence, coffee cups in hand. A gang of boys on bicycles—Sam recognized most of them: the Murphy twins, Molly Drake's kid, the Bigelow boy—were congregated at the corner where his street intersected with Main.

Sam had always had excellent peripheral vision. It had helped make him a star quarterback in high school and had earned him a four-year athletic scholarship to Purdue. Maybe that's why the glint of sunlight reflecting off the lenses of Goldie's binoculars caught his eye. He would've waved to her, but he was already a hand short.

It took several attempts to get through the front gate. The door of his house was standing wide open, but the screen door was hooked. Sam knew because once he managed to get the crook of his little finger wrapped around the handle and tugged, nothing happened.

He took a step back, managed to keep his balance, and called out, "Gillian."

She appeared almost instantaneously as if she'd been expecting him, or maybe even listening for the sound of his footfall on the porch steps. "Ohmigosh, Sam." She unlatched the screen door and opened it for him. "What should I take?"

"Pizza."

She relieved him of the pizza, and he followed her through the house into the kitchen, dodging paint cans, decorating paraphernalia, sacks, boxes, and Max scampering back and forth between the two of them as if he couldn't quite decide which one was his very favorite human being in the whole wide world.

Sam set the bottle of wine on the table beside the Papa Tony's Pizzeria pizza, dispensed with his briefcase—business could come after food; he was famished—and held the flowers out to Gillian.

"Shasta daisies." She broke into a smile that was a little bit shy and very attractive.

Then she dug around under the kitchen sink and came up with a vase he'd never seen before. With a minimum of fuss, she filled the clear glass container with tap water, added the simple flowers with their distinctive bright yellow centers, and set them in the middle of the table. Sam had to admit they looked perfect.

"How did you know that shade of yellow is my favorite color?" she asked.

"I figured it might be since you bought three gallons of yellow paint to redo my kitchen and laundry room."

"How in the world . . . ?" Gillian laughed that laugh of hers that made him want to smile. She planted her hands on slim hips. "Have you been talking to Doodles?"

"Nope."

She reached out and brushed at his sleeve. "Dried mud," she said by way of an explanation.

He'd suspected as much. "The Explorer's pretty well covered with the stuff." He was holding off getting his SUV cleaned until Saturday; that was when the local Boy Scouts were washing cars to raise money for a new troop hut. He thought to add, "Thanks."

"You're welcome." Apparently her curiosity wasn't satisfied. "So how did you find out I'd bought yellow paint for the kitchen?"

"Margie."

Her bafflement was clearly evident in the expression that skittered across her face. "Margie?"

Sam took off his suit jacket and tossed it over the back of a chair. Then he started in on his tie. "Margaret—aka Margie—Hoyt is one of the clerks recently hired at Wal-Mart. Her mother works at the bank next door to the Bagley Building."

"I see."

He ticked off her activities one by one on his fingertips. "You also went shopping at the antique mall this afternoon. You purchased a wheelbarrow load of flowers at the nursery. You had tea with Minerva Bagley. Three very large trunks arrived from New York with your name plastered on them. And you tipped Doodles a hundred bucks for driving you around town today."

A hint of color slowly crept up her neck and onto her cheeks. "I didn't know what the going rate was. And Doodles was so patient with me." A small but distinct crease formed between her eyes. "I'm surprised he told you, though."

"He didn't." Sam figured she may as well learn how it worked in Sweetheart. "You don't see a lot of one-hundred-dollar bills in a small town. In fact, a lot of businesses won't accept anything larger than a twenty."

"I didn't know."

"No reason you should. But Doodles took the hundred you gave him to the bank for change." He leaned back against the counter, rolled the sleeves of his dress shirt up to his elbows, and tugged on his tie until he was finally free of the thing. "People simply put two and two together and came up with four." He pitched his tie onto the same kitchen chair as his jacket. Then he shrugged and casually crossed his arms. "Or in this case, a hundred."

"Quite the detective, aren't you?"

Sam shook his head. "Like I warned you last night, Gillian. You're news."

"That makes you news as well, I'm afraid. You do realize people are under the impression that you and I are—"

"An item?" he said, deadpan.

She bit her bottom lip and nodded. "That's a rather nice way of putting it."

It sure sounded classier than saying they were screwing each other's brains out. He'd overheard that crude remark from a couple of teenage punks hanging out at the corner gas station. He had made it his business to set them straight, but in his gut Sam knew nothing was going to stop the talk. "Does the gossip bother you?"

She had to think about it for a minute. "I suppose not. It's convenient."

He wasn't altogether certain he liked being described as a convenience. "In what way?"

"I don't have to skirt around the issue of why I'm staying in town for an extended visit," she said without inflection. "Everyone just assumes it's because of you."

"And when you eventually leave and return to New York?" There was no doubt in Sam's mind that Ms. Charles would skedaddle the minute her six-month sentence was up.

"They'll think it didn't work out for us. Again." She reached down and scratched the top of Max's head as if it were the most natural thing in the world for her to do.

"You've got it all figured out, haven't you?"

Gillian laughed, but this time she didn't sound in the least bit amused. "Far from it." Her stomach growled several times, loud enough for both of them to hear. She pressed a hand to her midsection; her skin was pale, almost ghostly white against the black silk of her T-shirt. "I'll function better once I've had something to eat. How about dinner?"

"Took the words right out of my mouth," he said.

* * *

Why did this feel more like a date than a business meeting
between attorney and client?

Maybe it was the bottle of wine. Or maybe it was the
unexpected bouquet of flowers. Sam was right. She loved
anything yellow, especially flowers, especially a simple
arrangement like daisies wrapped in damp tissue paper, especially *not* the predictable long-stemmed roses sent to her
in the past in expensive Baccarat crystal vases, usually several dozen or more stems at a time.

Maybe it was the fact that it was seven o'clock on a
summerlike evening, and the sun was an iridescent orange
ball hanging miraculously on the horizon.

Maybe it was because they were standing in his house,
in his kitchen, with his personal belongings all around
them, and his bed—the beautiful antique mahogany sleigh
bed handed down from his grandparents—right upstairs in
his bedroom.

Maybe it was the suit jacket and tie nonchalantly tossed
over the back of a kitchen chair. Or perhaps it was the funny
kind of way the bungalow had gotten both larger and smaller
since the moment he'd walked through the front door.

Or maybe it was the man.

Don't think of him as a man, Gillian.

How was she supposed to think of Sam, then?

*Don't think of him at all. If you do, you'll live to regret
it. You knew he was trouble the minute you laid eyes on
him. You'll be sorry if you forget that even for one second.*

Every instinct she possessed warned Gillian that a
woman could fall in love with Samuel Law, have her heart
irreparably broken into little pieces, and he might not even
be aware of it.

She distracted herself by opening the cupboard doors

overhead and taking down two dinner plates and two salad bowls. Silverware was in the drawer next to the tea towels, which were right next to the sink. Napkins were kept in a wooden holder on the counter beside the toaster; that was before the small kitchen appliance had gone haywire this morning and turned her toast to cinders.

She opened the refrigerator and reached for the bag of romaine lettuce she'd already washed and dried. "I hope you like Caesar salad," she said with forced cheerfulness.

"I do."

She made herself very busy finishing up the salad. "I wish I'd had the time and the ingredients to make my homemade pizza."

Sam pushed away from the kitchen counter and went in search of wineglasses. "You mean you really can cook."

She made a sound in the back of her throat. "Don't tell me you've heard rumors otherwise."

Sam rooted around in a utensil drawer and came up with a corkscrew. "The subject of cooking didn't enter into any of my conversations today," he said with an air of innocence. "Well, except for the one I had with the kid working behind the counter at Papa Tony's."

"Anchovies on your salad?"

"Sure. Why not?"

She moistened her lips before asking, "What did the kid behind the counter say?"

"He wondered who I was 'cooking' for tonight." Sam tacked on, "It was meant as a joke."

Gillian held up a fresh clove. "Garlic?" If he was indulging; so was she.

"Garlic is an absolute must in a Caesar salad," said Sam.

With one good whack of a kitchen knife, she flattened the clove of garlic, then reached for the bottle of extra virgin olive oil. "Why would the kid ask you that?"

"I usually get a large pan-style pizza with extra pepperoni and cheese."

"What did you order tonight?"

"Extra-large."

She glanced over her shoulder at the pizza box he was popping into the oven to briefly reheat its contents. "Extra-large?" She snickered. "It's huge."

Sam made a movement with his head that was something akin to a nod. "Don't tell me size doesn't count." He gave an exaggerated sigh and uncorked the bottle of red wine. "With women it's always about size, isn't it?"

Gillian couldn't tell if he was teasing her or not, so she remained as straight-faced as he was. "The salad is ready," she announced several minutes later as she finished tossing the romaine with her special salad dressing. She grated fresh Parmesan on the top.

"The wine is poured." He opened the oven. "And the pizza is piping hot."

It was also delicious.

"My compliments to Papa Tony," said Gillian, surprising herself by devouring three pieces instead of her usual one. "So far the food I've had in Sweetheart has been amazingly good."

"What we do, we do well," Sam said, sitting back and taking a sip of his wine.

She wasn't going anywhere near that one. "I almost forgot." Gillian put her glass down and reached for the small pile of mail on the kitchen counter behind her. "You got a postcard today." She handed it over. "I didn't read it."

"It wouldn't have mattered if you had. I'm sure everyone else in town has." He held the picture postcard at eye level and read the printed message across the front. " 'Greetings from Cheyenne, Wyoming: Where the Old West comes alive during our annual Frontier Days.' " Sam felt an explanation was called for. "It's from my parents."

"The ones who are—"

"Gallivanting around the country," he said, finishing the sentence for her.

"How long have they been gone?"

He tapped the edge of the postcard against the tabletop. "Let's see. They took off the first week of January."

"When are you expecting them back?"

"Thanksgiving." He was noncommittal. "Maybe."

"Are they having fun?"

"The time of their lives." The prospect brought a smile to Sam's face, and in the space of a heartbeat he went from plain-old-ordinary handsome to steal-your-breath-away gorgeous.

Gillian filled her lungs with air and slowly exhaled. "What about your siblings?"

"Scattered to the four winds." He slipped the postcard into the breast pocket of his shirt. "Allie and her family live in Chicago. Serena's out West. California. Eric works for a big-time law firm in Boston." The mention of his younger brother brought a frown to Sam's face.

"What?" said Gillian, before she could think better of it.

"Eric's marriage is on the rocks. Hell, it's out to sea. The divorce was final this past fall."

The subject of family was often like a land mine. Gillian tiptoed. "How long was he married?"

"Less than two years."

"I'm sorry."

Sam blew out his breath. "So am I. We all are." He stared down into the glass of deep red wine for a moment, then glanced up and inquired, "What about you?"

"Me?"

"Your family?"

"All gone." She fingered the stem of her wineglass and avoided his eyes. Her voice was a little softer when she said, "My grandfather was the last."

Sam sat there quietly, without moving and yet without making her feel in the least self-conscious. She didn't get the impression that the usual questions concerning her family and its tragic history were on the tip of his tongue.

"My parents were killed in a car accident when I was eleven. My mother was pregnant at the time." There. She'd said it. She'd told him what he hadn't asked her.

Sam reached across the table and placed his hand lightly on hers. His touch was warm, personal, yet impersonal. He managed to convey compassion, even understanding, without the pity that usually followed that news.

She went on. "My father was an only child. Losing him broke my grandparents' hearts."

Sam's voice was soft but firm. "Your grandparents were saved by having you in their lives."

"And I was saved by having them." She wasn't uncomfortable confiding in Sam. In fact, just the opposite was true. "In the beginning we were stunned. Shocked. Unbearably sad. There were a lot of tears shed." She reminded herself to breathe. "Then we seemed to take turns being very angry." She didn't think she'd ever feel that angry again. She had been angry with her parents, with the driver of the other car, with anyone and everyone who was still alive, even with God. Gillian took a sip of her wine and held it in her mouth for a moment before she said, "Somehow we survived and eventually I think we learned to make peace with what we couldn't change. And the three of us did it together: my grandparents and me."

"That's what family does," Sam said quietly. "They

celebrate the good times together and somehow they help each other through the tough times."

"Together," she echoed. It was a little time before she said, without looking at him, "You're a good listener."

"A lawyer has to be."

"I know plenty of lawyers who aren't."

"A *good* lawyer, then."

"And you are a good lawyer, aren't you?"

"Yes, I am."

She nearly blurted out, *"You're a good man, too, Samuel Law,"* but thought it might sound patronizing or embarrass him; although something told her that little could embarrass the man at this point in his life. He seemed so unruffled by it all.

She looked up from her glass of Pinot Noir. "This wine is like a truth serum."

" *'In vino veritas.'* "

" 'There is truth in wine,' " translated Gillian. "Although I'm not sure I agree."

Sam went on to recite: " 'Wine comes in at the mouth, and love comes in at the eye; that's all we know for truth before we grow old and die.' "

"Now that sounds like an old drinking song."

There was a nod. "It's also Yeats."

"Do you know any more words of wisdom on the subject?" she inquired, not altogether serious.

" 'Wine is a peep-hole on a man.' "

That brought a raised eyebrow. "Who in the world said that?"

"Alcaeus. Around 500 B.C." Sam gave it another go. " 'What is man, but an ingenious machine for turning wine into urine?' " He cleared his throat. "In the immortal words of Isak Dinesen." Then he made a sound under his breath that was half-chuckle, half-laugh. "Just a few of the many and relatively useless things I learned in Mrs. Longerboner's eleventh grade English class."

Gillian kept a straight face. "Mrs. Longerboner?"

He tipped his chair back precariously. "Mrs. Dick Longerboner, née Alice Adcock."

"Oh, dear." Gillian had to cover her mouth. She was finally able to swallow. "Poor Alice."

"Yes," Sam agreed, moving his head up and down. "It was from the frying pan into the fire for Alice."

They sat there in his ridiculous pink kitchen laughing—Gillian realized it felt so damned good to laugh—and talking and sipping the last of their wine.

Small, familiar noises could be heard in the background: boys calling to one another as they pedaled by on their bicycles; the sound of a small motor running, a door slamming shut somewhere nearby, a dog barking in the distance.

Then they heard a car—it could have been an SUV or a pickup—coming slowly down the street. There was a distinct thud as something hit the front of the house, then the sound of an engine being gunned and tires screeching as it took off again.

Max was suddenly on alert and barking.

"I wonder what that was," Gillian said, pushing back from the kitchen table.

Sam held up his hand. "I'll take a look. Why don't you stay here and keep Max calm?"

Chapter

fourteen

"Damn," Sam swore under his breath. He'd moved pretty fast—it was those old quarterback instincts; they had never completely deserted him—but the speeding car had been faster. By the time he'd reached the front door, sprinted across the porch, and peered down the street, there was no one in sight. He was left without so much as a license plate number, color of the vehicle, or make.

He looked around for witnesses. As far as he could tell, there weren't any. In a town where everybody made it their business to know everybody else's business, it was ironic that not a single person on his street was around when he needed them to be.

It was a strange take on Murphy's Law. Sam was convinced that God had not only an appreciation for irony, but a slightly warped sense of humor, as well.

So, what had made the heavy thud as it had hit the front of the house?

He began a systematic search. The results turned up in the darkest corner of the porch, where the overhead light cast only a faint glow. It was an old-fashioned gunnysack, coarse, brown, mud-splattered, the top tied shut with a piece of twine. The sack was weighted with a rock—no doubt to give it the necessary heft to reach the front porch from the street, a distance of maybe thirty-five feet.

Sam carried the sack to the light, untied the cord, and peered inside. Then he dumped the contents onto the porch floor.

It was a bird.

A dead bird.

A very large, very dead black crow. Actually, it was huge even by crow standards, measuring at least two and a half feet in length. It was the common American variety, *Corvus brachyrhynchos,* cousin to the raven and the jays, and was part of the family *Corvidae,* in the order of *Passeriformes* (another of those relatively useless things he'd learned from Mrs. Longerboner, who had been—she still was, for that matter—president of the local Audubon Society).

He had seen hundreds, even thousands, of crows congregate on farms and in open fields. Those birds, of course, had been very much alive. This one had taken a bullet straight through the heart. Whoever had done the shooting was lethal with a small-caliber rifle.

Sam rocked back on his heels.

Was tossing a dead bird onto his porch meant as a stupid practical joke? He'd always thought practical jokes weren't practical or a joke. They were, however, definitely stupid.

Maybe it was supposed to be a prank. The kind some

punk might play. Punks like the two mouthy teenagers he'd encountered at the gas station this afternoon.

Was someone trying to send a less than subtle message to Gillian: letting her know that she was definitely out of her element and should hightail it back where she came from? If so, this was the second message in as many days.

He was well aware that there were already three strikes, maybe more, against Sweetheart's newest resident. She was a stranger. She was city folk. She was beautiful, rich, *and* thin. And she'd inherited most the town. Bad feelings could result from any of those.

In his day Jacob wouldn't have won any popularity contests, either. Not once he'd started buying up properties left and right. In the process he'd saved a lot of people's businesses, or at least their jobs, and sometimes their butts, but that tended to be overlooked.

On the other hand, Sam supposed the dead bird could be intended for him. Crows weren't picky eaters. In fact, they were scavengers that pretty much devoured everything in their path: other birds, insects, small reptiles, road kill, carrion, even crops. Especially crops. Farmers considered them pests at best and frequently shot the birds to save their fields from destruction.

Some people in Sweetheart had a similarly low opinion of lawyers. They regarded anyone in the legal profession as an ambulance chaser and a bottom feeder. And he'd had his share of disgruntled clients—no attorney could avoid them altogether—including the so-called Sheila, Max's former owner.

Then there were the rejects; those prospective clients he had declined to represent for any number of reasons. He didn't do divorces since the infamous case involving Max. Divorces were a no-win situation in his opinion. He refused to defend criminal cases since the Dunbar incident.

And he always trusted his instincts. Some people, his gut told him, were simply bad news from the get-go.

"Find anything?"

Sam turned and looked over his shoulder. Gillian was standing in the doorway with Max at her side. Her hand was resting lightly on the top of the sheepdog's head. She appeared perfectly calm. So did Max. "It's a bird."

"What kind of bird?"

"Common crow."

"That's the same as a raven, right?"

He shrugged. "More or less. It's the same family on the evolutionary tree."

With an unexpected and decided flair for the dramatic, Gillian flung out one hand and began to recite. " 'Take thy beak from out my heart, and take thy form from off my door!" She dropped her voice. " 'Quoth the Raven: "Nevermore." ' "

"Edgar Allan Poe."

"I had to memorize Poe's 'The Raven' for Miss Spade's fourth grade literature class."

"*Fourth* grade literature class?"

"I'm sure it sounded better than 'fourth grade reading class' to parents who were paying twenty thousand plus in annual tuition," she explained.

Sam grinned. " 'There comes Poe with his raven; like Barnaby Rudge, three fifths of him genius and two fifths sheer fudge.' James Russell Lowell. Plain old public school education, Sweetheart, Indiana–style."

She laughed. "I should have known."

"What?"

"You could go one better." Gillian craned her neck. "Is the crow hurt?"

"It's dead."

"Are you sure?"

"Yes."

"Did you check for a pulse?"

No, as a matter of fact, he hadn't.

Since he didn't want to alarm her unnecessarily, Sam decided to fudge a little on his answer. "Its neck is broken, Gillian."

"Poor thing." Max started licking her hand. "I wonder what happened."

He continued with the story he'd fabricated on the spot. "It must have flown into a window. Birds sometimes see their own reflection and mistake it for another bird."

"It didn't sound like a bird hitting a window." She bit her bottom lip; it all but disappeared. "Besides, wouldn't that usually occur during the daylight?"

Sam hadn't expected her to figure that out. "Every now and then it'll happen at twilight."

"It's not twilight," she said, peering out through the screen door. "It's nearly ten o'clock."

He looked around. It *was* dark. Where had the evening gone? "Time sure flies when you're having fun."

"Yes, it does," she said, agreeing with him. "What are you going to do now?"

"About what?"

"The bird."

Sam kept his body between Gillian and the gunny-sack, not to mention the crow with the bullet hole clean through its heart. "I'll give it a decent burial in the pet cemetery behind my parents' house."

"Pet cemetery." A funny look flitted across her face. "This doesn't have anything to do with Stephen King, does it?"

Sam chuckled and sought to reassure her. "No. Nothing to do with Stephen King. We've been burying family pets in the orchard for the past thirty years."

"Since you were a little boy?"

He nodded. "In fact, the first funeral was held in honor of Rocky's passing."

"Who was Rocky?"

"My pet turtle."

"Did you name him Rocky because of the movie?"

He shook his head. "It was because he spent all of his time sitting on the rock I'd put in his bowl of water."

It took her an instant to laugh. "I suppose there's a certain logic to that. How old were you when Rocky died?"

"Five going on six. Then after Rocky, we buried Petunia the parakeet."

"Don't tell me . . ."

"Nah, the name was Allie's idea. It was in some book my mother was reading to the twins at the time. Next was Moofie the Persian cat, followed by Buster the bulldog." There was no reason to list the entire roster of beloved family pets that had their final resting place in the orchard. She got the idea.

"So, that's where you'll bury the bird?"

"First thing in the morning."

Gillian seemed relieved. "Thank you, Sam."

"For what?"

"For not telling me you were going to do something like simply throw the crow in the trash." She heaved a sigh. "We're such a throwaway society."

Sam wasn't about to burst her bubble by telling her that putting a dead bird or any carcass in the garbage was a good way to attract scavengers and other unwanted creatures that came out at night.

He planned on digging a deep hole and then, before all was said and done, placing a good-size boulder on top of the grave. That way no animal could come along later and dig the crow up. He didn't want to see the expression on

Gillian's face if Max committed the ultimate faux pas: dropping a putrefying bird at her feet.

After Gillian had turned around, Sam carefully deposited the dead bird back into the gunnysack and retied the cord tightly. He hung it over the porch post. He'd pick it up on his way out.

"It's getting late. I guess we'd better take care of business," Sam said as he walked back into the house.

First, he thoroughly washed his hands with disinfectant soap. It wasn't wise to take chances with the carcass of a dead bird or any dead animal, for that matter. It could be carrying almost anything from parasites to West Nile virus.

He finally opened his briefcase and took out several booklets and forms. "I stopped by the BMV today." He kept his attention on his hands, then looked up at her. "That's the Bureau of Motor Vehicles. Are you still interested in getting your driver's license?"

"Absolutely."

"Do you mind if I ask why you haven't before?"

"I don't mind." Gillian crossed her arms in front of her. "When I was in high school and everyone else was getting their driver's license, my grandfather specifically asked me not to. He said he and my grandmother would worry themselves sick every time I got behind the wheel of a car." She hugged herself. "Considering what happened to my parents, I didn't see how I could refuse."

"So you made a promise."

"So I made a promise."

"And you kept it."

"Of course. But my grandparents are both gone now and circumstances have changed. Fortunately, I've spent most of my adult life living or traveling in cities where *not* driving wasn't a huge problem. But I can see why everyone does here. It's the only way to get anywhere. No taxis. No buses. No trains."

"No subways," he contributed, not altogether serious.

Gillian chuckled. "No subways." She unfolded her arms and reached for the booklets and forms. *"Know Your Road Signs,"* she read aloud. Then she glanced at the next one. *"Everything You Need to Know to Apply for a Learner's Permit in the State of Indiana."* She glanced up at him. "Catchy titles."

"Once you've thoroughly studied every fact and figure, you'll take a written test. If you pass—"

She interrupted him. "When I pass."

"I stand corrected. When you pass, you'll have your permit and we'll start driving lessons."

"Thank you, Sam."

"You're welcome." He took out a manila folder. "I've got some papers for you to take a look at, too."

"An heiress's work is never done," she said, unable to resist teasing him just a little.

It was some time later that he asked, "Any questions?"

"As a matter of fact, yes." Gillian gave herself a moment to think. It had been niggling at her since she'd arrived in Sweetheart. "How do I give this town back?"

The question caught Sam off guard. He frowned. "I'm afraid I don't understand."

"I don't want it."

"Sweetheart?"

She nodded. "Whatever local businesses or properties I own. I don't want them."

Sam drew a deep breath and straightened his shoulders. "Jacob made provision for that. You can do whatever you like, but not until your six months are up."

She propped her elbows on the table and dropped her

face into her hands. It was a minute or two before she looked up. "Why would my grandfather write that into a trust?"

"Maybe he figured you'd make better and wiser decisions after you'd gotten to know us."

She dropped her hands to her side. "Apparently he did want me to get to know you."

"Looks that way."

She blew out her breath. "I found out today from Minerva Bagley that my grandfather spent some time here while he was training to become an infantry officer."

"Nobody knows more about this town and its history than Minerva. Probably because nobody knew more about Sweetheart in his day than Bert Bagley."

"Bert and my grandfather were old friends," she said. "No doubt you were aware of the connection."

"Old friends. Lawyer and client."

"Bert was Grandpa's lawyer?"

Sam told her what he knew. "He handled local stuff only, of course. He'd done it for years. When she was cleaning out his office, Minerva found references to Jacob dating back to the early 1940s."

"I wish I could have talked to Bert Bagley."

"Bert was an exceptional man. Clear logical mind, yet a creative thinker. A brilliant lawyer with a big heart. A rare combination."

"You admired him."

"Most people did."

"Minerva mentioned there might be other older residents besides her uncle who would remember my grandfather."

Sam stuffed the legal papers back in his briefcase. "I can think of two or three off the top of my head."

"Anna Rogozinski?"

"She's one of the people I had in mind. Then there's Charlie Bushyhead. He's the local barber. Charlie's nearly ninety, but he still goes into his shop every day of the week except Sunday. And Walter P. You'll see him around town with a petition in his hand. He's lobbying against painting the water tower."

"Why?"

Sam sighed. "Somebody got the notion to paint a smiley face—the huge yellow twenty-five-foot kind—on the town water tower. Walter P. is a purist. He wants it to stay nondescript gray."

"I love the color yellow, as you know, but in this instance I may have to agree with Walter P."

Sam snapped his briefcase shut. "He'll be thrilled to hear that. Probably want you to sign his petition. You'll have a chance to meet them the weekend after next."

"What's the weekend after next?"

"Big May Dance. Held every year on the last Saturday of the month. It's a tradition for everyone in town to attend."

"Everyone?"

He moved his head. "It's held in the park by the bandstand. They'll start putting down the dance floor, hanging the lights, and assembling the booths in another week or so. Live music. Liquid refreshments. Homemade baked goods. You name it; we've got it. The barbershop is wall-to-wall for days ahead, and Blanche's Beauty Barn does a bang-up business because the women all get their hair and nails done. Everyone dresses up in their finery. It's *the* event to kick off the summer."

"I suppose I should go."

"I suppose you should."

"Are you?"

"I'll make an appearance."

"Do you dance?"

"As little as possible, but be sure to wear a comfortable pair of shoes," he told her.

Gillian stared at him. "Why comfortable shoes?"

"Everyone in Sweetheart will want to dance with you." Briefcase in hand, Sam sauntered toward the front door of his house. "And I do mean everyone."

Chapter
fifteen

"May I have this dance?"

No. Thanks, anyway, Gillian was tempted to say. *I don't want to dance even one more dance. Not one more rendition of the "Twist" or the "Mashed Potato." Not one more cha-cha-cha. Certainly not one more beer-barrel polka. My feet hurt. My head's pounding. I'm parched. I think there's a blister forming on my left heel. I know my toes have been stepped on more times than I can count, and I've heard confessions that would make a priest blush.*

She planted a smile on her face and looked up. Standing in front of her was an attractive brunette of "that certain age," as Europeans tactfully referred to a woman of mature years. She was well preserved, somewhere in her late forties or early fifties. There was something rather sweet and a little vulnerable about her.

Gillian groaned inwardly. She knew she didn't have the heart to refuse the woman.

"I'd love to dance," she said.

Sam had reminded her before the first waltz that everyone would ask her to dance tonight. Young and old. Male and female alike. Chatty housewives. Silent men with craggy, weathered faces. Farmers who were old enough to be her grandfather. Gangly teenagers with two left feet. Even curious children.

It was a tradition in Sweetheart dating back to the Second World War when most of the town's men were stationed overseas and male dance partners were at a premium. The custom had taken hold and ever since everybody danced with everybody else.

"I'm Mary Kay Weaver," said the woman decked out in layers of pale blue chiffon. "I run the Sweetheart Bed and Breakfast."

"I'm Gillian Charles."

"Yes. I know."

Small white lights strung along the bandstand, the refreshment booths, the dance floor, several nearby trees, even the public rest rooms, were a blur as the two of them began to twirl in a circle, somehow managing not to collide with anyone else. All the while they danced, the innkeeper regaled Gillian with stories about the guests who had stayed at her bed and breakfast.

Sam was right. Mary Kay Weaver *could* talk the ears off a field of corn.

Finally the woman moistened her lips and volunteered, "I was once married to Davison Weaver. Doodles, as everyone in Sweetheart calls him." There was a lengthy pause. "I understand he's been driving you around town."

Gillian wondered where this conversation was headed. "Yes. He has."

Mary Kay had something on her mind, although she seemed to be in no hurry to broach the subject. "Perhaps you've seen some of his drawings."

"I've glimpsed a few in a sketchbook he had in his car," she said carefully.

The attractive brunette smiled. "Back when we were in school together, he used to get in trouble for drawing caricatures of our teachers. He was really very clever." Her smile quickly faded. "We all wondered what Davison would do with it."

"It?"

"His talent."

Gillian was reluctant to ask, but in the end she said, "What did he do with it?"

Mary Kay exhaled on a long, drawn-out sigh. "Nothing. Absolutely nothing."

"You sound disappointed."

"I am. Well, I was. I guess I had dreams for Davison that he didn't have for himself." Shoulders draped in a matching blue chiffon stole rose and fell in tandem with another long sigh. "I wanted him to go to art school. But that would have meant leaving Sweetheart and he wasn't about to do anything so drastic. He claimed he was a hometown boy. Always had been. Always would be." Her mouth all but disappeared. "The truth is, he was afraid."

"Afraid he might fail?"

"Or afraid he might succeed. Either way, he was just plain scared. So, after high school he went to work full-time for his father in the family furniture store."

"Weaver's Emporium," Gillian said as they circled the dance floor a second time. "It's the antique mall now." A nod of a pretty head told her she had the facts straight.

"A few years ago my father-in-law decided he'd had

enough of the retail business; he'd been buying and selling furniture for more than five decades. He threw a Midnight Madness Sale and got rid of everything: lock, stock, and barrel, down to the last throw rug and mismatched bedside table lamp. He also tried to sell the building."

"Tried?"

Mary Kay shrugged; the stole slipped off her shoulders and down her arms, gathering in shimmering blue chiffon folds at her elbows. "No one wanted a century-old structure that had to be brought up to modern building code. The cost was prohibitive. In fact, there weren't any buyers until Jacob Charles came along."

The light was beginning to dawn. "That's when my grandfather bought the property."

"Yes." She gave Gillian's arm an appreciative pat. "I'll always be grateful to Mr. Charles. Thanks to his timely intervention, my in-laws were able to retire and spend their winters in Florida as they'd always planned. It also meant that I had the money to put a down payment on the Sweetheart Bed and Breakfast." Unfocused eyes stared right past her. "Davison, well . . ."

"What?"

"He had no interest in running either business." Her voice softened to a whisper. "Or any business, for that matter."

"I see." She was beginning to, anyway.

"In fact, that was about the time my husband seemed to lose interest in most things." Tears suddenly welled. There was no need for Mary Kay to say: *Including me.*

Gillian was at a loss for words.

The woman with the peaches-and-cream complexion, the leftover prom dress, and the chatty disposition brushed self-consciously at her eyes. "Everybody claimed it was a midlife crisis. They said it would pass. So I waited for

Doodles to snap out of it. But he never did. He just drove around in that damned car of his, listening to his music and doodling in his sketchbook. I finally gave up and filed for divorce." She sniffed. "I can't imagine why I'm telling you this." Her eyes were swimming with tears. "You're a good listener."

Gillian made one of those sympathetic yet nondescript sounds that had come in handy any number of times during the evening.

Her companion dabbed at her eyes. "Anyway, the divorce has been final for seven months, three weeks, and four days." Another watery sniff and another swipe of a lacy handkerchief. "Not that I'm counting, mind you."

Gillian realized she was skating on thin ice. "How long were you married?"

"Twenty-five years."

What could go so wrong between a man and a woman after they'd invested twenty-five precious years of their lives in each other? she wondered. "Do you and Davison have children?"

"Two boys and a girl. They're all grown up now, of course. Well, the youngest is still in college. He's studying fine arts at Cooper Union in New York."

Doing what Doodles didn't have the guts to try twenty-five-plus years ago, remained unspoken.

"Your son must be talented," said Gillian.

"He is." Mary Kay gnawed on her bottom lip. "To tell you the truth, the kids and I didn't think Davison would let me go through with the separation and divorce. I was just trying to get his attention, to force him to take an interest in something . . . someone. I wanted him to really look at me." The pretty woman pointed to herself and, in the process, stumbled over her own feet. Gillian caught her in the nick of time, preventing a six-couple pile-up right there in the middle of the dance floor. "Thank you," she said, steadying herself.

"You're welcome."

The brunette patted her head, although not a single strand of dark brown hair was out of place—no doubt thanks to Blanche's Beauty Barn. "Obviously my tactics didn't work. Doodles blithely signed the divorce papers and went on his merry way, never once looking back."

"Are you certain?"

"Yes." But her answer lacked conviction.

"He still calls his car by your name."

"Does he?" She looked at Gillian with a determined air. "Do you mind if I ask you something?"

"I suppose not."

"Why is Doodles driving you everywhere?"

Finally the question she knew Mary Kay Weaver had been dying to ask her all along. "Because I don't have a driver's license and Sweetheart doesn't have any taxi cabs."

The woman's expression was nonplussed. "You mean you don't drive?"

Sam had warned her that people would find that incredulous in a rural community where every kid was behind the wheel of the family car or the family tractor long *before* their sixteenth birthday.

Gillian raised her chin fractionally. "I passed the test for my learner's permit on Thursday. Next week we're going shopping for a car. Then I start my behind-the-wheel lessons."

"We?"

"Sam and I."

"I've heard that you and Sam are . . ."

"An item?" she supplied.

"Yes." Mary Kay Weaver exhaled at last. "So, Doodles won't be chauffeuring you around much longer."

"I'll soon be driving myself wherever I want to go." She added for good measure, "Doodles has been very nice about it, but it's still an inconvenience to have to rely on someone else for your transportation."

"I'll bet it is."

Gillian noticed that her dance partner seemed to be staring over her shoulder at someone. "What is it?"

"That hussy is up to no good," said Mary Kay, her lips thinning in disapproval.

Gillian pivoted. "What hussy?"

"The one forcing herself on Sam."

A rather pretty young woman—she certainly didn't appear to be a hussy—had hooked her arm through Sam's, and was half dragging, half cajoling him onto the dance floor. Once she'd succeeded, she turned and looked right at Gillian. There was no mistaking the surprisingly smug expression on her face. It was as if she were taunting her with: *NAH-nah-nah-NAH-nah. I've got your man, and there's not a blessed thing you can do about it.*

Gillian reminded herself that any relationship between her and Sam, other than that of attorney and client, of course, was only make-believe, strictly temporary, and for their mutual convenience. Still, she found she was curious. "Who is she?"

"Lynn Harrison."

Gillian cocked her head to one side. "Who's Lynn Harrison?"

"Our local librarian."

"Ah . . ."

"Sam's told you, then?"

"Yes."

"Some women don't know how to take no for an

answer. Lynn Harrison is one of them." Mary Kay lowered her voice. "You know what they say about librarians, don't you?"

Gillian managed to keep a straight face. "No. Actually, I don't."

Her companion moistened her lips before saying, "Don't judge a book by its cover." Then she added a friendly word of caution, "You'll want to watch your back."

"Thanks for the warning," she said.

The music stopped. While most of the couples went their separate ways, Gillian noticed that Sam's partner refused to relinquish her hold on him. She was glued to his side.

He's a big boy; he can take care of himself.

Gillian turned to the woman beside her. "Davison is hovering by Minerva Bagley's booth. He's pretending to study her selection of herbal teas, but he's really been watching you."

Mary Kay studied her ex-husband out of the corner of one eye. "He's traded in his blue jeans for a pair of khakis, but I see he's still got those godawful Jesus sandals on." A smile tugged at the corners of her mouth. "At least he appears to be washed and pressed." She added, "I think he's done something a little different with his hair."

Gillian bit her tongue—under the circumstances, she wasn't about to volunteer she was the one who had showed Doodles the trick with his ponytail—and quickly changed the subject. "I'm surprised he doesn't have a booth here."

"What would Davison do with a booth?"

"Set up shop; draw portraits and caricatures, and then sell them. We have artists doing it all the time on the streets of New York. They charge twenty-five or thirty dollars a pop." Gillian tapped a finger against her bottom lip. "He could even throw in a free picture frame and a mat as part of the asking price."

Apparently that got Mary Kay's mental wheels turning. "I don't know why someone hasn't thought of it before. It's a brilliant idea. There are dozens of fairs and festivals all over this part of Indiana through the summer and well into the autumn. Doodles could sketch to his heart's content." Color washed over her cheeks. "Why, I could even display some of his artwork at the bed and breakfast, with a discreet price tag attached, of course."

"Sounds like you two would make a good team: his artistic talent and your business sense."

Mary Kay's excitement quickly vanished. "What if he isn't interested? What if he turns me down flat?" What she really meant was: *What if he rejects me again?* "I suppose that's what I accused Doodles of, isn't it? Being afraid to even try?"

"I suppose it is."

She straightened her shoulders. "I'm going to do it. What have I got to lose besides my foolish pride and a little of my dignity? They sure don't keep you warm on a cold winter's night in Indiana." She gave Gillian's hand a squeeze. "I'm glad I asked you to dance."

"So am I." She called after her, "Good luck."

She watched as Mary Kay Weaver approached her ex-husband. Doodles leaned closer and appeared to listen intently as she talked. Then it was his turn. Mary Kay hung on his every word. The last Gillian saw of them, they were sitting together in a quiet corner.

She was feeling quite pleased with herself when someone tapped her on the shoulder. She turned. It was a tall, distinguished gentleman dressed in a suit, but no tie.

He introduced himself. "I'm Truman Hart, Miss Charles."

"The watchdog of the SPCA."

He chuckled; it was a deep-voiced rumble. "How in the world did you hear about that?" Truman held up one hand. "No. Don't tell me. I'll bet it was Samuel."

"Actually," Gillian said, lowering her voice to a conspiratorial whisper, "it was Max."

Chapter

sixteen

He hated being called Sammy.

He'd told Lynn that a number of times when they were dating, but she always turned a deaf ear and insisted on calling him Sammy anyway. No doubt she thought it was cute. It wasn't cute. It was annoying. In fact, damned annoying.

The song came to an end. The music stopped. The couples on the dance floor parted and went their separate ways. Sam stepped back. He figured it was his big chance to skedaddle.

"Sammy," the woman purred, sinking her claws into his arm and pressing her body up against his in a way that left very little to the imagination, "ask me to dance again."

He was tempted to remind Lynn that he hadn't asked her to dance in the first place. She'd asked him. But he decided to let it go this time. He didn't mind being blunt. He was famous for being blunt. But he did try not to be downright rude.

Of course, the line between blunt and rude was a very fine one sometimes.

As the band struck up a chord and segued into the next song, Sam went through the motions, moving his feet and letting Lynn do the talking. He simply tuned her out; listened without really listening. It was a technique he'd perfected long ago as the oldest of four siblings. He allowed his mind to wander to other things.

Cigar things.

Gillian things.

What had gone wrong tonight? His cigar was usually an excellent deterrent. Sam wasn't a smoker, but at the May Dance he always made sure he had a stogie or two in his coat pocket. He'd light up, lean back against a tree, and blow a ring of gray smoke around himself. It was an effective way to keep pests at bay: the flying insect kind and the two-legged female variety.

This time his tactics had failed. Cigar or no cigar, Lynn Harrison had cornered him and dragged him onto the dance floor. He'd left his Corona smoldering between the branches of a leafless tree where there was little risk of it starting a fire.

Glancing over his partner's shoulder, Sam spotted Gillian waltzing with Truman Hart. No doubt the gentleman was entertaining her with stories about the pair of injured barn owls he'd rescued and nursed back to health. The owls had been shot by someone with a small-caliber rifle, not unlike the one he suspected had been used to kill the crow that had been dumped on his front porch.

Hopefully Tru would remember *not* to mention to Gillian any of the theories the two men had discussed. For her peace of mind, as well as his own, Sam preferred she remain unenlightened about the exact cause of the crow's death. At least for the present.

Meanwhile, he'd decided to keep an eye on Ms. Charles, himself. That way if anything went wrong, he would be there to rescue her. So far—at least tonight, anyway—the only thing she seemed to need rescuing from were dance partners with two left feet. She'd had her toes stepped on repeatedly and her ear talked off, yet she had remained unfailingly polite to everyone.

She looked tired, Sam thought. Exhausted, really. And every now and then she limped. Maybe her feet hurt. Maybe he'd have to step in and rescue her, after all.

The knight-in-shining-armor thing.

He frowned. Gillian Charles was quite capable of taking care of herself, at least in social situations. Thank you very much.

Then why did he feel so protective of her? And why did he suddenly realize most of the women here tonight appeared overdressed—all fuss and frills and immovable bouffant hairdos—while Gillian stood out in a plain white sundress with her hair tied back in a simple ponytail? He wasn't sure she was even wearing any makeup.

Dammit, Sam, I know what you're thinking. It's not a good idea. In fact, it's a very bad idea. She's your client. You're her attorney. It's cut-and-dry. Conflict of interest. It's the reason you've always had a strict rule about not fraternizing. This is no time to start making exceptions to that rule. Besides, she's not your type.

Yeah, well, whatever his type was, there was something about Gillian that intrigued him. He didn't understand it, and he sure as hell couldn't explain it.

"Sammy," came a familiar and petulant female voice. He wondered if Lynn Harrison had any clue that whining was a surefire way to cool a man's interest. Probably not.

"Hm?"

"You stepped on my toes."

He glanced down at his feet. "Oh. Sorry." Then he stared off into space again.

Two minutes later. "Sammy." Her tone was more insistent. "You aren't paying any attention to me."

Sam practically bit his tongue off. He managed a brusque and unrepentant, "Sorry."

"You've already said you're sorry," she complained, her voice turning shrill. "Sorry just doesn't cut the mustard, Sammy. You'll have to do better than that."

Christ, the woman was nagging him as if she had a right to, as if they were a couple. Which they weren't. Which they'd never really been. Which they never would be.

Somehow he couldn't imagine Gillian nagging anyone. It wasn't her style. And she did have style, he thought. And class. Yes, she was definitely stylish and classy, unlike some women he knew. And she had the sweetest laugh he'd ever heard.

"I guess my mind is somewhere else tonight," he said to Lynn, without apologizing.

"No shit, Sherlock," she muttered inelegantly.

Ah, the well-read, academic type did have a way with words, he thought, then wondered for the tenth time in as many minutes what had ever possessed him to date the woman.

Rebound. You were on the rebound, buddy.

Of course, everyone in Sweetheart, including Lynn Harrison—*especially* Lynn Harrison—assumed Gillian was the reason he'd been on the rebound when he had hightailed it back to town three years ago. Maybe that explained why Lynn was being so proprietary tonight. It wasn't him she was interested in: It was seeing Gillian's reaction to the two of them together.

That's when it dawned on him. She was trying to make Gillian think there was something between Lynn and himself.

Damn, the idea was crazy. Ridiculous. Ludicrous. In fact, downright laughable. Sam couldn't help himself. He put his head back and let out a whoop. He wanted to tell Lynn there wasn't a snowball's chance in hell of her plan succeeding.

Gillian jerked in her partner's arms. The masculine laugh she heard from the far side of the dance floor was Sam's. She was absolutely certain of it.

When they'd arrived at the bandstand earlier that evening, Sam had done his civic duty, introducing her to the mayor and other local luminaries. Then he'd stepped aside while "His Honor" escorted her to the dance floor for the opening waltz. That was the last she'd seen of Mr. Law.

Until now.

Well, it was a two-way street. If Sam could ignore her, she was more than happy to return the favor. She made a point of *not* turning around and looking at him.

"You shouldn't be wasting your time with an old coot like me," said the man leading her in the current waltz. "You should be tripping the light fantastic with Sam."

Gillian had no intentions of being rude to Truman Hart since he had been unfailingly polite to her. "Sam is otherwise engaged. Besides, he seems to be enjoying himself."

"I'm sure Lynn Harrison hijacked him. He wouldn't have asked her to dance." When she didn't react to his statement, Truman tried a different tack. "You've heard about our town librarian, haven't you?"

Gillian nodded stiffly. "She dated Sam when he first moved back to Sweetheart."

"Briefly. It was of no consequence, I assure you. A passing flirtation. At least on his part." The distinguished gentleman looked down at her. "You ruined Sam for any other woman. Now that I've met you, I can understand why."

That was the problem with not sticking to the truth, Gillian thought. It always came back to haunt you. She and Sam had allowed local gossip about the two of them to go uncontested because it had served their own purposes. Now she'd just have to handle an awkward situation as best she could. It wouldn't be the first time, she reminded herself.

"I've known Sam all of his life," said Truman. "He's the kind of man you can rely on."

"Yes, he is."

"He's intelligent, as well. In fact, smart as a whip. I know. I was his teacher. I never had to explain anything to Sam twice. He always got it before anyone else in the class."

She didn't doubt Sam had brains as well as brawn.

Truman Hart continued to sing his former pupil's praises. "He's a man of integrity."

"Honest as the day is long," she said half in jest, then realized she meant it.

"Precisely."

As long as they were listing his virtues, Gillian said, "Kind to animals and small children."

Truman chuckled. "Now you're making fun."

"Perhaps a little."

Snowy white eyebrows formed a deep frown. "I don't know what went wrong between the two of you."

Gillian told him the truth. "Nothing."

The man shook his head from side to side. "I'm afraid it happens all too often: Couples decide to break up over nothing of any real consequence. When you reach my age, you realize the direction your life took was largely determined by those so-called inconsequential decisions you made along the way." It was some time before he went on to advise, "Don't make the mistake of underestimating Sam."

"In what way?"

"Beneath that cool and calm exterior of his, there is a caring, sensitive man."

"If you say so."

Truman grew deadly serious. "I'm talking about emotions that run deep, far beneath the surface like a subterranean river. Sam will do whatever it takes."

"Whatever it takes?"

"To protect what's his."

Gillian wasn't sure she understood his meaning. "I'm afraid I don't follow . . ."

He was blunt. "You, Ms. Charles. He'll do whatever it takes to keep you safe."

A tingle of awareness—*oh, good God, Gillian, is that excitement you're feeling?*—slithered down her spine.

The retired mathematics teacher went on. "Like the dead crow incident."

"The dead crow Sam found on my . . . his . . . front porch."

"Most men would simply dispose of the carcass and forget all about it. But not Sam."

"No, not Sam," she said, echoing his sentiment.

Truman left no doubt in either of their minds. "He'll get to the bottom of it sooner or later."

"I'm sure he'll find the prankster."

"If it was a prank. He's not taking any chances. The hunter was an expert shot."

The small, infinitesimal hairs on the back of her neck suddenly stood straight up on end. Gillian moistened her lips. "What makes you say that?"

"A single bullet straight through the heart. It takes skill to shoot like that."

It took every ounce of her self-control not to show her surprise. "Yes, it does."

As the band enthusiastically swung into the next song, her partner suggested, "Maybe it's time you rescued Sam from Lynn's clutches."

She casually glanced in their direction. "Sam doesn't look like he needs rescuing to me."

"That's the trouble: Sam never looks like he needs help. That doesn't mean it's true." Truman spoke plainly. "May I give you a piece of friendly advice?"

She hesitated briefly. "Yes."

"You may want to draw the line in the sand right here, right now, tonight. Otherwise, Lynn Harrison will have it all over town by tomorrow morning that she took your man away from you."

There was disbelief in Gillian's response. "You're kidding."

"I'm not kidding."

"But that's so"—she swallowed with no small amount of difficulty—"primitive."

"When you get right down to it, the relationship between a man and a woman always is," he said.

Gillian took a deep breath and drew herself up to her full height. "Thank you for the dance, Mr. Hart. And for the advice. If you'll excuse me, I believe it's time to draw that sandy line you mentioned." Besides, she had a bone or two to pick with her attorney. She didn't appreciate being left in the dark.

Truman made one last recommendation. "Keep your dukes up and come out swinging."

Gillian paused. "I beg your pardon."

He flashed her a cherubic smile. "I was the high school boxing coach as well as the mathematics teacher."

How had she gotten herself into this mess? Gillian wondered as she wended her way through the crowd on the temporary dance floor. She was about to force a showdown with a woman she didn't know over a man she wasn't engaged to, had never been personally involved with, hadn't even kissed.

Gillian felt as if several hundred pairs of eyes were boring into the back of her head. She took a sustaining breath, put her shoulders back, raised her chin an inch or two, fixed a confident smile on her face, and approached the couple.

Sam saw her coming.

She tapped Lynn Harrison firmly on the shoulder. The other woman turned. "Excuse me. I believe this is my"— Gillian allowed the remainder of the sentence to dangle in the air between them for a moment—"dance."

"Your dance?"

She stared the green-eyed creature down and declared, "They're playing our song, Sam's and mine."

Lynn snorted in an unladylike fashion. "'Blame It on the Bossa Nova' is your song?"

"Yes, it is." Gillian knew she'd have to play the cards she'd dealt herself. "Remember the first time we danced to this song, Sam, darling? We were at that intimate little nightclub down in the Village; the one with those cozy booths for two. You kept slipping twenties to the band so they'd keep playing the song over and over again. Finally we realized we were the only ones left in the place. So we went home, put 'Blame It on the Bossa Nova' on the stereo, and kept right on dancing through the wee, small hours. As a matter of fact, I seem to recall we danced all night long." She laughed seductively, way in the back of her throat. "How many times did we *dance* that night, darling?"

It was obvious what she really meant was: *How many times did we do the "horizontal rhumba"?*

Lynn Harrison stood there with her mouth hanging wide open. It was not an attractive look for her, in Gillian's opinion.

Sam was grinning from ear to ear.

Gillian took a step closer with an I-won't-take-no-for-an-answer attitude, and the other woman was forced to yield. Lynn muttered something under her breath that sounded like 'you witch,' turned on her heel, and stomped off the dance floor, conceding defeat.

"To the victor go the spoils," Sam said as he took her in his arms and swung her into the upbeat tempo of the music.

"Spoils just about describes it, Mr. Law."

That brought a raised eyebrow. "Mr. Law?" His mouth flattened. "What's wrong?"

"When were you planning to tell me about the crow, Sam?"

"Truman blabbed, huh?"

"Mr. Hart saw fit to inform me of the details, yes."

His hesitation was almost imperceptible. "That information was strictly on a need-to-know basis."

"Well, I need to know if it concerns me."

"We don't know that it does. The dead crow could have been a message for me."

"You?"

Sam nodded. "I'm not popular with everyone, you know."

He had her there. "I can understand that. I'm not too crazy about you right now, myself."

"See. Told you so." Then he gave her one of those heart-stopping smiles of his; the one that was all nearly perfect white teeth, the one that could charm the birds out of the trees and make a woman melt like warm, gooey caramel in his hands.

Gillian tried not to melt, but she couldn't help herself. First, she stopped frowning. Then she smiled back at him. Finally she started to laugh. After a few seconds Sam joined in. The tension between them began to dissolve into thin air.

"I don't know why I can't stay angry with you," she said as they danced.

"Why would you want to stay angry with me?" he asked. "Anger is such a waste of time."

"Yes, it is." But it was also safer. "I'm not sure I want to like you," she admitted.

"Why not?"

Because liking him complicated things. Because liking him meant trouble for her. Because she had to protect herself, look out for herself, keep herself—and her heart—safe. There was no one else left to do those things for her.

Not now. Not anymore.

"This is a good time—in fact, it's an excellent time—to change the subject," she said, without answering his question.

Apparently Sam could take a hint. He quickly retreated to neutral territory. "I hope you don't think I abandoned you earlier this evening. It's traditional for the mayor to dance the first waltz of the evening with the honored guest."

"Is that what I am? And here I thought I was simply the object of communal curiosity."

"Well, that, too," he said, moving closer.

Too close.

Gillian was aware of his breath on her skin like a warm breeze blowing in from the ocean. No, not warm, more like a hot and sultry tropical breeze. Intimate: the way he was holding her was far too intimate. A little scary, more than a little. It felt as if his lips were burning a pathway across that sensitive spot just below her earlobe, yet she knew Sam wasn't touching her. She shivered and goose bumps formed on her flesh.

Her breathing suddenly became swallow. "I'm sorry. What were you saying?"

"I said you're the biggest news to hit this town since the F3 tornado that blew through a couple of summers ago. People are bound to be curious about you."

"I suppose so." She willed herself to concentrate. "I don't think I've ever been compared to the weather before."

White teeth flashed. "I'll bet the mayor took you by storm."

She spun in a circle. "Is he always so . . ."

"Mayoral?"

She nodded. There was a slight buzzing in her ears. And she was feeling light-headed.

Sam seemed oblivious to his effect on her. "The mayor lives and breathes politics."

She heaved a sigh. "The first thing he asked me was whether I was registered as a Democrat or a Republican. I told him I considered myself an Independent."

Sam clicked his tongue in disapproval. "That's where you made your mistake."

"I realize that now. His Honor lectured me for the next five minutes about sitting on the proverbial fence. He said I'd have to dig down deep inside myself and decide what I stood for if I wanted to vote in the next primary."

Sam gave a chuckle. "Sounds like the mayor."

"Thank goodness Walter P. cut in. I was so grateful I promised to sign his petition."

"Ah, the water tower controversy."

"After Walter P., it all becomes kind of a blur of names and faces." She gave another long, drawn-out sigh. "I think I met every single person in town tonight."

"Did you have a chance to talk with Anna Rogozinski?"

She nodded. "It was the oddest thing, though. Almost immediately after we were introduced, Miss Rogozinski said she wasn't feeling well and her companion, Esther somebody or other—I didn't catch the last name— whisked her away home."

"Esther Preston," said Sam, filling in the blank. "Sadly Anna has crippling arthritis, among other physical ailments. She tires easily. And sometimes the excitement of a social gathering gets to be too much for her."

"I see."

"I know how important it is for you to find the answers to your questions, Gillian. I'll make sure you have a chance to talk to Anna about your grandfather."

"Thank you, Sam."

"You're welcome." Then he stopped in his tracks. "Damn, I forgot all about my cigar."

She gave him an inquiring look. "I didn't know you smoked."

"I don't."

She arched one eyebrow quizzically.

"The cigar is strictly for self-defense," he explained. "A smoke screen."

"To keep the mosquitoes away?"

"Something like that. Pests, anyway. It usually works."

"But it didn't tonight."

"Some pests won't take no for an answer."

"Where is your cigar?"

Sam jerked his thumb over his shoulder. "Wedged in one of those trees. It seemed like the safest place to put it at the time. I didn't expect to be gone so long." He suddenly grabbed her by the hand and headed into the park. "C'mon, you, too, can prevent forest fires."

" 'A woman's only a woman, but a good cigar is a smoke,' " Sam said as they headed into the park. He hastened to add, "Not that I personally agree with Rudyard Kipling, of course."

Obviously Kipling didn't know diddly-squat about women, he thought. About a real woman. A woman like the one walking beside him as they searched for his Corona.

Damn, which tree *had* he left it in?

" 'Sometimes,' " Gillian said as she checked the nearest Japanese maple, " 'a cigar is just a cigar.' "

Sam paused and peered over a moss-covered branch at her. "Who said that?"

She shrugged. "It's attributed to Sigmund Freud." He watched as one strap of her sundress slipped off her shoulder—*a Freudian slip?*—and down her arm, leaving lovely bare skin behind.

"Freud, huh?"

She pushed the thin strap back up. "So they claim."

Sam snickered under his breath. "Well, that's one line I wouldn't touch with a ten-foot pole."

"Why?"

"Because of the sex scandal involving a certain modern-day President and the unorthodox use of his cigar."

Gillian groaned and went on to the next stand of trees.

"Hey, cigars aren't just cigars or even good smokes in the public's mind anymore, thanks to who-know-who," he called after her. "It's a crying shame, too."

Her blond head popped up some distance away. "I thought you weren't a smoker."

"I'm not." Sam brushed away a cobweb from in front of his face. "I do, however, have an appreciation for what was once a time-honored tradition: brandy and cigars in the library. Now the idea is distasteful. If you'll pardon the pun."

Gillian wrinkled her nose and triumphantly held up the Corona. "The lost is found."

"Thanks." Sam took the stone-cold cigar from her. "I guess it wasn't much of a fire hazard."

"Better safe than sorry," said Gillian.

Sam discarded the stogie in a nearby trash receptacle. *Same time next year.*

The thought was suddenly oddly depressing. Would he be leaning against a tree in this same park, blowing cigar smoke into the air to avoid dancing with the same women he wasn't even remotely interested in at this same time next year? And the year after that? And the year after that, ad infinitum, ad nauseam?

If he didn't make some significant changes in his life—

like having a life—he could end up a pathetic caricature of himself at some point, Sam realized.

He leaned back against the tree behind him. "How do you feel about it?"

Gillian circled the century-old sycamore and came to a standstill in front of him. She reached up and tugged on her ponytail until her hair fell down into soft blond waves around her face and shoulders. "About cigars?"

Sam shook his head and nonchalantly crossed his arms. "About better safe than sorry."

She gave him an inquiring look. "I suppose that depends. Do you mean when it comes to taking foolish risks like crossing a busy city street against a green light? Or eating fried foods every day when scientists think they may contain a carcinogen that causes cancer in rats and maybe in humans? Or white-water rafting after a torrential downpour? Or climbing Mount Everest during a snowstorm? Or heading down a dark, narrow alley in Timbuktu when you don't know where you're going and don't speak the language?"

He decided to make it easy for her. "I was thinking more along the lines of dancing with me."

Gillian glanced down at his feet. "Do you have two left ones?"

His eyes followed hers. "Nope. One of each." He uncrossed his arms and pointed them out in turn. "A right and a left."

"So, it's unlikely you'll trample on mine," she said, apparently feeling it was necessary to double-check.

He gave her question the attention it deserved. "I can't make any promises, but I've always been considered fairly agile and pretty light on my feet."

"Do you have any proof of that?" she asked, her tone of voice not altogether serious.

It took him a second to come up with an answer. "I played quarterback in high school."

"Were you any good?"

Not that he was one to toot his own horn, *but* . . . "Good enough to earn a four-year football scholarship to Purdue."

Gillian's mouth curved up at the corners. "You were a jock."

"I prefer the term 'athlete,' " he said, showing his teeth.

"In that case, I'm willing to take my chances." Her features formed a telling frown. "You can't be any worse than half of the people I've danced with tonight."

Oh, but he could be much, much better, thought Sam.

A pained expression flitted across her face. "Do you mind if I go barefoot?"

"Of course not."

Gillian slipped her shoes off, wiggled her toes in the grass, and gave a huge sigh of relief. Then she went into his arms.

She fit perfectly. She shouldn't have, but she did. For one thing, she wasn't as tall as she appeared to be. It was the high heels; they literally added inches to her height. This was the first time, to Sam's knowledge, that she'd been without them.

They'd been dancing for only a minute or two when he felt her shiver. "Cold?"

"A little." Gillian turned and glanced over her shoulder. "I left my sweater and handbag with Minerva."

It was the knight-in-shining-armor thing, after all.

Sam shrugged off his suit jacket and draped it around her shoulders, his knuckles brushing against her bare skin. "We'll kill two birds with one stone. I'm warm. You're cold. You get the jacket." He slipped her arms into the sleeves. "Better?"

"Better." Gillian trembled again and snuggled deep into his coat. "Much better."

"Not quite your size," Sam observed with a wry smile. His coat had swallowed her up; even her hands had disappeared. He reached down and began to roll up the sleeves.

"Your suit jacket will get wrinkled," she said.

He kept on rolling. "Then I'll get it pressed."

When they began to dance again, Sam noticed that the top of Gillian's head was more or less level with his chin. A wisp or two of her hair was tickling his throat. His nostrils were filled with her scent. It wasn't a heavy perfume smell, but a mixture of night air, something faintly floral, and something he couldn't even begin to describe.

Maybe there weren't any words for it; only images. A sliver of silver moon. A sky filled with starlight. Cool, damp grass. Beckoning warmth and then a strange erotic heat.

Ah, the scent of a woman.

Sam rested his hand on her waist just above the small of her back. He could feel her body pressing against his as they moved. She was slender but surprisingly shapely. Or as he'd overheard down at the gas station this afternoon from the same pair of mouthy punks he'd run into before: She was built like a brick outhouse.

She was stacked.

She had a body that wouldn't quit.

His teenage years came back to Sam in a flood of memories. Hot summer days and even hotter summer nights. Dances at the lake. Girls in bikinis. Crisp autumn evenings. The adrenaline rush after winning a football game. Making out hot and heavy in the backseat of his car with a girl just bad enough to be good.

Thank God he had more control over himself, and his hormones, than he'd had at seventeen. Still, to be on the safe side, he forced himself to concentrate on the music.

He recognized the song being played. "I was hoping we could dance for a while."

"Why can't we?" Gillian asked, her voice muffled against the front of his shirt.

"This is the last dance."

Her head came up. "How do you know?"

"It's traditional for the band to play 'Goodnight, Sweetheart' at the end of the evening."

"That's the song they're playing now?"

Sam nodded. "His Honor, the mayor, always makes sure these events end right on time, too. Considers it part of his civic duty." He held his wristwatch up to the faint light coming from the direction of the dance floor. "The stroke of midnight," he announced just as the clock on the courthouse began to toll the bewitching hour.

Gillian laughed a little nervously. "You aren't going to turn into a pumpkin on me or anything, are you?"

Or anything?

Did she mean anything like a horny thirty-five-year-old man who hadn't felt this sexually attracted to a woman for a couple of years, maybe longer, maybe far longer?

Or anything like the images that had been bombarding his brain while the two of them danced? Images of her in his hands? Images of his hands on her?

Or anything like the fact that he could almost touch her, taste her, feel her as if their bodies, slick with sweat and sex, were tangled up in the sheets of his huge mahogany bed?

Sam swallowed a groan of arousal. Damn! Double damn! This was exactly the kind of trouble he'd been trying to avoid. *Trouble's your middle name, buddy. Remember?*

He stared down into Gillian's eyes. Their color was an ever-changing montage of green and blue and all the shades in between. They reminded him of the famous impressionistic painting by Monet—the one with the water lilies.

Sam didn't brush away the strand of silky blond hair that had caught on his bottom lip. He smiled lazily and said, "We could always dance without music."

Careful, Gillian.

Sam's eyes had been a soft gray color; the same soft gray as the lamb's ears she'd planted with Sylvia's help as a border around his flowerbeds the week before last. But something happened while they were dancing. His eyes suddenly changed, grew darker, hotter, became molten lava.

Gillian wasn't naive. She knew it was sex, pure and simple. Although she couldn't imagine any relationship with Samuel Law, especially a sexual one, being either pure or simple.

The truth was she was no longer dancing with her attorney. Had she ever been? She was in the arms of a man she had known was trouble from the minute she'd laid eyes on him.

"Here be dragons," she said, and shivered within the warmth of his jacket.

Sam didn't take his eyes off her. He lowered his voice to an intimate level. "Here be what?"

"Dragons." Gillian quickly went on to explain. "That's what they used to write on ancient maps to show any unexplored or uncharted region of the ocean."

"Who did?"

"Sailors. Sea captains. Navigators. Well into the Middle Ages many people still believed the earth was flat. They were afraid if they got too close to the edge, they'd fall off into the Great Abyss."

"So 'here be dragons' was meant as a warning?"

She nodded.

Sam searched her face. "Is that what you think: that

we're poised on the edge of some kind of precipice? That we're headed for trouble?" His voice dropped another half an octave; the sound resonated along her nerve endings. "That we're flirting with danger?"

She moistened her lips. "Yes." He made her a little nervous. Okay, he made her a lot nervous.

"Nervous?"

Apparently he was also a mind reader. "A bit," she said, willing to concede that much to him.

"Me, too," he admitted.

Gillian wasn't going to be coy about this. She made herself breathe in and out, and then she took the plunge. "I don't want to be attracted to you, Sam."

His eyes were black fire. "Ditto."

"In fact, it's the last thing I'm interested in."

"*It* meaning sex?"

"Of course, I'm interested in sex."

His smile was sudden, bewitching, beguiling. "At least we agree on one thing. So am I."

Gillian forced herself to concentrate on the point she was trying to make. "*It* meaning I'm not interested in getting involved with anyone right now."

"Then we agree on two things. I'm not either."

"I've got a lot to deal with in the next few months. I don't need for this to get messy."

"Ditto again," he said emphatically.

She only hesitated briefly before saying, "I've had messy before and I didn't care for it."

Sam returned her gaze unflinchingly. "I couldn't agree more. Messy is . . . well, messy."

She licked her lips. "Besides, someone could end up getting hurt." Someone meaning her.

"There's always that chance."

"You understand, then?"

"I understand completely." Sam slowly swung her around in his arms. "We'll keep it nice and simple. No complications. No involvement. No messiness."

"How?" she said, challenging him.

Sam gave a half-shrug. "We'll just dance."

He began to move his feet and softly hum a tune Gillian didn't recognize. She swayed with him, her hand tucked in his, both resting on his chest directly over his heart.

Gillian could feel—she swore she could even hear—its rhythmic beat intermingling with her own until she couldn't separate one from the other. Eventually she relaxed in his arms and allowed her eyes to drift shut. Maybe that's why she was so surprised when she opened them again a few minutes later and discovered they were in a section of the park she'd never seen before.

They were surrounded by a small grove of Norwegian spruce and a lush undergrowth of azaleas and rhododendrons. It was quiet. Dark. Intimate. Their own private bower. Sam leaned back against the trunk of the nearest tree and Gillian went with him.

They never knew who made the first move. One moment she was gazing up at Sam; the next he was kissing her.

Or was she kissing him?

Chapter
eighteen

Coup de foudre.

The literal translation was lightning strike, and it described that instant in which a man and a woman meet, kiss, fall in love, make love for the first time; the moment when everything changes.

In the space of a single breath, Gillian's whole world shifted on its axis. From the start she'd found Sam attractive, known he was dangerous. What she hadn't fathomed, or even imagined in her wildest dreams, was that a kiss could make her feel as if she'd been struck by lightning.

The kiss never had the chance to start the way a first kiss usually does: sweet and slow. There was no trial and error. No tentative or polite positioning of hands, lips, bodies. No hesitation. No exploration. They came together, and the kiss exploded in their faces. It went from nothing to something to everything in a single heartbeat.

The air sizzled with electricity. Mouths were open. Tongues were intertwined, exploring, thrusting, sliding in and out. Gillian had never been kissed with such blatant sexuality before. But then she couldn't ever recall kissing a man as if she wanted to devour him, gobble him up whole; as if she couldn't resist him, as if she were desperate to have him and wouldn't be satisfied until every last scrap of clothing had been torn from their bodies, until they were naked flesh against naked flesh, needing, craving, demanding release from this exquisite torture.

It was the hottest sex she'd ever experienced, and all Sam had done was kiss her.

"This is insane."

Had she said the words out loud? Or had Sam?

"Bad idea." That time it was definitely Sam.

Gillian thought she nodded.

"Good idea." He immediately corrected himself. "*Great* idea."

She moved her head again.

Fiery dragon eyes stared down into hers. "But what the hell was it?"

Gillian shrugged her shoulders beneath his suit jacket. Both straps of her dress started to slide down her arms and there wasn't a darned thing she could do about it; her hands were gripping his waist as if she were hanging on for dear life.

He made another suggestion. "Beginner's luck?"

Were they beginners? Not really. Not entirely. Perhaps with each other.

Sam was still seeking answers. "A one-time fluke?"

Gillian finally found her voice. It didn't sound quite like her. "Possibly. Probably."

He brought his face closer to hers; so close she could count the individual eyelashes that framed his quicksilver eyes. "Care to put it to the test?"

It was a challenge. He'd thrown down the gauntlet and now he was waiting to see if she'd pick it up, or turn and walk away. If she was half as smart as she gave herself credit for, Gillian knew she should run in the opposite direction just as fast as her legs would carry her.

Her feet didn't move. Her mouth did. "Put it to the test?"

His expressive eyebrows rose a fraction of an inch. "Give it another go."

Caution, along with every other semblance of common sense, was tossed aside. She heard herself say, "Why not?"

Gillian knew there were dozens of reasons why not, but she couldn't articulate a single one fast enough to stop herself from leaning toward Sam, into Sam.

Their mouths collided. She felt an electric charge coursing through her body, igniting nerve endings one by one. An erotic explosion followed; it made her breasts tingle and her nipples itch at their very tips. There was a fine sheen of perspiration on her upper lip, in the hollow between her breasts, and farther down, in the highly sensitive and intimate places between her thighs.

If only Sam didn't taste so good, smell so good. If only he didn't feel so good. If only she didn't find herself drawn to him in ways she couldn't begin to put into words.

On some elemental level she now understood what had been missing in her previous relationships. Sam's kiss opened her up, revealed her to herself and to him. His kiss, his touch, made her brain turn off and her body turn on.

She'd always considered herself to be sophisticated, worldly. She had traveled extensively. She had met and mingled with the wealthy, the powerful, the titled; the poor, the sick, and the less fortunate. She'd stayed in palaces and stately homes, lived in tents and hovels that barely provided a roof over her head. She had seen the world and its wonders, its humanity and sometimes its inhumanity. But she had never truly comprehended what it was all about between a man and a woman until now.

Now she'd caught a glimpse of that other world: the world of the senses, where it was all taste and touch and smell and desperate need. The world of physical passion, and what it could do to a woman, how it made her feel: vulnerable. Uncertain of herself. Naive. A little lost. A little foolish. A lot crazy.

Sam tore his mouth away and rested his forehead against hers. He was breathing like a runner at the end of a marathon. His skin was covered with a musk-scented sweat that drew her in as if they were wild animals and it was mating season. His body was solid and muscular. His erection was rock hard.

"I must be crazy," he muttered under his breath.

"You are," she agreed.

His laugh had dark undertones. "Gee, thanks."

Heart racing, she quickly went on to explain. "I'm crazy, too. This is crazy."

"*This* is simply a kiss between a man and a woman who suddenly realize they're attracted to each other and act on that attraction. It's not the first time it's happened in the annals of human history. It won't be the last." Sam's voice was full of disbelief. "Christ, what went wrong?"

"Wrong?"

"What went right?" He cracked under the strain. "I don't have a fucking clue what's going on here, do you?"

She shook her head. No, she didn't have a clue, either. She had to ask. "Now what?"

His eyes were like black ice. "Beats me."

She only hesitated briefly before saying, "Maybe we're overreacting. Maybe it isn't what we think."

It was some time before Sam responded. "Think? I'm not thinking and I don't want to." Curiosity, and something beyond mere curiosity, clung to his sharply drawn features. He took in a ragged breath and said, "Come here."

He was nuts. A glutton for punishment. He was asking for trouble. Hell, he was already in trouble. Big trouble. He was a man who had just discovered that kissing a woman—well, this particular woman—could bring him right to the razor's edge. It was that dangerous precipice she'd warned him about earlier. The one he should have paid closer attention to.

He'd told Gillian there would be no complications. No involvement. No messiness. They would merely dance. Nothing more. Nothing less. It had sounded innocent enough.

He'd lied. Not intentionally. Not to her. But to himself. The truth was they'd ventured into the unknown and dragons turned out to be the least of their problems. They were up to their necks in trouble. There was danger everywhere.

How could he be so sexually aroused by a kiss? Or two kisses? Or even a hundred goddamned kisses? It certainly wasn't his habit to go around with an erection—let alone a painfully hard and trigger-happy one—as a result of what was usually deemed casual contact.

Okay, maybe he'd been "Quick Draw McGraw" back in high school. But that was eons ago when he was a hormone-driven teenager. Now he was a mature man of thirty-five, and this kind of thing just didn't happen to him.

Oh, yeah, buddy. Well, guess again.

It wasn't him. It wasn't Gillian. It was something about

the two of them together. They were the diametric opposite
of apples and oranges, oil and water. They mixed too well.
They liked the taste and touch of each other too much. The
kiss had been unexpected, brand-new, yet instantly addictive. And he needed another fix.

Sam brought his mouth down to Gillian's. She rose up
on her tiptoes. Under the suit jacket he'd draped around her
for warmth, his palms rested on her shoulders. She was all
soft, fragrant, bare skin.

Where were the straps of her sundress?

The top of her dress slipped a little farther, helped by
hands that skimmed along the soft swell of breast that rose
above her bra. It was all hot flesh, wants and desires. Sensations. He stroked her through the next-to-nothing bit of
lace. She shuddered and moaned indistinguishable words
into his mouth.

He needed no encouragement. For two cents he'd get
rid of the dress, the bra, the panties, and anything else she
was wearing and lick her from head to toe. Hell, he'd do it
for free.

Over the wild beat of blood pumping through his body,
Sam groaned an admission. "Sweet Jesus, I'm losing it."

She'd already lost it. She had to have his hands on her. His
mouth. His tongue. If he didn't do something to ease the pain,
exquisite as it was, she was going to go stark raving mad.

Sam, please.

She must have said it out loud. Either that or he'd
tapped into Miss Cleo's psychic hotline and had somehow
divined her unspoken entreaty. His hand covered her
breast. His fingers dipped beneath the lacy edge of her bra.
The itch had to be scratched. He squeezed gently; the first

gentle thing he'd done since they entered the bower. It wasn't enough. The itch was worse than ever.

"Harder," was a near-desperate plea on her part.

He caught her nipple between thumb and finger, and squeezed until the breath caught ragged and raw in her throat. It was a step in the right direction; it distracted her and provided momentary relief.

"More," came out low and husky.

He knew exactly what to do. His fingers were replaced by his teeth and tongue. Sensations swirled around her in the night. The darkness closed in. She tried to open her eyes, managed to at last, stared down at the contrast of his black hair against her pale skin, watched, transfixed, as he took her between his lips and sucked her into his mouth.

She felt her nipple harden on his tongue and she couldn't stop the moan of pain-pleasure. Her head was thrown back. She was unsteady on her feet. Her skin was damp and cooled by a midnight breeze, yet she was burning up. The itch eased, but now there was an awful ache settling lower in her body.

Was there no end to the needing and the wanting? How would it end? Where would it end?

Sam stopped, released her abruptly, and raised his head. He remained unmoving for an instant. Then he straightened, placing a hand under her elbow to help steady her before stepping away entirely. The blaze in his eyes quickly faded to annoyance.

"Christ, we've got company," he said.

Gillian dropped her arms to her sides. She could just imagine what she must look like with her breasts exposed, her skin flushed pink with sexual arousal and from the natural abrasion of Sam's beard, her bra scrunched up under her rib cage, and the bodice of her sundress pulled down around her waist. And to top it all off: She was wearing a man's suit jacket with the sleeves rolled up.

Pinpoints of light came closer. Voices in the distance grew nearer and louder.

"I think I've found her shoes, Minerva." There was a pause and then a tentative, "Ferragamo."

Sam attempted to tug the lacy bra over her breasts and made a hash of the job.

Gillian had difficulty getting her brain to function, or her mouth to work properly. "M-nerva?" she said, stumbling over the name.

He tried to put her dress to rights. "From the sounds of it, Minerva and Goldie."

Even with trembling hands, she managed to rearrange her clothing and make sure everything was covered that should be covered for modesty's sake. How ironic—and in some ways how utterly ridiculous, she thought—to be concerned with modesty at this point.

She combed her fingers through her hair before pulling it up into its usual ponytail. There wasn't anything she could do about her makeup. Thank goodness it was minimal.

"Why are they out there?" she said, still not comprehending the finer details of the situation.

"Maybe Minerva got worried when you didn't come back for your sweater and handbag. After all, you were dancing one minute and gone the next."

"Vanished." Gillian tried to snap her fingers. "Just like that. Into thin air."

"Something like that." Sam took both her hands in his. "Are you all right?"

She wondered if he could see the color staining her cheeks. "I'm fine."

He was solicitous. "Think you can walk on your own?"

"Maybe with practice," she said saucily and with far

more gumption than she was actually feeling. Her gaze dropped to the front of his trousers. "What about you? Presentable for company?"

Self-deprecating humor filled his eyes. "I will be by the time they find us." Then he softly muttered, "Hopefully." Taking her by the hand, Sam guided her out the far side of the pine grove.

"So, what's our story?"

Before he could answer her, two beams of light converged on them and they froze in place like a pair of deer caught in a car's headlights, and Goldie was calling out to her companion, "The lost is found, Minerva. Here she is safe and sound. And Sam, too."

Apparently the appearance of the women was the human equivalent of a cold shower on Sam's libido. He sounded in control—cool, calm, and collected—when he said, "Good evening, Goldie." He looked past his neighbor's shoulder and acknowledged the presence of the second intruder, "Minerva."

"Sam. Gillian."

Gillian smiled and tried to speak. She finally managed a simple, "Ladies."

Sam wouldn't let go of her hand. "Are you looking for us, by any chance?"

"Gillian, actually," Minerva said. "But I wouldn't have been concerned if I'd known she was with you."

Goldie was unaware—or perhaps just plain ignorant—of the adage "Silence is golden." She opened her mouth and put her foot in it, sensible two-inch heels and all. "What in the world are you two doing out here in the dark, anyway?"

"As a matter of fact," Sam said, "we were taking a walk."

Goldie was a tenacious old busybody. "Didn't you hear the music stop?"

He gave a noncommittal shrug.

"Well, the band played 'Goodnight, Sweetheart' a good half hour ago. Just about everybody else has gone home." Apparently she felt it was her duty to add, "Minerva was worried sick."

"So were you, Goldie."

"So was I."

"I'm sorry to have upset you both," Gillian said, collecting her handbag and sweater from Minerva with a polite thank-you. "I was so warm from dancing that I decided to take a stroll."

Goldie handed her the pair of Ferragamo stilettos she'd found in the grass. "In your bare feet?"

"These darned shoes were rubbing my toes." And she had the blisters to prove it.

"Gillian did dance every dance tonight," Minerva gently reminded her friend.

Gillian rattled on, trying to regain her composure as she went. "Sam kindly offered to walk with me. I suppose we went farther than we'd intended."

Understatement of the year.

Minerva was ready to put the incident behind her. "Well, no real harm done," she said. "All's well that ends well."

Elvira Goldman was another matter altogether. Nothing, it seemed, escaped her ever-vigilant eye. "If you're warm, why are you wearing Sam's suit jacket?"

Having learned her lesson earlier with Truman Hart, Gillian stuck as close to the truth as she could. "I *was* warm. I got chilled strolling in the night air. Sam came to my rescue."

"Perfectly understandable," piped up Minerva.

"Well, the party's over for another year. It's time we were all home and in our beds," Sam managed to say with a straight face. "May I escort you ladies to your cars?"

A few minutes later, having bid good night to Minerva and Goldie and sent them on their way, they climbed into Sam's SUV. He didn't utter a word on the short drive to his house. Neither did she.

Sitting there in the passenger seat beside him, still wearing the jacket to his gray pinstriped suit, Gillian tried to think of something clever, witty, and sophisticated to say.

Her mind was a blank.

Sam walked her as far as the front porch.

"Oh, here, before I forget," she said, and started to take his jacket off. In the process the rolled-up sleeves came undone and ended up hanging down past her fingertips.

He waved the offer aside as if he were swatting at a pesky insect. "You don't have to return my coat right now. I'll stop by sometime in the next day or two and get it."

Gillian dug around in her handbag for the key to the front door, found it, slid it into the lock, and then turned back to him for a moment. "Sam, about tonight . . ."

He brought his teeth together. "I know."

She wasn't sure what she should say to him. Wasn't sure what she wanted him to say to her.

He raked a hand roughly through his hair. "We agreed: No complications. No involvement. No messiness."

"Yes, we did."

Breath whistled out between his teeth. "I'm sure we can put what happened to us back in the park in some kind of perspective. After all, we're both adults."

"Yes, we are."

"We kissed. We made out." He laughed sharply. "Hell, we even got a little carried away."

Or a lot.

"It's no big deal," he said.

"No big deal," she echoed. Then why did she feel strangely deflated, even disappointed?

Gillian reached behind her. Her hands were like ice on the antique brass doorknob. "Good night then, Sam."

He stood there and watched her for a minute with enigmatic eyes. "Good night, Gillian." Then he turned on his heel and walked away.

"You seem plum worn out, Miss Rogozinski."

"I am tired," Anna admitted to her companion.

She was exhausted. Events like the annual community dance were getting to be too much for her. All the commotion and loud music. All the people laughing and talking, eating and drinking. The bright lights. The traffic coming and going along Main Street, headlights flashing, horns blaring in a cacophony of noise.

You've never lied to yourself before, Anna. This is no time to start. It was the girl. You hadn't expected it to be such a shock to see her, to talk to her.

Esther Preston hovered in the doorway of her lady's bedroom; for that was how she thought of Anna, and Anna knew it. More than once during the afternoon nap recommended by her doctor—when her housekeeper thought she

was asleep but when she was merely resting her eyes—
she'd heard Esther answer the telephone and inform the
caller: *"My lady is resting right now. Can she ring you
back later?"*

The woman hovered at a respectful distance. "Would
you like me to take your jewelry off for you?"

"I could use a little help tonight." Anna sank onto the
cedar chest at the foot of her bed.

She glanced down at the hands in her lap. The skin on
their backs appeared to be paper thin and splotchy with
age. The fingers were gnarled and bony. The joints were
disfigured with arthritis. The nails were clean and clipped
short. But then, as a concert pianist, she'd always kept
them trimmed.

Surely these couldn't be her hands, Anna thought.
These were the hands of an old woman. Where had her
hands gone?

She'd once been known, by music critics and potentates
alike, for her beautiful hands.

*Miss Rogozinski's hands, with their long, elegant fin-
gers, are perfection against the ivory keys of a Steinway.
And while the lady may look like an angel, she plays with
the ferocity and the heart of a concert virtuoso.*

*"Your hands, my dearest Anna, like the rest of you, were
made to be adorned with jewels and precious gems."*

"Miss Rogozinski, are you all right?"

Anna made herself come back to the present. "My
hands do seem particularly stiff tonight."

Her housekeeper-companion clicked her tongue in gentle disapproval. "It's no good for you to sit out in the cool
night air like that. Does a body harm. Especially an older
one with arthritis."

Esther knew nearly all there was to know about older

folk's troubles. During the last—if not the best—years of their lives, she had cared for her parents, her grandparents, even several elderly aunts and uncles before becoming a paid companion.

"If you like, once you're ready for bed, I'll massage some of the special cream into your hands that the doctor prescribed," she said, laying out her lady's nightgown just the way Anna preferred.

"I'm sure that would help. Thank you."

"Earrings first?"

Anna nodded.

Esther carefully removed the sapphire earrings one by one and placed them on the dressing table. The matching sapphire necklace followed and then the diamond ring.

"These sure are pretty things," she said. "I had sparklers once, but the stones came loose. Even lost one or two. So I put them away for safekeeping. I still take them out on special occasions or when my heart is feeling kind of heavy. Just looking at pretty things cheers me up no end." The solidly built, usually no-nonsense woman straightened and urged, "Tell me again about yours."

They'd been down this pathway before. Esther asking for the stories and Anna telling them, and both women deriving immense pleasure from the ritual.

"The earrings and necklace were a gift from a *conte* who heard me play in Venice," Anna recalled, carried along by her memories. "He called my music *magnifico,* and came to hear me perform every evening for an entire month."

"Imagine that," said Esther, shaking her head in wonder as she bent down to remove Anna's shoes.

"The ring was bestowed upon me by a maharajah after I agreed to a single performance at his summer palace. I'll never forget that night. He came up after the concert, inclined his regal head ever so slightly, and then presented me with what he called a 'tiny bauble' in appreciation of the pleasure my music had given to him and his guests."

Who but a maharajah would consider a flawless five-carat diamond a mere bauble?

"The sparklers I lost weren't half the size of the stone in your ring," said the housekeeper as she hung Anna's dress up in the closet.

It was a simple statement of fact. There was no envy in the woman's voice, even though Anna suspected Esther's jewelry was actually set with crystals or rhinestones rather than genuine diamonds. The pleasure the two women derived from their "sparklers" was the same, either way. One of life's little ironies.

"Where was the maharajah's palace?" the woman asked, placing her lady's undergarments in a lingerie bag to await laundering.

"Near Darjeeling, in the north of India," Anna said, slipping the clean nightgown over her head.

Esther finished tidying the bedroom. "That's the kind of tea you sometimes drink, isn't it?"

Anna nodded and went into the adjoining bathroom to brush her teeth and remove what little makeup she wore at this stage in her life.

She gazed at herself in the mirror above the sink. Admittedly her hair was snow white now where it had once been the color of honey, but her complexion was still good. Even enviable for her age. Apparently she'd avoided any extensive sun damage, and the wrinkles that went with it, by spending years sleeping half the day away and performing during the evening.

Esther was turning down the covers when she returned

to her bedroom. The housekeeper was meticulous by nature; she smoothed out a single wrinkle in the top sheet before looking up. "Have you seen the Taj Mahal?"

"Oh, yes."

Next, pillows were plumped. "I always imagined it would be the loveliest spot on earth. Just think of it: a beautiful palace built by a man in memory of his beloved wife." The woman gave a wistful sigh. "I've seen pictures of the Taj Mahal. I wonder if it's as clean and sparkling white as it looks."

"It was when I last saw it." Of course, that had been forty years ago. Or was it fifty now? Anna wondered briefly if Esther realized the Taj Mahal was a tomb.

"My, but you've traveled to some strange and wondrous places, Miss Rogozinski. Places I've only seen pictures of in books or on television. I don't expect I'll ever get to Venice or Dar-jelling," the housekeeper said, stumbling over the pronunciation.

Anna's eyes began to drift shut.

"Enough of my chatter. I see you need to be tucked in your bed for the night."

She agreed and tried not to fuss. "I don't want the earrings and ring left out. My jewelry box is in the bottom drawer of the dresser. The key is in the vanity, under the powder puffs."

This was the first time Anna had trusted her hired companion to put her jewelry away. But the woman had more than proven herself to be reliable and trustworthy, punctual and a hard worker. For the past year Esther had looked after her with patience and kindness, and with the proper respect.

There was no pretense to Esther Preston. She wasn't a formally educated woman, but she had certainly learned life's lessons the hard way as a widow who'd had to make it on her own in the world. Anna not only sympathized with her, but respected her for it as well.

"You go on and climb in. I'll put your jewelry away where it belongs," Esther said. "And I won't forget to rub the cream into your hands before you fall asleep."

She was as good as her word. Anna watched through heavy lids as her jewelry was safely locked up. Then Esther sat on the edge of the mattress and began to gently massage the soothing ointment into her aching joints. Warmth and relief spread up her hands and into her arms. She couldn't seem to keep her eyes open.

The last words she remembered hearing before the room went dark were, "Good night, my lady. Sweet dreams."

Was she dreaming? Or was she suspended in that timeless place between waking and sleeping? The place where the old were young again, and the young saw their lives stretched out before them like a winding road on the horizon?

Jacob.

She remembered another time—a long-ago time—and another dance in the park. She had been young and beautiful then. Men had vied for the chance to take a turn on the dance floor with her. But she had eyes only for Jacob Charles: tall, handsome, heroic, and resplendent in his officer's uniform.

Jacob fascinated her. He'd been everywhere. He knew everyone. He moved freely and confidently in New York and London society. He attended the opera and the ballet on both sides of the Atlantic. He endowed museums and supported charity galas. He spoke four languages fluently, besides English. He'd studied at Oxford and had hitch-hiked through Italy one summer, learning the local customs, eating the native cuisine, drinking their wine.

He had done all the things she'd only dreamed of, or so it seemed. In her eighteen years, Anna Rogozinski had traveled no farther from home than Chicago. Even then it had been for a piano recital, and she'd been chaperoned by her music teacher and her parents.

Jacob had been honest with her. He'd told her right up front that he was engaged to a girl back home in New York. She'd informed him that it didn't matter one iota to her. She was planning to become the greatest concert pianist of her generation. After the war she was going to travel the world, performing in every major city and in every legendary concert hall, and she never intended to marry anyone.

They'd both been true to their word.

Still, sometimes as she lay in her bed at night, not altogether certain if she were awake or asleep, Anna wondered what her life would be like if she had made other choices, if her ruling passion had been for a man instead of her music.

She only wondered briefly, of course, because regrets were for the weak-minded and the weak-willed, and her mind and will were like tempered steel.

Then she would think of the last words Jacob had said to her before he'd boarded the eastbound train that day. "Water from the moon, Anna. That's what I am to you, that's what you are to me."

"Water from the moon," she'd repeated. "That's lovely, but what does it mean?"

"It means something we can never have."

He'd kissed her right there at the train station in front of half the town of Sweetheart. She'd kissed him back, then had stood on the platform and watched as his train pulled away.

She'd forgotten to wave and she had refused to cry.

Anna brushed a hand across her cheek. She was vaguely aware that both her face and the pillow were damp.

Water from the moon.

"You silly old fool," she muttered to herself. "It's too late for tears now."

Chapter
twenty

No one was home. No one but the damned dog, that is. Most people in town were still at the dance.

The dog started barking as soon as the handle on the back door was rattled. It didn't take any time or skill to get the door open. The lock was old. A standard skeleton key and a little luck had taken care of the rest. It was a piece of cake.

The house wasn't much different than the last time the intruder had been inside. Well, at least the laundry room and the kitchen weren't. The walls were the same pukey pink. It was the same flecked linoleum on the floor. Same old countertops. Even the table and chairs were the same. Some things never changed.

The dog wouldn't stop barking. Thank God, dogs were always barking in Sweetheart. Still, getting the mongrel out of the way for a few minutes would make the job go a lot faster and a lot easier. The animal was lured outside and tossed a juicy bone brought along just for the occasion. Then the pet door was blocked shut with a chair.

It was time to get to work.

There was a full moon tonight. That was both good news and bad news.

The bad news had come first. Even dressed in camouflage, trying to sneak across the backyard and up to the house left the trespasser clearly visible if a neighbor happened to look out their window. Fortunately the old biddy who lived across the street wasn't home from the dance yet. Not that she had an unobstructed view of the back door even with her binoculars.

The good news was that the moonlight streaming in the kitchen window meant the job could be done without a flashlight.

The intruder stood in the middle of the room. Then drawers and cupboards were opened one by one and their contents eyed. Experience was always a good teacher. There was a right way and a wrong way of doing this.

A small foil bag finally caught the uninvited guest's attention. It was held up to the moonlight. There was a label on the front and printed lettering.

"Sweet Dreams," was read out loud. "What in the hell is Sweet Dreams?"

The top of the bag had been folded over and secured with a plastic clip. The clip was carefully removed and placed on the counter. The foil bag made a crinkling noise as the top was opened; it seemed to echo through the whole house since the dog had suddenly decided to stop barking.

The intruder froze for a minute or two, then leaned over and took a sniff.

Tea?

It smelled like tea. Tea with something a little extra added. Maybe it was one of those fancy blends. Or maybe it was some of that herbal crap Minerva Bagley sold all over town.

The tea smelled funny already. Maybe it looked funny, too. A small amount was poured out into a gloved palm.

"That's the ticket," came a satisfied whisper.

The grandfather clock in the entranceway chimed the quarter hour. It was getting late; already past midnight. It was time to finish up and get the hell out of Dodge.

The tea was dumped back into the sack. A small packet was removed from a pocket, torn open, and poured into the tea. There was a knife in the drain rack by the sink. It was used to stir up the contents, so the tiny crystals wouldn't be noticed. Then the sack was meticulously refolded, the plastic clip replaced, and the tea put in its proper place in the cupboard. The empty packet went into a shirt pocket. The knife was wiped off on a pant leg and returned to the drain rack.

There was a soft snicker in the moonlit kitchen.

It hadn't been so hard to slip a little Demolition Insecticide in somewhere, after all. It was doubtful anybody would notice until it was too late. The dose had been guesswork. It might make her sick. It might make her real sick. All there was left to do now was wait and see.

Poisoning someone took a heap of patience. It might be a day or a week or even longer before Miss Charles made herself a cup of Sweet Dreams. But when she did, her dreams would be anything but sweet; that was guaranteed.

Maybe if she got real sick, she'd realize Sweetheart was bad luck for her. Maybe then she'd see it was better for everybody if she got back into her big, black, shiny limousine and took the first road out of town. They'd all done just fine and dandy without her. There was no reason for her to stay. Those who'd worked hard deserved the rewards, not some Johnny-come-lately.

The intruder was removing the chair blocking the doggie door when sounds could be heard coming from the other end of the house.

Someone was home.

She was here.

Maybe Samuel Law, too.

The key turned in the front door. The intruder quickly slipped out the back and past the dog chewing on its bone.

Blood pumped hard and fast through legs and arms as the backyard was crossed at a gallop. A hand was planted on a fence post for leverage as first one leg and then the other were swung over the back fence. It was time to skirt the pond. Then a final burst of energy and it was into the cornfield and home free.

Air was gulped into lungs starved for oxygen.

Skin was drenched with sweat.

Muscles trembled from exertion.

Pulse was pounding wildly.

Plastic gloves were slipped off and stuffed into a pocket. No reason to get sloppy at this stage of the game.

There wasn't a single shred of evidence that anyone had been in the house, except for the Demolition in the tea. No fingerprints. No mishaps. Nothing out of place.

A smug expression transformed into a grotesque grin.

No one would ever know who. Or why. Or even when Miss Charles had been poisoned . . .

Chapter
twenty-one

The clock on the bedside table said 2:45. The small red dot beside the A.M. was blinking. It was the middle of the night. Gillian shifted restlessly and punched at her pillow. She'd been lying here since midnight. Insomnia was rearing its ugly head again.

A psychologist-friend had once told her that insomnia was no more than a bad habit. If he was right, then like most bad habits, this one was hard to break.

In the end, Gillian wasn't sure which was more disturbing. To lie in bed hour after hour, eyes wide open, unable to sleep. Or to fall asleep only to dream dreams—nightmares—that woke her as if she'd been plunged headfirst into the waters of an icy sea.

On those nights, she shot straight up in bed, her heart racing like a runaway train, and her hair, her pajamas, her body drenched in a cold sweat. She felt as if she were jumping out of her skin, as if she were suffocating, unable to breathe, as if her lungs were starved for oxygen.

In her dark dreams, as she called them, she was always running away from someone, some*thing*. There were menacing footsteps right on her heels. There was the stench of someone's—some*thing's*—breath on the back of her neck, stirring the tiny hairs there and raising the gooseflesh on her body.

She tried to turn around and see who it was or *what* it was, to finally put a face or a name to the terrifying unknown, but it was always at that precise moment she woke up.

Gillian knew a little about dream interpretation. Being chased supposedly stemmed from feelings of anxiety, stress, fear. Running away was an instinctive reaction to a physical threat in waking life; the "fight or flight" response that had evolved in human beings over thousands of years. And with good reason, it had probably meant the difference between survival and extinction. She just wasn't sure she believed the same was true for dreams.

She'd recently watched a documentary on a local public television channel about dreams. One theory was that neurons fire off during deep REM sleep and the result was dreams formed out of random bits of memory, rather like the odds and ends of leftover cloth used to sew a crazy quilt. A patch here. A patch there. No pattern. No logic. No meaning. Certainly no need for interpretation.

Of course, then there were her *other* dreams.

In those dreams a man was holding her, kissing her, caressing her, making love to her. She'd never seen his face and she'd never known who he was until the past several weeks. Since the night of the community dance, since the night they'd kissed in the park, the face in her dreams was Sam's.

"Oh, great, now you're dreaming about your lawyer." Gillian gave her pillow another good punch. "Nobody has dreams about their lawyer. Nightmares, yes. Sex dreams, no." Her self-amused laughter bounced off the walls, creating an eerie echo in the bedroom. The sleeping dog at her feet suddenly lifted his head and stared at her. His eyes were huge shiny pools of black. "Sorry, Max."

The sheepdog heaved a great sigh—she'd never realized dogs sighed before she met Max—and rested his head on her thigh. She reached down and scratched him behind the ears.

Being wide awake, while the rest of the world slept, wasn't nearly so lonely or frightening when someone was there to share it with you. More than ever, Gillian wished she'd had a dog when she was a girl, especially during those difficult months after her parents had been killed. The warmth and comfort of someone beside her at night would have been an immense help.

"When I have children, Max . . ." She stopped and, with the back of her hand, wiped away unexpected tears. Then she took a deep breath and cleared her throat. "If I ever have children, I'll make sure they have a dog like you." She caressed his smooth black head. "I'm going to miss you more than I can say."

Maybe once she was back in the city, she'd pay a visit to the local animal shelter and adopt a dog who needed her as much as she needed him. Not that it would ever be the same.

"You'll always be my first, Max," she said, pushing herself up into a sitting position.

Maybe it was time to admit defeat and get up, read awhile, watch some TV, make herself a cup of that special tea Minerva had given her for nights like tonight.

Gillian switched on the lamp on the bedside table. It was an Arts and Crafts style, complete with its original leaded glass shade. She'd bought it at the antique mall last week. The dealer had also been willing to part with the table, a very nice Frank Lloyd Wright reproduction, for a surprisingly reasonable price.

It wasn't until she'd gotten the lamp and the table home that she'd realized the furniture not only was perfect for the space, but reminded her of Sam. That settled the matter. When she left in a few months, whatever improvements she'd made to his house, including any furniture, would be her parting gift to him.

"The most I could ever get out of Jacob was: 'It's my last gift to Gillian.' "

"Last gift," she said softly.

For the hundredth time since arriving in Sweetheart, Gillian wished her grandfather had left some clue, some hint as to the reason behind his so-called gift to her.

"What in the world were you thinking, Grandpa?" she said, swinging her legs over the edge of the mattress. "Why didn't you confide in me while you were still alive?"

Most people who had known Jacob Armand Charles were aware that he'd been a stubborn man. He'd liked getting his own way. And he'd always preferred—in fact, he'd needed—to be in charge.

As a man of wealth, power, and social position, her grandfather had control over most areas of his life, but he'd felt—*been*—tragically out-of-control when it came to the accident that had claimed his son's life. He hadn't been able to do anything to change that. No amount of money or influence or power had mattered then. The frustration of being powerless to save his family had understandably driven her grandfather a little crazy for a while.

Gillian sighed and slipped her feet into the slippers that matched her silk pajamas.

Maybe she was asking herself the wrong question. Maybe the right question was: *Why Sweetheart, Indiana?*

What did she know about this place and her grandfather? Well, it was a town he'd had connections with dating back more than sixty years. It was a town where he'd apparently had lifelong friends like Bert Bagley. It was a town he'd felt so strongly about that he had bought up dozens of businesses and properties during the intervening decades since the war. In fact, he'd purchased a farm on the outskirts of town only six months before his death, according to Sam.

And it was a town that her grandfather had never mentioned to her. Not once.

Gillian reached for her cashmere robe. Max immediately jumped down from the bed and took up his post by the door. He waited patiently, tail swishing back and forth across the floor.

She gave him an affectionate pat as she walked by. "How about a doggie treat, boy, while I have a cup of tea?"

He answered with a soft woof.

She tramped downstairs, Max at her heels. After living for the better part of a month and a half in this house, she could now find her way in the dark. She paused and gazed out the window. The porch light over Sam's front door was a beacon in the night. The only other illumination was cast by the streetlight on the corner. Otherwise, the world was dark and quiet and asleep.

Gillian flipped on the light switch in the kitchen and immediately felt a sense of gratification, even pride, at the sight that greeted her. A bright, cheery, sun yellow kitchen was a definite improvement over a Pepto-Bismol pink one.

Thanks to Sylvia—a young woman of many talents, as it turned out, not the least of which was a variety of home improvements skills that Gillian sadly lacked—the job of painting the kitchen had been done in a fraction of the time it would have taken Gillian on her own.

The two of them had formed a friendship during the hours they'd worked side by side. In fact, they had decided to start painting the upstairs bedrooms together the day after tomorrow.

Max plopped down in the middle of the kitchen floor. His eyes followed her every move as she filled the kettle with water and put it on the stove. She took down a cup and saucer before rooting around in the cupboard for the chamomile tea Minerva had given her weeks ago for when she had trouble sleeping.

Well, tonight was the night.

Gillian was just opening the bag of tea when something caught her attention. Across the side yard between their two houses, a light went on in Sam's kitchen. Well, in his mother's kitchen.

She watched as Sam, bare-chested and wearing only a pair of briefs, sauntered over and opened the refrigerator. Rubbing his abdomen with one hand and holding on to the fridge door with the other, he stood there and studied its contents, head bent, hair ruffled, as if he'd been running his fingers through it. She could even make out the errant strand that had a tendency to fall across his forehead.

Gillian moistened her lips with the tip of her tongue, and tried to swallow.

Sam was half-naked.

More than half, actually.

She thought of the snapshot she'd seen of him back in the offices of Dutton, Dutton, McQuade & Martin the first time she'd heard his name, learned of his existence; the snapshot she'd studied in the limo on the drive into town.

Gillian blew out her breath. Sam's shoulders *were*

ridiculously broad. His masculine features *were* too handsome, but he was definitely *not* too pretty.

His build was athletic. His arms were muscular. His jawline was chiseled. His ears were flat against his head. His nose was in perfect proportion to the rest of his face. There was a small bump on the bridge of his nose; she wondered if it had been broken playing football. And he had that careless, tousled, incredibly sexy look of a man who has just crawled out of bed.

What color were his eyes at 3 A.M.? Was his skin still warm? Did he smell of clean sheets and a man's sleep? Did he have a nighttime erection?

Gillian groaned out loud. She couldn't help but remember what it had felt like to have his body—tough as nails and twice as hard—pressed up against hers.

Heat flamed her cheeks. Her breathing was quick, shallow, erratic. Her pulse was throbbing in the small hollow at the base of her throat. Here, in the flesh, was the reason she couldn't fall asleep. The devil in disguise. That's what he was.

Not much of a disguise.

"Get a grip, girl," she said, chastising herself.

The kettle on the stove began to whistle like a freight train. Gillian quickly set the bag of tea on the counter and reached over to turn off the burner. When she looked up again, Sam was standing at his kitchen window watching her.

He raised his hand.

She slowly raised hers.

Then he suddenly disappeared.

The stillness of the night was shattered by the shrill ring of the telephone on the wall behind her. She jumped straight up in the air. Her elbow connected with the bag of tea. It went flying off the counter and hit the floor with a soft thud, scattering loose tea leaves everywhere.

"Damn-sam," Gillian muttered under her breath as she picked up the receiver.

"Guess that means you don't want to talk," came a husky male voice, a voice that sent hot prickles down her spine.

"It was just an expression. Nothing personal." She glanced up and saw him framed in the kitchen window, a cell phone held against his ear. "Hi, Sam."

"Hi, Gillian." Her heart thumped in her chest. "Are you okay?" he asked.

"I'm fine." She brushed at the sleeve of her bathrobe. "I spilled some tea, that's all."

"I didn't mean to startle you."

Well, he had. "You know what they say," she said, looking in his direction.

"What?"

"There's no use in crying over spilled tea."

"You're having a cup of tea at"—Sam paused, raised his left arm, and stared at the watch on his wrist—"three-oh-seven?"

"You're digging in your fridge for something to eat at"—Gillian glanced at the clock on the kitchen wall—"three-oh-eight?"

"I was hungry."

"I was thirsty."

Fingers were dragged through thick dark hair. "Truthfully, I couldn't sleep," said Sam.

She hesitated. "Neither could I."

"Food sometimes helps." He cleared his throat and said, "My favorite middle-of-the-night snack is Ritz crackers, topped with cottage cheese and . . ."

"What?"

"Ketchup."

She shuddered at the thought. "You actually put ketchup on cottage cheese?"

Sam sniffed as if her question was an affront to his dignity—or at the very least his taste in food—but Gillian could hear the laughter in his voice. "Doesn't everyone?"

"Not everyone," she said.

"Have you ever tried cottage cheese with ketchup?"

She shook her head.

"Didn't they teach you anything at that fancy cooking school you attended?"

"How did you know I went to Cordon Bleu?"

"I have my ways," he said mysteriously.

"It was Trace Ballinger, wasn't it? You two went to Harvard Law together. I'll bet you're still as thick as thieves." She made a sound that was halfway between annoyance and amusement. "And I'll bet he blabbed."

Sam cleared his throat. "I'm taking the Fifth on that one. Anyway, back to the cottage cheese and ketchup. Do you know the best way to prepare the dish?"

She put her hand on her hip. "I don't think it was covered in the curriculum at Cordon Bleu."

"Just as well. I'm sure gourmets wouldn't have a clue whether to serve a red or a white wine with it."

Okay, that was fairly droll, she thought, and laughed out loud.

"Anyway, first you mash the cottage cheese with your fork. That gets out all those large lumps that tend to collect in the bottom of the container. Next you drizzle ketchup on the top. Personally I prefer Heinz, but any brand will do, I suppose. Then you stir well until it's a kind of salmon pink color. The last step is to heap the mixture onto the Ritz crackers."

"This helps you sleep?"

"No. But it's the only thing I've got in my fridge besides cold beer and what looks like a piece of cheese."

"Only *looks* like a piece of cheese?"

She could hear the bafflement in his voice. "There's a bluish-gray mold growing on what was once a chunk of extra-sharp cheddar. I guess I'd better ditch it, huh?"

She gave the matter some thought and then shrugged. "Do you like blue cheese or Stilton?"

"Sure."

"Well, the blue vein in those cheeses is a deliberate form of mold. I recommend you scrape off the blue-grayish stuff and eat the cheese. *Bon appetit.*"

"If you say so," Sam said, sounding less than convinced.

"Trust me, I know my cheese," she assured him. "Europeans make hundreds of varieties of cheeses. It's a national passion in most countries on the continent."

He was none too subtle in changing the subject. "What are you having?"

She glanced down at the mess on the kitchen floor. "I was making myself a cup of something Minerva calls 'Sweet Dreams.' Max is nibbling on a doggie treat."

"You spoil him rotten."

"Do you mind?"

"Not in the least."

"I mean do you mind that he's staying with me?"

Sam made a sound in the back of his throat. "Hell, you take better care of him than I do. Than I did. He wouldn't have me back even if I wanted him to come back." He took the conversation in a different direction. "Ready for your driving lesson tomorrow?"

"I think so."

He ran his hand back and forth over the smattering of dark hair on his chest. "We'll drive out into the countryside and see how you manage on rough terrain instead of paved city streets. If all goes well, you'll be ready to take your behind-the-wheel."

Her stomach flipped over. "Just the thought of driving

with someone else sitting in the front seat beside me watching my every move makes me nervous."

"Believe me, everybody's jittery when they take their first driving test," Sam said, obviously in an attempt to reassure her.

"Were you?"

There was a pause. "No." He snorted. "But I was a cocky, overconfident sixteen-year-old at the time. At that age I figured I was pretty much invincible."

"Most people do when they're sixteen," she said, suddenly thoughtful.

"But you didn't, did you?"

"No."

"What were you doing at sixteen?"

She opened her mouth and the words came out unedited, uncensored. "Wishing I could be like everyone else. Wishing I could learn how to drive." She gave a small sigh. "Better late than never, I guess."

" 'It's never too late to be what you might have been,' " Sam quoted softly.

"Who said that?"

"George Eliot."

"Then George Eliot was very wise."

"Yes, she was."

There was something she'd been wanting to say to him for several weeks. "You've been a very patient teacher, Sam."

"You're a good driver. In fact, you're a natural. You took to it like a duck to water."

Her cheeks warmed with pleasure. "Do you really think so?"

"Yup."

"Well, I know you're a busy man. I appreciate the time you've taken out of your schedule."

"Hey, I can always make time for you," Sam said, his voice dropping lower.

The night suddenly became very intimate.

"I'll find some way to pay you back," Gillian said, noticing that her mouth had gone dry.

"That's not necessary. I know you're making major improvements to the house. Sylvia can't stop talking about it. Or you. She thinks you're an amazing woman."

"I like her, too."

"Want to know what else she said to me when she was cleaning my parents' house last week?"

Probably some of the same crazy, romantic drivel Sylvia had been spouting to her over the past several weeks.

Gillian segued into another topic of conversation. "Speaking of your parents: You got a postcard from them today." She reached for the stack of mail.

"Where from this time?"

"An amusement park in California. There's a picture of a roller coaster on the front and it says: 'Take a wild ride on The Prehistoric Beast.' Then: 'We dare you not to scream.' "

"My mother loves amusement parks. She also loves roller coasters. Not so sure about my dad." Then Sam urged, "You can read what she wrote to me."

So she did. " 'Dear Sam, I had to bribe your dad to go on the roller coaster. He prefers the Ferris wheel, which we rode six times today. Next we plan to drive up the coast along Highway 1 toward the wine country. Hope you're having a great summer. Give our best to Gillian. Love, Mom and Dad.' " She looked up and stared at him across no-man's-land. "How does your mother know my name?"

He snickered. "Are you kidding? Every time they call to chat with one of their friends in town—even my secretary— all they talk about is you."

"Your parents know I'm not your ex-fiancée Nora, right?"

"My mom has figured it out. She's too smart to put anything private on a public post card, of course." He cleared his throat. "Which brings me back to my original question."

She didn't want to ask, but wasn't sure how to get out of asking, "What question?"

"Know what else Sylvia said to me when she was finished cleaning my parents' place?"

Gillian's heart was drumming in her ears. "No, I don't."

"She thinks we're perfect for each other."

There was dead silence.

Finally she forced a response and said, "Sylvia is a romantic and a natural born matchmaker."

"Yes, she is."

"I guess she doesn't understand that you and I are very"—in a split second any number of words were considered and rejected—"different."

"We are that."

"In fact, we're opposites."

"That's for damned sure." She could see Sam's smile and knew he'd meant that as a double entendre.

"You know what they say about opposites?"

He cocked his head to one side and dropped his voice even lower. "Sure. Opposites attract."

"I was thinking more along the lines of that quote—I can't remember who said it—'A bird and a fish may love, but where will they live?' "

Silence.

"Ah, *that* quote."

Gillian realized she'd been hoping for a clever comeback from Sam. There was none.

"It's getting late," he finally said, his voice altering slightly. "I should let you go."

She stood there in front of the window and nodded. "I have to clean up the mess I made."

"Just sweep the tea out the back door."

"Okay."

There was another awkward silence.

"Well, good night then, Sam."

"Good night, Gillian. Sweet dreams."

The phone went dead. Ten seconds later the light went out in his kitchen. The night suddenly seemed lonely again.

Gillian went to the utility closet, took out a broom, and began to clean up the spilled tea. She unlocked the back door and did as Sam had suggested.

Since she wouldn't be enjoying a cup of Minerva's chamomile blend tonight, it was time to take a different approach to the insomnia problem.

"C'mon, Max, maybe one of Mozart's *sotto* sonatas or Liszt's *Liebestraume* will soothe the savage beast. I'm pretty sure it will put you to sleep."

Max trotted along behind her as she turned off the kitchen light and went to her piano.

Sam stood in the dark, watching.

He'd been upstairs at the window of his old bedroom when he'd first seen the light go on in her kitchen.

On impulse he'd jogged downstairs.

On impulse he'd waved to her.

On impulse he'd called her on his cell phone.

Now it took every ounce of self-control he possessed not to pull on a pair of jeans and run across the yard to his house . . . to Gillian's house. It took every ounce of his self-control not to call her back. Not to tell her that he couldn't sleep and she couldn't sleep so, what the hell, why didn't they not sleep together?

There were all kinds of things they could do together in the middle of the night. They could listen to music. They could read. They could watch TV. They could sit and talk. They could share a cup of tea or a cold drink. They could even dance.

Sam smiled to himself. Yeah, or they could do the "horizontal rhumba" and put him out of his misery. Take his mind off the one thing that had been keeping him awake: Gillian.

He'd read somewhere that there were three kinds of moments in life: Yes. No. And Wow!

Gillian was Wow!

He rubbed his hand back and forth across his bare chest. No future in Wow!

Didn't have to be.

Wow! moments weren't expected to last.

The kitchen went dark. A minute later a light came on in the front of his house. He was willing to bet Gillian was going to her piano. He couldn't see the alcove. There was a tree in the way. But he could imagine her sitting there in the middle of the night, playing some beautiful piece of music, her back straight, her hair flowing around her shoulders, her lovely hands flying across the piano keys, Max stretched out at her feet.

He realized he'd be willing to trade places with his dog any day of the week and twice on Sundays.

"It's a dog's life, Max, old boy," Sam muttered under his breath as he headed upstairs for a shower. "I sure as hell hope you appreciate it."

Chapter
twenty-two

"Don't I get any credit for missing the pig?"

Sam sat slumped in the passenger seat, his legs stretched out in front of him, his elbow propped up on the edge of the open window. He was wearing dark aviator sunglasses to conceal bloodshot eyes. His throat was scratchy and his head was pounding from way too much coffee and far too little sleep. His beard was like sandpaper; he hadn't bothered shaving this morning.

What the hell, he thought, it was Wednesday and he was taking a rare weekday off.

He was also in a foul mood and only half joking when he snapped at Gillian, "If you'd hit the pig, it would have meant a demerit on your driving record and a sizable dent in your front bumper." He paused and then added, "Plus, you'd be required to compensate the farmer for the loss of his animal."

"Are you speaking now as my driving instructor or as my attorney?" she inquired.

"Both."

Gillian gave him a sidelong glance. "I thought you said I own the Flying Pig."

"You do."

She swallowed and hurried on with the point she seemed determined to make. "Doesn't that mean I own the land, the duck pond, the houses, the outbuildings, the grain silos, the farm equipment, and the livestock, including the pig I almost hit?"

His jaw clenched. He gave her a reluctant, "Yes."

Gillian looked like a million bucks this morning in designer jeans that fit her derriere like a glove, a T-shirt with the word BABE emblazoned across the chest in silver glitter, and a pair of sandals that were a concoction of skinny straps and impossibly high heels. Her shoes were totally impractical for driving, or anything else for that matter, but they did show off her fine-boned ankles.

Sam also noticed her toenails were painted the color of Big Reds—those extra-sweet, oversize Texas grapefruit—and looked good enough to eat.

He wondered if she'd mind if he nibbled on her.

She was single-minded, even tenacious. "Can I be held liable for hitting my own pig?"

He ground his teeth. "Probably not."

"So, other than for humanitarian reasons, I can do whatever I like to the pig."

"Yeah, that's right, you can. You own the pig." He took a small bottle of aspirin from his shirt pocket, lined up the arrows, flipped the top off, tapped four pills into the palm of his hand, snapped the bottle shut again, then popped all four aspirin into his mouth, and chewed them up dry. The bitter aftertaste suited his mood perfectly. "I'd be hard pressed to find something in this town you don't own, Ms. Charles," he muttered under his breath.

"I think somebody got up on the wrong side of the bed this morning," Gillian said, as if she were humoring him.

Geez, I wonder who, Sam thought as he turned and stared out the window of the vehicle.

The wind was blowing in his face, ruffling his hair, but bringing with it some relief from the sledgehammer banging against the back of his head. Unfortunately, the breeze also brought with it the distinctive odors of the barnyard.

There were fields on either side of the road. The corn on his right was well on its way to being "knee high by the Fourth of July." There was a white frame farmhouse on the left. Trumpet lilies were in full bloom; they cascaded over a weathered fence in a splash of vivid orange. An American flag blew majestically in the wind. Laundry dried on an old-fashioned clothesline. Red barns dotted the landscape, along with a flock of Canadian geese, a herd of dairy cows, the odd horse or two, and the occasional mud-covered pig.

In fact, Gillian had just missed hitting a two-hundred-pound sow that had somehow gotten out of its pen and was wandering across the road into the adjoining field.

Make the most of your freedom, pig. Life's a bitch and then you're bacon.

The woman beside him was unrelentingly cheerful. "Maybe you didn't get enough sleep last night, Sam. We can postpone my driving lesson, if you like."

"Sleep, or the lack thereof, has nothing to do with it," he said stubbornly.

"Do you want to tell me why you're angry?" She sounded just like his third grade teacher.

"I'm not angry."

"Yes, you are."

He counted to ten—twice—and then pitched his voice a

little louder and enunciated even more clearly, as if that would somehow convince her where his words had failed to. "No. I am not."

Apparently his anger was a foregone conclusion in her opinion. "You said anger was a waste of time." She barely paused for a breath. "You said . . ."

"I know what I said." Sam rubbed his jaw as if he were scrubbing it with his hand. "I've got a lot on my mind, that's all." He blew out his breath in exasperation. "Maybe it was a mistake to let you buy a pickup truck."

Gillian's eyes were fixed on the dirt road in front of them. "I thought you said if I can drive a pickup with a stick shift, I can drive just about anything."

On occasion the woman drove him nuts, Sam decided. For one thing, she had this annoying habit of remembering everything he said and then quoting it back to him.

For another, she was usually right.

He slouched in his seat, plucked a nonexistent speck of lint from the pant leg of his blue jeans, and drummed his fingers on the edge of the window. "It's true."

"Then why the change of heart?"

He scrambled for an answer. "A pickup is a lot for a woman to handle. Especially a delicate woman like you." It sounded pretty lame even to him.

"I'm not all that delicate," Gillian said in that sweet, self-deprecating, and at the moment, irritating way she had of laughing at herself. "I've handled bigger things than this."

"I'll just bet you have."

He was being a real pain in the ass, but he didn't care. He was pretty much pissed at the world in general and at himself in particular. He'd broken one of his cardinal rules. He gotten involved with a client—assuming a few kisses and feeling Ms. Charles up that night in the park consti-tuted involvement—and he was paying the price. He hadn't had enough sleep. He wasn't eating right. His concentration was shot to hell, along with his patience.

And he wanted to hit something.

"Turn north on County Road 400. That's right at the next intersection for you city folks," he said in a snide tone.

She knew which direction was north. That's what the compass on her dashboard was for.

She also knew Sam was in a foul mood. What she didn't know was why. But it had been apparent the minute he'd shown up on her doorstep this morning with his face unshaven, his shirttail hanging out, and his eyes hidden behind dark glasses. One-word responses had also been a dead giveaway.

"Would you like a cup of coffee before we go?" she'd asked.

"Nope."

"Have you had any breakfast?"

"Nope."

"Hungry?"

That time he'd simply stood there in the doorway, shaken his head, and skipped the "nope."

"Are you feeling all right?"

"Yup."

"You're sure you want to do this?"

He'd nodded.

"Well, I guess I'm ready if you are," she'd said, grabbing her handbag and car keys off the table in the front hall and calling out to Max that she'd be back later.

"Head straight down Main Street," Sam had said. From there, his instructions had quickly reverted to one-word orders. "Right." Followed a few minutes later by, "Left." He'd even pointed in one case and said nothing at all.

He made her nervous, sitting there all broody and silent, displeasure radiating from every pore. She wasn't the type to automatically assume it was something she'd done, but she wondered if it was something she'd done.

Gillian drew in a deep breath and let it out slowly. While men in general were fairly transparent, in her opinion, this man was a complete and utter mystery to her. Even after spending countless hours in his company over the past six-going-on-seven weeks, she wondered if she knew anything about him at all.

Oh, sure, she was aware that Sam's favorite pizza was triple pepperoni and his beer of choice—well, ale of choice—was Guinness. She knew he preferred going to the movies over watching television, and reading over going to the movies. His favorite books were nonfiction: an eclectic mixture of history, science, and true crime. She knew his bookshelves also contained a collection of lawyers-turned-best-selling fiction writers: David Baldacci, John Grisham, Scott Turow.

The radio in his SUV was usually tuned to a country-and-western station or to old-time rock 'n' roll. He was addicted to pistachio ice cream. He hated the color chartreuse. He had no time for ostentatious or pretentious people. He had a killer smile he used on rare but appropriate occasions, and always with the desired effect. He was a good listener. A great listener, in her opinion. He went down on his haunches and put himself at eye level whenever he was talking to small children. He worked hard and he believed in justice.

Half the women in the county under the age of fifty thought they were in love with Sam. The other half lusted after Sweetheart's most eligible bachelor. None of them was likely to turn down a tumble in the hay with the man.

He was also a loner. Which she found intriguing since

he lived in a small town where literally everyone knew his name and oftentimes his business.

And he was a great kisser.

Don't go there, Gillian, she cautioned herself. There be dragons. She flicked on the directional signal—*clickety-click, clickety-click*—and turned north at the next intersection.

Of course, this morning Sam was being a real pain in the butt. She'd never seen him like this before. There was, she supposed, a first time for everything.

Five minutes later she headed east, skirted another cornfield—funny how they all looked alike after a while—and started back toward town, slowing to a snail's pace as she approached the city limits.

"This is a one-way street," the man beside her said, growling like a bear with a burr in its paw.

She knew that.

Interjecting a sunny tone into her voice, Gillian said, "By the way, did you know that the first one-way street was established in New York City in 1791?"

Sam acknowledged he was still in a pissant mood when Gillian pulled up in front of her house—well, *his* house, not to put too fine a point on it—stepped on the brakes, turned off the key in the ignition, and released the clutch.

"Emergency brake," he barked.

"I know," she said, giving him a smile he didn't deserve.

He got out of the pickup, slamming the door shut behind him. The sound reverberated along the nerve endings at the back of his neck, reminding him that the aspirin hadn't put a dent in his headache. Plus, he was suddenly hungry. Starved. Never mind breakfast or lunch, he'd never gotten his 3 A.M. snack.

A craving for Ritz crackers and cottage cheese à la ketchup wasn't the only hunger that had been left unsatisfied last night.

No good ever came from a man being at the mercy of his Johnson. That bit of sage advice had been handed out every fall at the start of the football season by Sam's high school coach. It had always been followed by the recommendation to: *Work hard, boys. Exercise. Self-control when it comes to sex. Cold showers, that's the key. Never met a man yet that regretted taking a cold shower.*

"If I take any more cold showers, I'm gonna shrivel up like a prune," Sam said, muttering to himself as he opened the gate and waited for Gillian to precede him down the sidewalk.

If she heard him, she ignored it.

Piano music came from an open window. It was highly unlikely but, "Sylvia?"

Gillian shook her head and pointed to the black limousine parked just beyond Sylvia's vintage cherry red Beetle. "Mr. Biaggi insisted on tuning my piano again this month."

The man who greeted them in the front hallway was not the same Mr. Biaggi whom Sam had first met back in late April. That man had been of short stature. He had also been white-haired, bespectacled, and seventy if he was a day.

This man was tall, dark, and handsome. Too tall and too handsome. His slightly graying-at-the-temples hair was perfectly groomed and perfectly coiffed in a Fifth Avenue kind of way. He was mid-forties, give or take a year. And he was wearing an ascot.

Sam was willing to bet the farm, and every last pig on it, that the guy knew full well the blue silk tied around his neck matched the blue color of his eyes.

"Edoardo, what a lovely surprise."

"*Cara mia,* how good to see you," he said, dropping a

kiss on each of Gillian's cheeks in the European fashion, then kissing her on the mouth in a totally American fashion.

"I wasn't expecting you."

The man chuckled intimately and called her *cara mia* again, and then murmured something in Italian that raised the color on Gillian's face to a becoming pink.

"You are naughty, Edoardo," she said, looking up into his eyes and laughing.

Sam cleared his throat.

Gillian took half a step back. He noticed that Edoardo slipped an arm around her waist as she did so. The message was clear and less than subtle: *Two's company; three's a crowd.*

"This is Samuel Law, my attorney and part-time driving instructor." She moistened her lips. "Sam, Edoardo Biaggi."

"You're the piano tuner," Sam said, reaching out to shake the other man's hand.

Edoardo Biaggi winced and took his hand back, checking to make sure there hadn't been any permanent damage done. "Actually I'm a concert pianist."

Yeah, whatever.

An elegant brow arched above clear, ascot blue eyes. "Part-time driving instructor?"

Gillian positioned herself between the two men. "Sam's been teaching me how to drive."

"He teaches you how to drive a"—Edoardo glanced out the front window—"pickup truck." His cultured voice was full of amusement. "I teach you how to play Mozart."

Sam's lips curved in a parody of a smile. "Well, no offense, Ed, but driving is a necessary skill in these parts. Playing Mozart isn't."

"I don't doubt that for a minute," said the urbane man.

Sam opened his mouth again to say something slightly

sarcastic and definitely adolescent. Something like, "Where'd you get the pretty scarf, piano boy?" when Gillian interjected, "I was expecting your father. I hope he's well."

"He's very well. He sends his regards and his apologies. He was called to Milan, so I volunteered to come take care of your piano myself." He drew her closer. "Anything to have a chance to see you, darling." He gestured with the other hand. "But why are you burying yourself out here in the middle of nowhere? From Newport, it took three planes and a long drive just to get to the place."

"This is not the middle of nowhere," said Sam. "This is the crossroads of America."

"Right," the man agreed, laughing in that sophisticated way of his. "I think I saw that printed on a sign at the airport." He managed to make Sam feel like the outsider. "We have a lot of catching up to do, Gillian. Madge sends her love. Pamela and Biff wonder when you're returning. At a party last weekend the gang all said summer in Newport just isn't the same without you there. Let me see," he said, tapping his perfectly manicured finger against his lower lip, "I have so many messages for you." One hand disappeared into the breast pocket of his navy blue blazer. "I actually jotted them down in my appointment book."

"Would you like a cup of tea?"

"I would love a cup of tea," Edoardo said.

Time to exit stage right, Sam thought. "Well, I'd better be going and let you two play catch-up. Nice to meet you, Ed," he lied. Then he looked directly at Gillian. "I'll be by tomorrow morning around ten to take you to the test site."

"Thank you, Sam."

He nodded. "I'll let myself out."

"Ciao," said the elegant man standing beside Gillian, smiling his Rolex smile.

Sam was out the door and halfway down the sidewalk when he realized Max was trotting along beside him. "You didn't like him either, did you, boy?"

Max gave a soft woof.

"The guy probably keeps poodles. You know, the froufrou kind that prance around at those fancy dog shows."

Sam closed the gate behind him and started for home, shuffling his feet and occasionally kicking a small stone in his path with the toe of his boot.

He ran his hand along the top of the white picket fence and came away with half a dozen small bits of wood embedded in his flesh. He raised his hand to his mouth and pulled out the largest splinter with his teeth. A spot of blood oozed on the pad of his thumb. Sam spit out the first one and went after a second splinter.

Apparently Gillian and Edoardo moved in the same social circles, had the same friends, summered at the same expensive cottages at the shore. No doubt they played a set or two of tennis together every morning in their designer tennis whites. Went sailing and yachting. Played a round of golf at the club. Picnicked along a private stretch of beach. Took afternoon tea in the conservatory. Drank cocktails at seven sharp. Stood around discussing the latest hit show on Broadway, the sold-out concert at Lincoln Center, the marvelous exhibit at the Guggenheim.

On the other hand, what did he and Gillian have in common? Max. Sexual attraction. Guinness and Reubens. Sexual attraction. Laughing at the same jokes . . . sometimes. Sexual attraction.

What the hell difference did it make? Any personal relationship with a client came under the heading "Conflict of Interest." It was the reason he'd always had a strict rule about not fraternizing.

Besides, it seemed inevitable that Gillian would end up

with a guy like Edoardo Biaggi, and he would eventually settle down with one of the women who threw themselves in his path.

Damned depressing thought.

Sam stopped in front of his parents' house, wiped his bloodied hand on his jeans, and glanced down at his companion. "Wanna go for a walk, Max?"

Max wagged his tail and fell into step beside him.

At least he had his dog back.

Chapter
twenty-three

It was the "dog days" of summer. Hot. Humid. Hazy. Not a breath of air stirring. At twilight a mist formed over the land, softening its sharp edges and muffling its sounds.

Summer nights, on the other hand, were a cacophony of noise: chirping crickets, a chorus of frog songs rising from ponds choked green with lily pads and algae, yipping dogs, children's laughter, the occasional backfiring of a car muffler.

At the bewitching hour, the whole world seemed to suddenly fall silent. Far off, on the horizon, heat lightning split the midnight blue canopy in two.

Mornings came early, a wash of pink spilling over sky and land alike. It was the time of year when farmers claimed if you stood in the middle of a field at daybreak and listened carefully, you could actually hear the corn growing.

It was well past noon on a Thursday. Anna Rogozinski was sitting on her front porch, her cane in one hand and an antique ivory fan in the other. She was rocking back and forth, trying to cool herself and trying to buck up her courage to tell Jacob's granddaughter the whole story.

Screw your courage to the sticking-place, Anna. This is no time to lose your nerve. You've been afraid before, but you have never been a coward.

In some ways, it was getting harder and harder not to tell Gillian since the young woman had taken to stopping by several times a week for a visit. At first, their conversations had been polite, courteous, impersonal. Gillian had asked about the old days, the World War Two days, and about Jacob. Anna had answered her questions with great care. In return, she'd been discreet but curious about Gillian's life.

Almost immediately they'd discovered a mutual love of classical music and the piano. The beautiful vintage instrument in her living room was the first thing Gillian had noticed on entering the house. She'd laughed (she did have a lovely laugh; Minerva hadn't exaggerated about that) and said she had a similar Steinway in her front room.

Well, in Sam's front room.

A bond, perhaps even a friendship of sorts, had grown up between the two of them, despite the difference in their ages. She liked Gillian very much, and Gillian seemed to like her. But their relationship was new, fragile, untested. Maybe the time to tell her was never. Maybe she should just leave well enough alone.

Anna brought the tip of her cane down hard on the porch floor. "Damn it, Jacob, you must have suspected this would happen." It was a rare display of temper—for time, age, and experience had mellowed her; had rounded off the sharp edges of her once legendary artistic temperament. "You've thrown the whole thing in my lap and I don't know what to do about it."

She had been so sure of herself at one time. She'd had all the answers. She had known exactly what she wanted and how to get it. But it had been a vastly different world back in the forties. Decisions were either black or white, rather than infinite shades of gray. So was right and wrong.

Then, on December 7, 1941, the war had hit home. Every person of her generation remembered where they were when they'd first heard the news of Pearl Harbor. Suddenly dreams and plans were put on hold, and she had become just another young woman caught up in the passion and the drama of the times.

Against the horrific backdrop of a world war—not knowing from day to day who would live and who would die— she and Jacob had been confident they were doing what was best for everyone involved. Now she wasn't so sure. Now she had so much more to lose.

Or perhaps she had *nothing* left to lose, Anna thought.

She made up her mind. She was going to tell Gillian today, this very afternoon. For a moment she considered beginning with "Once upon a time," but she knew her story had been no fairy tale and she had certainly been no princess.

When her guest walked out onto the porch with two glasses of lemonade, Anna opened her mouth and said, "Will Edoardo be coming back this summer?"

Gillian set the tray down between them. She took a seat and had her glass in hand before she said, "I don't think so. Sweetheart wasn't quite his cup of tea."

"Pity. He seemed like such a nice man."

"He is a nice man."

"He was interesting to converse with, too." Then Anna laughed at her own transparency and at the remnants of her own conceit. "Of course, he was well acquainted with my concert career, had all my records in his personal collection, even the earliest and the rarest, considered me an icon, and worshiped at my feet."

Gillian's mouth curved up at the edges. "I suppose a little hero worship never hurt anyone."

Anna rocked back and forth. Age did have its advantages, she'd discovered. One could blurt out indiscreet and inappropriate questions, and simply be mistaken for being eccentric. Or a bit dotty. "Is there something between you and Edoardo Biaggi?"

"I thought there might be. Briefly."

"But not now?

"Not for some time, actually."

"Would he still like there to be?"

Gillian's answer was succinct. "Yes."

Anna took a sip of lemonade; it was cold and tart on her tongue. "He seems perfect for you."

A lovely mouth in a lovely face all but disappeared. "At least on paper."

"Only on paper?"

There was a shrug of fine-boned shoulders under an expensively tailored Egyptian cotton shirt. "Edoardo should be everything I want and need in a man. We grew up in similar, privileged circumstances. We've spent our lives living in the same world. We know the same people. We travel in the same circles and to the same places. We enjoy the same things."

"Especially music?"

Gillian had nodded.

Anna sensed her companion's hesitation. "But . . . ?"

It was a moment before Gillian said in a thoughtful tone, "Something is missing."

"Do you know what it is?"

A nod sent Gillian's ponytail swishing back and forth against the collar of her shirt, while a few damp tendrils of blond hair clung to her neck. "Passion."

Anna put her glass of lemonade down on the wicker table at her elbow. "I see."

"I'm not sure I can explain it, but I find Edoardo predictable. It's as if I know beforehand what he'll say, what he'll do, even what he's thinking and feeling." Gillian made a sudden and emphatic gesture with her hand. "With Edoardo there are no challenges and no surprises."

And consequently, no passion.

Anna had to admit she'd been of a similar temperament as a young woman. Even in high school she could wrap the local boys around her little finger without even trying. They had been familiar, too familiar, utterly predictable and utterly boring. It was Jacob who had attracted her, intrigued her, captivated her.

"The predictable quickly becomes boring," Anna said, picking up her glass again.

"Exactly," said Gillian.

"I remember one long-ago beau of mine." Anna laughed at the memory and, in the process, nearly spilled her lemonade. "I called him bubble-gum boy."

The younger woman's delighted laughter joined her own. "Bubble-gum boy?"

Anna relished telling the story. "I met Adam the summer I was seventeen. He was beautiful; the most beautiful human being I've ever seen, then or since. He was tall and athletic. His features were like sculpted Carrara marble. He had sun-kissed hair and eyes the color of the Mediterranean Sea. He was delicious—flawless—to look at. I thought he was everything a young woman could desire in a young man. I thought I was in love with him." She paused, remembering, the fan in her hand frozen in midair.

"I soon discovered, however, that beneath Adam's beautiful and perfect exterior there was nothing."

"Nothing at all?"

She moved her head. "He'd never bothered to develop a personality or any intellectual curiosity or social skills—not even a sense of humor—to go with his God-given physical attributes. He thought his beauty was enough. He thought it would last forever."

"It wasn't nearly enough, of course."

"Not by a long shot. I realized he was bland and boring, like a piece of old bubble gum that had lost all its flavor." Anna waved her fan back and forth as if she were swatting at an annoying insect. "I quickly lost interest in him."

Gillian leaned forward in anticipation. "How long did you think you were in love with Adam?"

She sighed dramatically. "One week." The summer breeze dropped a leaf onto the bodice of her dress. She picked the leaf up and twirled the stem between her thumb and forefinger. Her arthritis seemed much better today, she realized. "Edoardo may be predictable and familiar, but I assume he isn't entirely bubble gum."

"Not entirely. We share a mutual passion for classical music, if not each other."

Anna played with the small leaf, and waited.

Gillian reached back and lifted her hair away from her neck. "When I was growing up, I saw the kind of love and passion my parents shared. It was an almost tangible force between them. I don't know if I fully understood what it was at the time, but I certainly did as I got older. I also discovered how rare their relationship had been. But I knew that was the kind of love I wanted. I knew I could never settle for less." Her eyes seemed to focus on something in the distance; her voice softened. "I want to be the one thing a man can't live without. I want him to be the one thing I must have. I'll put him first. In return, I want to be first in his life." She unceremoniously dropped her ponytail. "With Edoardo, I know I'm not. I never would be."

"His music comes first."

"His music. His career. His fans and their adoration. A wife, and by extension any family they'd have together, would come in a distant fourth. At best."

It was some little time before Anna said, "I understand Edoardo's situation better than most people."

"Of course you do." Gillian reached out and patted her hand. "I'm sorry, Anna."

"There's no need to apologize. I knew at the age of eighteen, perhaps even younger, that music would be my grand passion, the ruling passion of my life."

"Well, it is for Edoardo, too. A woman—any woman— is an afterthought for him."

She placed her hand over Gillian's, noticing, not for the first time, that the young woman had long, lovely, elegant fingers. "It's understandable why you don't want to be fourth on anyone's list. None of us want to be an afterthought."

They both sat back, sipped their lemonade, and nibbled on fresh chocolate chip cookies, courtesy of Minerva Bagley. Minerva was very generous with her baked goods, bestowing them on her friends and neighbors on a regular basis.

Out of the blue Anna heard herself say, "I hear you and Sam have had a falling-out."

Beside her, Gillian stiffened. "Who told you?" She speculated, "Mrs. Goldman?"

"Goldie and just about every other person in town," Anna said, finishing off the cookie and sweeping the crumbs from her lap. "This so-called estrangement between you two wouldn't have anything to do with Edoardo, would it?"

Her visitor passed her tongue over her lips. "I don't see why. Edoardo is just an old friend."

"Does Sam know that?"

"I assume so." Gillian blew out an expressive breath. "It isn't as if Sam and I are engaged." She found and held Anna's gaze. "As a matter of fact, we never were."

"I know."

Surprise created a momentary silence. "How?"

Anna steeled herself for what was to come. "Your grandfather wrote to me last winter just before he died. He told me you would be coming to Sweetheart. He said Sam was going to be appointed as your attorney, but there was no mention of any engagement or broken engagement between the two of you."

Green eyes darkened to a shadow-filled forest. "Why would my grandfather write to tell you I was coming to town? I didn't even know until after his death."

The perfect opportunity had just presented itself, Anna realized. "That's a rather long story."

"I like long stories," Gillian said, putting her iced lemonade down on the table between them and moving her chair a little closer.

Anna had a change of heart. She opened her mouth and began with, "Once upon a time there was a young woman—she was no more than a girl really—who'd lived her whole life in a small Indiana town. It was May of 1942 and Sweetheart was throwing its annual community dance. The girl went that evening, reluctantly, and only at the insistence of her friends." The words came from Anna almost unconsciously. "There she met a young man, a soldier, who was stationed at a nearby army base. They danced and they talked and they laughed. Then they danced and talked and laughed some more. She was fascinated by the young officer. He was intelligent and witty and mature beyond his years. And it seemed to her that he'd been everywhere and seen everything she had only dreamed of." One hand brushed aside a wisp of white hair as she turned her head. "I'm sure you've guessed I was the young woman."

Gillian nodded. "And the soldier was my grandfather."

Anna took a fortifying breath and said, "That was the night I met and fell in love with Jacob Charles."

Chapter
twenty-four

 It was ancient history, Gillian thought as she climbed into her pickup truck an hour later. She shifted into gear, released the clutch, and drove due west out of town.

So, why had Anna told her?

Because you asked, that's why.

Well, she hadn't really asked. She'd simply been curious why her grandfather had written to a woman he hadn't seen in over sixty years; why he had told Anna about his plans for sending her to Sweetheart when she'd found out only after his death and through his lawyers.

The answer was more than Gillian had bargained for. Not that she was shocked—or even surprised, she realized now—to learn that an eighteen-year-old Anna Rogozinski and a twenty-two-year-old Lieutenant Jacob Charles had had a brief love affair in the summer of 1942.

Maybe it was something she'd glimpsed in the vintage black-and-white photograph Minerva had given her. Heaven knows, she'd looked at it often enough during the past several months. Maybe there had been some subtle body language between Anna and Jacob that made her think of them as a couple, although there were three people in the snapshot.

Or maybe it was the way Anna said her grandfather's name . . . even after all these years.

Discovering her grandfather had only been human—he'd always seemed so much larger-than-life to her, especially as a girl—flooded Gillian with feelings of sadness and compassion for the young soldier he'd been so long ago.

"They were all young in those days with young men's dreams and young men's passions," Minerva had said to her that first afternoon when they'd had a cup of tea together.

Or in Anna Rogozinski's case, a young woman with dreams and passions of her own.

Anna hadn't said the affair meant nothing. She'd said it hadn't meant enough.

"It was wartime, Gillian. Everyone and everything seemed to change overnight. We were young. Jacob was lonely. I was infatuated with him. We were both searching for something. We thought we'd found it in each other."

Apparently they'd soon realized there was no future for them. In the end Anna had stayed and Jacob had gone. He had returned to his world and his fiancée, a debutante named Emily Windsor Farnsworth. He'd known Emily all his life. Emily would make him the perfect wife. He would be happy with Emily.

"I would have made Jacob utterly miserable," Anna had

admitted to her as they sat side by side on the front porch, sipping their lemonade. "I was obsessed with my music. I practiced for hours every day, oblivious to the world, to the passing of time, to anyone else's wishes or desires. It would have driven a man like Jacob crazy. Besides, I had my own plans and my own dreams, and they didn't include marriage. I was determined to succeed, to have a concert career, to travel the world, to see London and Paris and Rome, to play before kings and queens."

"And you did."

"And I did."

"So you went your separate ways."

A snowy white head had nodded. "Jacob told Emily about the affair when he returned to New York that fall. Your grandmother was gracious and forgiving and wise beyond her years. Emily was the quintessential lady."

"Yes, she was."

"They were married some months later. And I returned to my life and my first love: music." Anna had stared off into the distance. "I don't believe I trust the kind of passion that erupts between a man and a woman. It always seems so fleeting to me, and it never ensures happiness." Her eyelids had lowered. "Perhaps William Penn was right when he wrote that 'passion is a sort of fever in the mind, which leaves us weaker than it found us.' "

"A fever in the mind," Gillian said aloud as she turned north at the next crossroads.

Passion might not be enough to ensure happiness, but a relationship without passion was equally doomed. Look at her and Edoardo. They were a perfect example.

And what about Sam?

"I'm not going to think about Sam," she said, pushing the button for the window on the driver's side. What she needed was fresh air to clear away the mental and emotional cobwebs.

There was a long stretch of deserted road in front of her. Cornfields had grown to six or seven feet in height on either side, creating a slightly claustrophobic landscape. The sun was an unrelenting ball of fire in a pale blue sky. Heat rippled up from the black top. The only sounds were the engine of her truck, the wind in her hair, and the occasional screech of a bird overhead.

Gillian took in another deep breath. It was filled with familiar odors: sun beating down on hot metal, damp earth, musky vegetation, dust raised by her tires, animals in a nearby barnyard. She wrinkled up her nose. That was one smell she'd never get used to.

She flicked on the radio. It was tuned to a local country-and-western channel. A man and a woman were singing a duet; it was all about a man's anger.

Gillian let out a slow breath. Sam was angry with her. She was pretty sure it dated to the morning of her last driving lesson when they'd returned to find Edoardo in her house. Well, in Sam's house.

For that matter, Sam had been unhappy with her the night of the community dance. It was the eternal paradox: finding yourself attracted to someone you don't want to be attracted to.

She knew how he felt.

Maybe it went back even farther to that May evening when she'd driven into town and met him at his office. He'd been upset with her for not understanding the power and control she had over his hometown and its residents.

Well, owning most of Sweetheart, Indiana, and being forced to live here for six months wasn't her first choice, either. She and Sam were stuck with each other. So he'd just have to deal with it.

She randomly pushed the buttons on the radio until she heard James Taylor singing "Handy Man."

She had no intentions of allowing her heart to be broken, so she didn't need a man—handy or otherwise—to fix it, thank you very much. She reached out and pressed the tuner button again.

The dial settled on another channel just as the announcer was saying, *"Our six o'clock news broadcast has been brought to you by Demolition. Remember, nothing works better to wipe out corn borers than Demolition Insecticide."* Then the announcer had gone on to say, *"Fact is still stranger than fiction, folks, especially in the agricultural arena. Especially when it comes to agriculture and the law. It seems the farmers in the United Kingdom are now required by law to give their pigs toys to play with or face a fine."* The male broadcaster chuckled. *"It could happen here, folks . . . when pigs fly."*

Gillian started to laugh along with the newscaster. She was still laughing when she glanced in the rearview mirror and discovered another pickup truck was directly behind her, hugging her rear bumper, filling her range of vision.

"Go around, go around," she said as she stuck her left hand out the window and waved them on.

The pickup stayed right on her tail. She motioned again. Whoever was behind the wheel either hadn't seen her gesture or got their kicks from tailgating. The driver seemed determined to close the gap between their two vehicles to mere inches.

Gillian pressed her foot down on the accelerator and watched as the speedometer on the dashboard edged up five, ten, fifteen miles an hour. The other pickup truck kept pace.

It was time to try a different strategy. She took her foot off the pedal and allowed her white Ford Ranger to coast. The speedometer plummeted. Thirty-five. Thirty. Twenty-five. Twenty. Fifteen. Surely at this snail's pace the other driver would grow impatient and finally pass her.

The oversize pickup truck slowed and maintained its intimidating presence behind her.

Gillian didn't recognize the make of the vehicle, only that it was big and black with tinted windows. She could barely make out a form behind the wheel. It could have been a man or a woman.

"This is a silly game of cat and mouse," she said, muttering to the idiot on her rear. "I've never cared for those kinds of games." A road or farm or two-bit town would come in handy right about now. Any place where there were other people. Unfortunately there was nothing but cornfields as far as the eye could see.

Gillian sped up.

The black pickup followed suit.

She slowed down.

The driver behind her appeared to do the same. Then there was a definite thud as the bumper of her pickup was hit from behind. Surely it was an accident. Surely it couldn't have been deliberate.

Gillian licked her lips, checked to make sure her seatbelt was secure, then pressed her foot down hard on the accelerator. Before she could manage to speed away, there was another thud and her Ranger lurched forward again.

This is crazy, she thought.

This was no longer a game or a practical joke, if it ever had been. This was serious business. The driver of the black pickup seemed determined to force her off the road.

Mouth suddenly dry, Gillian found she had no saliva to swallow. There was a large lump wedged in her throat. Her heart was racing. Her stomach flipped over with an awful sick feeling in its pit. She felt as if she was going to throw up.

For a split second she wondered if her parents had seen the accident coming all those years ago. Had there been time for them to be frightened? To say any last words to each other? Or had they been happy and alive one moment and gone the next?

Gillian gripped the steering wheel with both hands. There was a sharp curve in the road just ahead. She slammed her foot down on the accelerator.

The engine roared.

She shot forward.

The black menace was left eating her dust.

Just when she thought escape was within her grasp, the rear bumper of her pickup was struck again and again, harder and harder. The steering wheel slipped in hands damp with nerves and sweat.

The Ranger veered right. In a blink of an eye Gillian saw the ditch in front of her and then the cornfield coming up to meet her. Stalks of corn, their silky tassels whipping wildly back and forth from the impact, slapped across the windshield. She tried to remember what she'd learned from Sam during her driving lessons.

Stay calm.

Don't slam on the brakes.

Downshift into a lower gear.

Turn into the slide.

Focus on keeping control of the vehicle.

The Ford Ranger bounced along on uneven ground. Clumps of mud, small rocks, and bits of cornstalks were spewed into the air. The muscles in her arms and shoulders strained under the physical effort. Her heart was in her throat. Breathing was no longer an involuntary response.

At the last moment the terrifying black creature flew past her and disappeared down the road. She finally pumped the brakes and came to a stop. Gasping for air, Gillian had to remind herself to breathe.

Just breathe.

Then she got the shakes. Delayed shock. She put her head down on the steering wheel and the tears flowed.

It'd been one hell of a day, Sam thought as he tossed his briefcase and suit jacket onto the seat beside him. The judge had thrown his case out of court. The hard drive on his office computer had crashed before lunch. Then he'd missed lunch entirely thanks to an ex-client who wanted to cry on his shoulder . . . for free. Carol was on vacation. Max was moping. Sylvia wasn't speaking to him. And Gillian was avoiding him. Not that he blamed her. He hadn't exactly been Mr. Sunshine lately.

"Well, ain't life just hunky-dory?"

The Explorer was stifling hot. He'd forgotten to roll down the windows this morning. It was like an oven after sitting in the sun all day. His shirt was already damp and clinging to his back from the short walk from his office to the parking lot.

He put the key in the ignition and turned on the air-conditioning full blast. Then he reached up, loosened his tie, and jerked it from around his neck. It ended up in a careless heap on top of his jacket. He unbuttoned his shirt-sleeves and rolled them up to his elbows.

The phone in his shirt pocket began to jingle. He took it out and glanced at the caller ID. It read *Charles, G.* For an instant he was tempted to ignore the call.

He pushed the button. "Hello, Gillian."

"Sam?"

"Yes."

"Where are you?"

What, no hello, Sam? No how are you, Sam? No have you been getting any sleep, Sam? No I miss you, Sam? Just a where in the hell are you, Sam?

"I'm in the parking lot outside my office." He nudged dark glasses up the bridge of his nose; they settled on the permanent bump, courtesy of a linebacker named Tom Robinson, that he'd acquired during the final quarter of the state championship football game his senior year in high school. At least he had something to show for his broken nose, he supposed. The Sweetheart Bulldogs had won the game and the trophy. It only seemed polite for him to inquire in return, "Where are you?"

"In a ditch."

A blast of lukewarm air from the vent hit Sam square in the face. "Are you all right?"

There was a momentary hesitation. "Yes."

She didn't sound all right. "Are you hurt?"

"No."

His lips thinned to a single slash of disapproval. "Why are you in a ditch?"

"Someone ran me off the road." Gillian's voice broke. "Someone in a big black pickup truck."

A slightly sick sensation twisted his guts. "Who?"

"I don't know who. I couldn't see the driver's face. The tinted glass in the windshield was dark."

"Where are you?"

No answer was forthcoming.

He broke out in a cold sweat. "Gillian?"

She sounded different when she said, "I don't know where I am, Sam."

Her answer wasn't reassuring. "Are you sure you're all right? Did you hit your head or anything?"

"I'm fine. It's the cornfields. They all look alike. That's why I don't know where I am."

Muscles in his back and shoulders knotted with tension. "Do you remember what road you started out on?"

"Road?"

"Retrace your steps this afternoon."

"Well, I was visiting with Anna. Then I decided to go for a ride. I took the main road going . . . west, yes, I went west out of town. I turned a couple of times and just kept driving until I ended up here." The words seemed to be sticking in her throat. "Wherever here is."

Sam realized he was gripping the steering wheel so tightly his knuckles were white. "Stay calm."

"I am calm."

His hands had fallen asleep. He gave them a vigorous shake and willed himself to relax. "Can you see an intersection?"

"I'll look." Then she said, "I'm up on the road now."

"Paved or dirt?"

"Paved. Kind of. There are a lot of potholes. I think there's a railroad crossing and maybe another road about a mile away."

"What shoes are you wearing?"

"Shoes?"

Sam could hear the bewilderment in her voice, and realized he'd have to clarify his reasons for asking about her footwear. "Can you hike a mile in the shoes you're wearing?"

"Oh, I see what you mean."

For the first time today he felt a hint of a smile coming on. "I don't suppose you have a sensible pair of shoes with you."

With her usual spunk, Gillian informed him, "I don't buy shoes because they're sensible."

Of course not.

"Any chance of getting your truck out of the ditch?"

She heaved an audible sigh. "That's what I've been try-ing to do for the past fifteen minutes. The incline is pretty steep. And the tires just keep spinning in the mud."

Time to take a different tack with her. "Do you see anything that will help me locate you? A farmhouse? A grain silo? Any kind of landmark at all?"

"I can't see anything. Nothing but cornfields." She sounded discouraged. Then she said, "Wait a minute."

There was a lengthy silence.

He didn't like the sounds of silence. "Gillian?"

"There's a sign. Several actually. They're too far away to read with the naked eye. I'm going to climb down the embankment and retrieve my binoculars from the truck."

"I'll wait," he said, trying to be patient and not entirely succeeding. Then he muttered, "Binoculars?"

She was back. "Didn't I tell you? I joined the local Audubon Society a few weeks ago. Mrs. Longerboner ad-vised me to keep a pair of binoculars handy at all times. 'Be prepared, Gillian,' she said to me. 'You never know when you're going to spot a beautiful or rare bird, and wish you had your field glasses with you.' "

"Sounds like Mrs. Longerboner."

Then he heard her exclaim incredulously, "I must have driven a lot farther than I realized, Sam."

"What makes you say that?"

"The first sign says, 'Peru: fifteen miles.' The second, 'Mexico: ten miles.' And the third reads, 'Chili: twelve miles.' " She snorted softly into her cell phone. "They spelled 'Chile' wrong."

He cleared his throat. "Local legend has it that Chili was originally settled by a chef and his family from a small town somewhere in Texas. Wink, I think. Anyway, the chef's specialty dish was—"

"Chili," she said, finishing his sentence.

"Yeah. The good news is I know where you are. Old State Road 5. I'll find you. It might take me a little while. Stay with your pickup truck. And stay on the phone."

"Okay, Sam."

"I'm on my way, Gillian."

It was that knight-in-shining-armor thing again, Sam thought as he pulled out of the parking lot and headed west.

Chapter
twenty-five

"I don't see why we have to involve the police."

Sam scowled at her. "Because someone tried to run you off the road, Gillian. Hell, they didn't just try; they succeeded." He pointed to the rear bumper of the Ranger. "Take a good look at the damage done to your vehicle."

She licked her lips. "We both know that a few dents and scratches don't prove anything. I've got no license plate number to report. No description beyond a black pickup truck with a tinted windshield. How many of those are there in Sweetheart County? Fifty? A hundred? A thousand?" She threw her hands up in frustration and continued pacing back and forth. "I can't even tell the authorities if it was a man or a woman behind the wheel."

Sam frowned at her and said, "Is there some reason why you don't want to call the police?"

"There are several, actually. For one thing, I'm afraid nobody will believe me."

"I believe you."

She lifted her chin. "Thank you."

"You're welcome."

"However, not everybody in town knows me as well as you do," she was quick to point out.

"I suppose that's true."

Of course it was true.

Sam raised his right arm and used his shirtsleeve to mop up the perspiration beading on his forehead. "Whew! It is hotter than hell out here."

Gillian agreed, but she wasn't about to allow herself to be distracted by the weather. She had a point to make and she was darn well going to make it. "For another thing, I don't want to look like a fool. I've only had my driver's license a little over a month. I can just imagine what the official attitude will be." Lowering her voice, she tried to sound as authoritative as possible. " 'Ms. Charles is a new driver.' Or 'Ms. Charles is a typical woman driver.' Or 'Ms. Charles is from the Big City. We all know *they* can't drive.' "

Sam gave her a sharp glance. "I didn't realize you cared so much about other people's opinions."

"I don't. But I also don't want this incident to become a matter of public record and get into the newspapers. There's always a chance one of the wire services could pick up the story, and then all the two-bit paparazzi on both sides of the Atlantic will descend on Sweetheart."

"Ah, the dreaded 'p' word."

"Yes, the dreaded 'p' word." She reached back and lifted her loose hair from her neck with one hand—Sam was right; it was hot—and wrote in the air with the index finger of her other hand. "I can just see the headlines now: HIGH-WAY TO HELL HEWN OUT OF THE HEARTLAND. Or how about: PHANTOM PICKUP TRUCK TARGETS HEIRESS."

"Not to mention: LIGHTS OUT IN SWEETHEART FOR AMERICA'S SWEETHEART," said Sam, chiming in with his two cents' worth.

He wasn't taking her concerns about the tabloid press seriously. "Okay, I admit it sounds silly, but trust me, it could happen. If has before. I'm sure you don't want that kind of publicity any more than I do."

Sam crossed his arms, and in the process his shirt was pulled taut across his back and shoulders, outlining hard muscles and a trim waistline. She noticed there was a wedge of sweat up his back, giving the material a two-tone appearance of white on damp white. "I don't want publicity of any kind."

She drew a deep breath. "No police; no publicity. I'll have the Ranger fixed with my own money. That will keep the insurance company out of it." She delivered her final argument. "Besides, telling the local authorities won't get us any closer to identifying whoever it was, will it?"

There was a short, wary pause. "I guess not."

"Please, Sam. I want this to stay between the two of us." Gillian looked him right in the eyes; today they were the color of storm clouds. "If I'd been able to get the blasted pickup out of the ditch on my own, I wouldn't have told even you."

His gaze narrowed in warning. "Promise you'll tell me if anything happens. Big or small."

"Why?"

He made an emphatic gesture. "Because I'm not sleeping all that well as it is, okay? If I think you're keeping secrets from me, if there's a threat you haven't told me about, I won't get any sleep."

He did look tired. Weary. Ragged around the edges. Even a little gaunt.

"All right, I promise," she said at last.

Of course, she had her secrets, but they were the kind of secrets Sam didn't need to know anything about.

Like how shaken she'd been after her Ranger had landed in the ditch. Like how relieved she'd been to see him drive up a few minutes ago. Like how excited, how right-down-to-her-toes thrilled she'd felt at the sight of him climbing out of his Ford Explorer, removing his dark glasses, and then walking toward her looking as if he couldn't decide if he wanted to cross-examine her or take her in his arms and kiss her.

Gillian wasn't sure how a man could be reliable and rock solid on the one hand, and exciting and unpredictable on the other. But that described Sam to a T.

He raked fingers through hair that was black and shiny against the setting sun. "All right, let's make a deal."

It was her turn to be wary. "What kind of deal?"

He laid his cards out on the table for her. "You allow me to alert my cousin; he was elected sheriff of Sweetheart County after my dad retired. I'll tell him I'm uncomfortable with some of the stuff that has been happening since you arrived in town. I'll ask him to keep an eye out. He'll arrange for a patrol car to drive by your house a couple of times during the day and again at night. Maybe the presence of that kind of security will discourage any more 'incidents.' "

"No formal police report."

"No formal report. Strictly off the record. Nothing in the papers. No publicity. No paparazzi. No headlines."

She sensed there was more. "And . . . ?"

"And you let me know the next time you decide to take a drive by yourself in the country. Or anywhere else, for that matter," Sam said. "Deal?"

Gillian finally agreed. "Deal."

He started down the embankment. "Now let's hope I can get your pickup out of the ditch. Otherwise, we'll have to call for a tow and Ernie is a notorious blabbermouth."

"Who's Ernie?" she called after him.

"Owner, proprietor, and sole employee of Ernie's Towing and Tattooing." Sam added, "Ernie is also the one who came up with the motto on the side of his tow truck."

"Which is?"

" 'We meet by accident.' "

She chuckled. "I don't suppose Ernie owes you any favors?"

" 'Fraid not." He tossed over his shoulder, "But you could always offer him hush money."

She stared after him. "Is that legal?"

His laughter floated back to her on the evening air. "I was only joking, Gillian."

In the end Sam succeeded where she'd failed. Using the corn that had been knocked over during her wild descent into the farmer's field, he spread a few flattened stalks under the tires. On his third attempt he managed to get the pickup turned around and out of the ditch.

"I didn't think of using cornstalks for traction," she admitted, once her vehicle was back on the road and Sam had scraped the mud off his shoes.

"No reason you should," he said. "It's the kind of knowledge that comes from living most of your life in a rural area."

She quirked an eyebrow in his direction. "Not your first experience with a ditch?"

"Not by a long shot," Sam said, digging around under the front seat of his Explorer. He surfaced a few seconds later with an old towel, which he used to wipe the muck off his hands.

Gillian stared at the devastation left in the wake of her accident. Clumps of mud, tire tracks, chewed-up turf, and ruined corn were strewn everywhere. "What about the damage to the field?"

"This is Jim Dennison's farm. I'll give him a call tomorrow. Tell him I represent a client who swerved to avoid hitting a deer that darted across the road in front of her vehicle. Under the circumstances, and for the greater good, I think we can both live with that white lie. I'll also let Jim know you're willing to compensate him for any ruined crops; not that I think it will amount to much."

"Thank you, Sam."

"You're welcome." He flashed her a reassuring smile. "Like I said before: I'm a full-service attorney." On the heels of the smile came a questioning glance. "Are you sure you want to drive yourself back to town?"

She nodded. "I understand it's always best to get right back up on the horse." Besides, she refused to allow anyone—especially a coward and a bully who hid behind a dark windshield—to take away her hard-earned confidence and the pride she'd felt in getting her driver's license.

"I'll be right behind you. If you experience any problems, just pull over to the side of the road."

"Okay. Sweetheart is that way," she said, squinting into the sun and pointing in one direction.

Sam gently took her by the shoulders and turned her around in the opposite direction. "Sweetheart is this way."

"I knew that."

"Remember: At the next crossroads take a left, then right, and then right again. Go three miles and turn left at the stoplight. That will get you back to the main drag."

"Left. Right. Right again. Three miles. Left at the stoplight. I've got it." Gillian climbed behind the wheel of her

Ranger, fastened her seat belt, and through the open window, said to him, "I'll meet you back at my house . . . your house . . ." She finally gave up and settled on, "*Our* house."

Forty-five minutes later Gillian was standing on the front porch of *their* house, looking cool, calm, and collected in spite of the heat and despite her recent run-in with a bad-ass pickup truck and its demented driver. Sam wondered how the *upper* upper class managed to instill that kind of self-control in their offspring. Might be interesting to see what it took for Ms. Charles to *lose* control.

Gillian paused with her hand on the doorknob. "Thanks again for coming to my rescue, Sam."

"Anytime."

A moment passed before she said, "Are you hungry?"

"Starved," he said, realizing it was true. He was hungrier than he'd been in days. Weeks.

"Would you like to stay for dinner? I've got a couple of steaks I can grill. And I'll make one of my famous salads."

"Sounds great," he said appreciatively. "I'll just run home and feed Max."

"Dinner is in half an hour." Gillian closed the screen door behind her, then turned. "By the way, how do you like your steak cooked?"

"Rare."

"So do I."

Something else they had in common, Sam thought, and then he volunteered, "I'll bring a bottle of wine."

A shower, a shave, and a change of clothes later he showed up at the front door, Max beside him.

Gillian unlocked the screen door. "You look . . ."

"Cleaner?"

"I was going to say better." She reached down and gave Max an affectionate pat, then preceded Sam down the hallway to the rear of the house.

"I feel better, too," he said, leaning back against the counter and watching as she washed her hands before placing a Roma tomato on the cutting board and slicing it into perfect wedges. The tomato was followed by a seedless cucumber, an orange-colored sweet pepper, an avocado, a handful of scallions, and a chunk of cheese. "Speaking of better," he said, looking around his kitchen, "it's amazing what a coat of paint did for this room."

"Yellow is the perfect color for a kitchen that faces east," she said. "You should see how bright and cheerful it is in here first thing in the morning with the sunlight streaming in the windows."

Sounded like an invitation to him.

"Dinner is ready if you'd like to pour the wine," Gillian said as she added her homemade salad dressing to the bowl of spring greens and lightly tossed.

Sam dug in. "This is delicious." In between bites he added, "You really are a good cook."

"Thank you. More Cabernet sauce for your steak?"

"Sure."

It was sometime later that he became aware of Gillian studying him across the kitchen table. "What?"

"Would you like the rest of my steak?"

"Don't you want it?"

She shook her head. "I can't manage another bite." When he hesitated, she said, "It'll just go to waste."

"Not with Max and me around," he assured her.

He could still feel her eyes on him. "How long has it been since you had a decent meal?" she asked.

"Define decent," he said, using his fork to spear what was left of her filet. He plopped it down on his own plate.

Gillian took a sip of her wine before she said, "Not fast food. Not a microwave dinner. Not something that comes out of a box or a can. And not one of Papa Tony's Pizzeria pizzas."

In that case, when was the last time she'd cooked for him? Not since Piano Boy had been in town. He shrugged and gave her an inconclusive answer. "A while."

"Not eating. Not sleeping."

"Not asking," he said.

After the best dinner he'd had in weeks, Sam figured the least he could do was clear the table and deal with the garbage while Gillian loaded the dishwasher.

"By the way, I had a deck built in the backyard," she said, drying her hands after they'd tidied up.

He topped off their wine. "That would explain the lumber and the hammering."

"Yes, it would. Why don't we try it out while we finish our Pinot Noir?"

"You might want to bring something to put around your shoulders. As hot as it was this afternoon, it's really cooled off outside. In fact, the night air smells like fall."

Gillian reached for a sweater. "Summer's nearly over."

"Yes, it is."

They both knew what that meant: Her time in Sweetheart was nearly over, as well. According to the provisions in her trust, in a few short weeks she'd be legally free to leave.

Gillian said, "If you can manage our wineglasses, I'll bring the after-dinner chocolates and a lighter."

He frowned. "A lighter?"

"For the outdoor lanterns. They're supposed to keep the mosquitoes and other insects away."

"I hope your lanterns work better than my cigar did."

"So do I."

Sam approached the plain wooden deck. "This is similar

to Minerva's moon-watching platform. Well, the one Bert had put in his backyard a long time ago."

"As a matter of fact, it's identical. That's where I got the idea," she said.

"You enjoy sitting and staring up at the moon?"

"And the stars." Gillian lit several of the lanterns behind them. "The world would be a better place if we all took more time to appreciate the wonders of Nature."

No argument there. "Hey, I'm all in favor of Nature's wonders. What could be more natural?" he said, laughing his earthy laugh. "Nice chairs." Bet she hadn't bought them around here.

"I had them shipped from the coast," was all Gillian said.

Bet they cost a pretty penny, too, but Sam didn't say so out loud. That would be crass. And he'd sworn while he was in the shower to be on his best behavior tonight.

He set their wineglasses on the set of matching side tables. Max plunked himself down between the chairs as they sat back and looked up at the heavens.

Sam was the first to break the silence. "I've always been fascinated by the infinite possibilities of what might be out there."

A soft-spoken, "Me, too."

A little while later, he said, "It's estimated that there are millions, maybe billions, of galaxies in space. Talk about immense." He raised the wineglass to his mouth and took a drink. "And unfathomable." Kind of like the woman sitting beside him.

He heard a rather wistful feminine sigh. "It certainly puts human problems in perspective, doesn't it?"

"It should, but I don't know that it does." He gazed up at the sliver of silver moon for a few minutes. "Another theory is that the moon was formed when a planet, which scientists have named Orpheus, collided with Earth. From that cataclysmic event came the Earth and moon that we know today. Well, after they both cooled off a few thousand degrees. At that time the moon was only fourteen thousand miles from Earth, and would have filled the night sky." He paused for a moment. "The moon has been slowly spinning away from us ever since."

"And here we are millions of years—"

"Billions," he said.

"Billions of years later looking up at the same moon in the same sky," Gillian said in a hushed tone.

Silence.

Sam raised his hand and pointed. "There's Polaris, the Pole Star. It lies almost directly above the North Pole."

"Where?"

"Find the Big Dipper first. See it?"

"I see it."

"The Pointers form the front of the Big Dipper and they point toward Polaris. Actually the Big Dipper is part of the larger constellation Ursa Major, or the Big Bear."

"There's the Little Dipper." There was genuine wonder in her voice. "I suppose it's part of the constellation Little Bear."

He nodded and said, "Ursa Minor. At the end of the long handle is Polaris."

"The Pole Star."

"The Little Dipper is always visible in the skies of the Northern Hemisphere on a clear night."

"How do you know so much about astronomy? No. Don't tell me. I'll bet it was Mrs. Longerboner."

He shook his head. "The Boy Scouts."

"You were a Boy Scout?"

He held up his right hand in the traditional salute. "Scout's honor, ma'am. May I carry your packages for you? Can I help you across the street?"

Gillian laughed and offered him a chocolate. They each took a piece and then fell silent again.

She stared straight ahead, and then finally said, "You've been angry with me."

He dragged a hand through his hair. "I haven't really been angry with you."

"You could have fooled me."

He shifted uneasily in his chair. "I've been angry with myself *about* you."

She turned her head. "Why?"

Yeah, why, Law? Explain it to her.

Sam licked the remnants of chocolate from his lips, cleared his throat, and said, "Anton Chekov wrote that 'women deprived of the company of men, pine; men deprived of the company of women become stupid.'" He took in a long deep breath and gradually released it. "I guess I've been pretty stupid."

She didn't say a word.

He went on. "I live my life by a few simple rules, Gillian."

Her hands were clasped very tightly in her lap. "I think we all do," she said.

"Well, one rule most honorable men try to live by is not getting involved with another man's woman."

She gave him a curious glance. "I don't understand."

In two words, "Edoardo Biaggi."

"What about him?"

"I assumed . . ."

"There's nothing to assume about Edoardo and me. We've been friends for a long time. That's all it was. All it is. All it ever will be," she said adamantly.

That cleared up one potential problem: At least he wouldn't be trespassing. "Another cardinal rule of mine is business is business. And pleasure is pleasure."

"Meaning?"

"Never get personally involved with a client."

"That seems like a reasonable rule."

His mouth curved humorlessly. "It does, doesn't it? Unfortunately reasonable, in this case, doesn't translate to easy. I've been trying not to break that rule and it's driving me crazy. It's the reason I'm not sleeping and not eating." And the reason he wasn't worth a tinker's damn to himself or anyone else.

"You're fighting with yourself over your own rule?"

"You can say that again." He turned toward her. "You've made it very clear you don't want any involvement, any complications, or any mess. But sometimes things get involved, complicated, and messy anyway, don't they?"

There was the merest hesitation on Gillian's part. "Yes."

This was no time to mince words. "You don't want to be attracted to me."

"I don't."

"But you are."

"I am," came out on a whisper.

"Believe me, I've got the same problem. I'm attracted to you, too. And I sure as hell don't want to be." "Attraction" was a piss-poor word for how he felt about her.

"Sam . . ."

"The truth is I want you so much I can taste it." There was no mistaking his meaning.

"And I want you," Gillian said, wrapping her arms around herself. "But being attracted to each other, wanting each other, isn't a problem if we don't act on it."

Maybe not for her. "Unfortunately I can't seem to forget that night in the park."

"Neither can I."

"What do you call what happened between us?" he said, dropping any pretense.

She swallowed hard.

"And if you say a mistake . . ."

"It wasn't a mistake," she quickly countered. "Well, maybe it was since I can't seem to forget how your hands felt on me, or how you tasted, or how you made me feel."

"Which was?"

"Desired and desirable. Excited and exciting. Hungry. Hot. Wild. Out of control."

Sam exhaled on a silent curse. "I'd better go before a little mistake becomes a big mistake, a huge mistake."

Gillian only hesitated briefly before saying, "Why does it have to be a mistake if two consenting adults consent?"

He stared into dark, dark green eyes and felt his blood heat. "Are you consenting?"

A breathless, "Yes." Then, "Are you?"

His heart was pounding. "Absolutely."

She nervously played with the buttons up the front of her cashmere sweater. "There's no reason we can't handle this like adults."

"No reason at all." *Crap.* "There's just one problem."

"What's that?"

"You're still my client."

A blond head nodded.

"And I'm still your lawyer."

"Yes, you are."

Sam stood and faced her. He reached down, took both her hands in his, and slowly brought her to her feet. "There's only one thing for you to do."

Gillian dug her teeth into her bottom lip. "What's that?"

"Fire me."

Chapter
twenty-six

"In that case, you're fired."

Sam leaned closer, his breath stirring the tendrils of hair around her face, leaving her covered with goose bumps, and whispered, "I never thought I'd say this, but thank God."

Of course, she fully intended to *re*hire him when this was all over. Whatever *this* was. Wherever *this* took them. But Sam didn't need to know that. Not right now, anyway.

Gillian realized she had butterflies; the kind that did a frenzied tap dance in her stomach. She was nervous. She was cold. She was warm. She was a little bit of everything really: excited, terrified, eager, expectant, certain, uncertain, definitely all hot and bothered. And Sam hadn't even kissed her yet.

"Come here," he said in that voice that was like crushed

velvet rubbing against her skin. She shivered when he touched his lips to the sensitive spot below her ear. "Cold?"

"Yes." She changed her mind almost immediately. "No." She turned into his shoulder. "I don't know."

"Maybe we should go inside," he said, leaving a scorching trail from her ear to the corner of her mouth.

Why don't you just kiss me?

His mouth came down on hers, stole her breath *and* her reason away in a single heartbeat. He tugged at her sweater and pushed it aside. She could feel his heat right through her cotton shirt. His hands cupped her breasts. Hers were pressed against his chest. Nipples tightened and became engorged. Sensitive to the slightest touch. Itchy, and itching to be pinched, licked, tongued.

They moved in a dance of their own creation and to music only the two of them could hear: off the newly constructed wooden deck, across the yard, stumbling up three steps onto the tiny back porch, kissing, touching, caressing, not wanting to separate even long enough to make a mad dash for the house.

Sam pinned her against the side of the porch, reached behind her, and grabbed the doorknob. They were inside. He groped for the kitchen light and flicked it off. They stopped by the table, fingers fumbling with buttons and zippers and straps. Her sweater disappeared altogether. His shirt. She kicked off her shoes. His landed with a distinctive thud. They were in the hallway. More lights went out. The house was quiet and dark, intimate and seductive.

"I don't think we're going to make it to a bed," he muttered in warning, dragon eyes burning into hers.

"Highly overrated," she said, slurring her words.

"What is?"

"Beds." Where had that come from? she wondered.

"Floor's too hard."

She put her head back and laughed a little feverishly "The floor has nothing on you."

Sam's body was pressed tightly against hers; his hard to her soft. She felt something give way inside her, melt. Perspiration formed on her upper lip, drizzled down into the small of her back, gathered under her breasts, wept between her thighs.

He backed her up against the wall. She wanted to climb the walls as his teeth nipped her, marked her, composed a wild, sweet song that sang in her blood.

Her blouse was next. His belt. Her legs parted and he planted himself between them. There no mistaking his intention. He was letting her know without uttering a word how much she excited him, aroused him, made him want to lose himself in her.

He set her free. She was free to kiss him, to touch him, to stroke him, to let him kiss and touch and stroke her. She was empty and craved the fulfillment he could give. She was screaming questions inside her head and needed the answers he possessed.

Then her mind went silent. Sometimes just doing—without thinking, without analyzing, without considering all the pros and cons—was the smartest thing a woman could do.

Just breathe, Gillian.

She forgot to breathe.

He reached for the zipper on her jeans; cool air wafted across her bare abdomen. She unbuttoned the fastening at his waist. Tugged. Jeans were kicked aside. Silk panties and male briefs followed. Then it was skin against skin. Soft, crinkly, damp hair. Hot flesh pressed to even hotter flesh.

In some far corner of her consciousness Gillian realized she was losing herself in his urgent heat, in the heat and urgency of the moment, and in the promise of what was to come.

This is a mistake, she thought. But it didn't feel like a mistake. It felt right. Very right.

This wasn't her. This wasn't the way she behaved. It wasn't like her to go crazy, to throw caution, or any semblance of common sense, to the wind, to trust a man so completely that she was willing to put herself in his hands.

This isn't just any man. This is Sam. Sam the Strong. Sam the Stalwart. Sam the Trustworthy. Sam the Exciting and Sexy. For once in your life, Gillian, just let go. You're not in control. It's okay. You don't have to be.

It was more than okay. Up until this moment the hottest sex she'd ever experienced was that night in the park: Sam kissing her; Sam feeling her up; Sam taking her into his mouth and . . .

She moaned deep, deep in her throat. He must have heard her. He wrapped his arms around her and lifted. She was aware of something smooth beneath her backside.

Where was she?

Then she realized she was poised on the edge of the pool table in his dining room, beneath the antique crystal chandelier, in full view of the bay window at the front of his house.

This was crazy.

His hands were on her; his fingers probed. She struggled to form intelligible words. "Someone may see us."

His masculine response came out low and intense and slightly edgy. "Who?"

Who? She said the first name that popped into her head. "Mrs. Goldman."

"It's pitch black and her binoculars don't have night vision," Sam said, sounding logical.

He had to be pretending, of course. How could he be sane and logical while she was going crazy, couldn't think straight, wondered what time it was, what year it was?

He slipped a finger into her, then two, stealing her breath, her brain, her sanity. "A . . ." became "Ahhhh . . . Peeping . . . Tom?"

He gave a raw laugh, the kind of laugh that made her wonder if he was in pain. "Never heard of any in the neighborhood."

"Max?"

"Wise dog. Took his bone into the study." Sam came closer still. She could feel the sensual heat emanating from his body. His voice dropped. "It's just you and me."

This was crazy, but she no longer cared.

She gave up thinking, heaved a long sigh that took her breath away and her resistance with it, realized her whole body was trembling, and lay back, spread her arms, and tried to clutch the sides of the pool table. He stepped between her thighs. She opened to him and the tip of his erection pushed against her.

She exhaled on his name. "Sam."

"Gillian," he said, and then his breath stirred wet, musky curls and the next thing she knew his tongue was pressing against the very place where she had expected him to enter her.

His name became an urgent query on her lips. "Sam?"

He lifted his head for a moment. "Relax, sweetheart. Just lie back and relax."

He had to be kidding.

She tensed, reached for him, grabbed a handful of his silky black hair. Moaned. Transformed into a creature of unnamed needs and desires. The intimacy was like a tidal wave washing over her, dragging her under, then forcing her to the surface before she was once more caught in the undertow. She was swamped by sensations, came up for air, gasped, went down again.

Time had no meaning. Neither did the past. Nor the future. There was nothing but the here and now, nothing but Sam. No thought beyond thoughts of Sam. No reality beyond the way Sam was making her feel. She cried out. Came utterly undone.

How strange, came the realization as she lay spread-eagled before him, that his mouth on her was the greatest intimacy she had ever known. He tasted her on his lips. He licked her. He took small sensual nips. He seemed to savor the feel, the smell, the texture of her. He thrust his tongue deep inside her. Again and then again. She had no secrets from him. He would know everything. He would know her more intimately than any other human being ever had.

She was slick with sweat and sex. Her pulse was drumming in her ears, in her head, in the sensitive veins along the pathway his mouth had forged. Her body throbbed. She felt like the strings on a pianoforte that had been strung too tightly. Something had to give. Something *must* give. Everything was spiraling upward, out of control, crescendoing toward some great explosive finale.

She couldn't see. She couldn't think. She couldn't breathe. Her world began and ended in the small and yet infinite space she and Sam occupied.

Her hips rose up, buckled, fell. Her mouth opened and closed on an indistinguishable word. Maybe it was Sam's name. Then her climax was upon her, improbably, inevitably, magnificently, gloriously. It overwhelmed and overpowered her. Still, she rose up to meet it, cried out hoarsely, then shattered into a thousand infinitesimal pieces.

It was some time later that she vaguely realized what a

vulnerable position she was in and how ridiculous she must look lying across the end of a pool table.

Her brain was mush. She laughed and said in a murmur, "That was much better than . . ."

Fiery dragon eyes gazed down into hers. "Than what?"

"Playing the piano."

A masculine snort of disbelief met her announcement. "Playing the piano?"

She reached for him, placated him, measured and stroked him. Her fingers feathered across his mouth, his tongue, his throat, down his neck, across his chest and ribs, along his washboard abs, dipping below his waist, brushing over a tangle of masculine hair until she clasped him in her hand. His penis was hard and smooth; fine marble with a velvet head and a bead or two of moisture on the very tip.

The whoosh of air he'd been holding rushed from his lungs. "Holy Hannah."

"I don't know about Hannah," Gillian said, teasing him, titillating him, "but I like your instrument much better than the Steinway I've been playing all these years."

Sam's laugh was pure male; it lived and breathed sex. It held the promise of things to come. "We're just warming up. Wait until we get to the actual performance."

"Are you a virtuoso, sir?"

"Bet your sweet patootie."

She was feeling very daring. "Show me."

"Yes, ma'am."

He reached down and took something from the pocket of his jeans. "We Boy Scouts always like to be prepared," he said, opening the small foil packet.

"How wise," she murmured, floating, drifting. "Although I don't feel wise. Maybe it's midnight madness." She turned her head and gazed down the length of the pool table. "Do you play?"

Sam was preoccupied and had failed to make the leap of logic with her. "The piano?"

She laughed in the back of her throat. "Pool. Billiards. Eight ball"—she reached between their bodies, found his, fondled them, cupped them in her palm—"in the corner pocket."

His breathing came hard and faster; his words slow and strained. "I play. At least I used to. I'm a little rusty." His eyes darkened as he stepped closer. "How about you?"

"I've played a few times. It was a while ago." She swallowed and tried to tell him something. "I was never very good, I'm afraid. Now I'm completely out of practice."

"Then we'll just have to make allowances for each other, won't we?" he said, his arms wrapping around her, muscles primed, nearer and nearer, pushing against her, finding her.

She was feeling giddy, intoxicated. "I see you have your cue stick with you, sir."

Sam laughed.

He was still laughing when he surged into her, and then it was all searing heat and incredible friction and exquisite tension.

Chapter
twenty-seven

Wow!

She was beyond anything he'd ever experienced, ever imagined, ever hoped or prayed for. Wow didn't come close to describing what it was like to bury himself in her right up to the hilt. Miraculously she took in every last inch of him, closing tightly around him, threatening to squeeze him dry with his first hard thrust into her body.

He desperately wanted it to last, to savor the feel of her, the feel of the two of them together. He was determined to make this good—great—for Gillian, and for himself. He wanted the moment to go on forever. But he knew the odds were against him. After all, he'd been living like a hermit for the past several years. And this woman had a singular ability to make him lose control.

Sam thrust into her a second time and then a third. "My God." He fought for enough control to say, "Amazing."

Gillian opened her mouth; nothing came out but a low feminine moan of pleasure.

In response, Sam heard himself groan out loud. He felt like he was going to explode, like he was Mount Saint Helens about to erupt, blow its top, spew forth a flow of hot molten lava.

Hell, he thought with culpable humor, at this rate he wouldn't last a nanosecond. He was right. He managed one, "Sweet Jesus," and then he came.

His mind, along with the proverbial slate, was instantly wiped clean. No doubt about it: He'd died and gone to heaven. What a way to go. The only way to go.

It was a minute or two or three before his brain jump-started. It was another couple of minutes before he mumbled against her breast, "Sorry about that."

"There's no need to a—"

He knew Gillian had been about to say "apologize," but the thought was interrupted when it became apparent to both of them that he hadn't lost his erection. In fact, he seemed to be growing harder by the second.

Coitus *not* interruptus.

"Again so soon?" she said, a little breathlessly, skin flushed, eyes, mesmerizing eyes staring up into his; eyes the unfathomable blue of the deep blue sea, eyes glazed over with desire.

Sam smiled, and tried to soften the sharply drawn edges of his features. "Again and again and then again until we can't move one bloody muscle."

"Please," was all she said, which pleased him immensely.

He began to slip in and out of her in an exquisitely, tortuously slow dance. She cried out his name, grabbed at his shoulders, sank her nails into his flesh. Her heat rose up to burn him. Her excitement excited him. Her scent filled his nostrils, his lungs, his mind.

He thrust harder, deeper, taking them both up and up, higher and higher. Skin sweaty and musky. Muscles strained to the limit. Hearts beating wildly. Hips pounding fast and furious.

Overhead the antique crystal chandelier swayed slightly; fine glass tinkling against fine glass. A billiard ball was accidentally knocked off the table and rolled across the dining room and into the front hall. The floor moved beneath his feet. Or maybe it was simply the way Gillian made him feel: as if his whole world had been rocked to its core. Then she began to convulse around him; her inner muscles gripping him in their velvet grasp and refusing to let him go.

His climax hit him like a ton of bricks. It tore the last bit of breath from his lungs. It quick-froze his muscles in place. It fried his brain. He thought he shouted her name, but he wasn't certain.

Sometime later—for the life of him he couldn't have said how much later—it occurred to Sam that he was probably the only man he knew who would happily spend his life bent over a billiards table without a rack of balls and without a cue stick. Except for the God-given variety, he thought, smiling to himself.

He took a moment to dispense with the sheath covering him, grabbed a couple of small packets from his jeans, kicked the rest of their clothes aside, and gathered Gillian up in his arms. He gallantly helped her off the pool table and said, "Bed?"

"Bed."

They ran hand in hand toward the stairs and made it

halfway up before pausing to take a desperately needed taste of each other. The next thing he knew she was gliding down his body, kissing his chin, his chest, lightly testing her teeth on his nipples. She followed the natural line of his sternum: flicked her tongue into his navel and across his abdomen, before heading lower into the danger zone.

She touched him in places he hadn't even realized he liked to be touched. He'd never thought of the backs of his knees as sensitive, let alone as an erogenous zone.

Then she was pressing hot, sweet, stinging kisses to the most vulnerable parts of his body. His erection was already painfully taut. He was as hard as he could ever remember being in his whole life. His muscles contracted, and he sucked in a rush of air when she touched the very tip of her tongue to the tip of his penis. His body twitched and moved toward her.

And when she took him into her mouth, his knees nearly buckled, and he knew he was in trouble.

Big trouble.

He was among that rare breed of men who actually looked better naked than clothed, Gillian thought as she lay beside Sam in the big beautiful bed that had once belonged to his grandparents.

The sheets were in an unholy tangle around their ankles. The summerweight comforter was in a heap at the foot of the bed. Her pillow was missing. Sometime during their lovemaking it must have been tossed aside: maybe onto the floor; maybe into the next county. She was using his chest as a cushion for her head; her face was pressed to the spot above his heart. She could clearly hear its strong rhythmic cadence; feel its powerful and steady beat.

Her hair was in a wild tumble around her shoulders. She

impatiently pushed at its unmanageable mass with one hand, trying to secure it behind her ears, but errant wisps kept escaping and brushing along his bare skin and hers, tickling them both.

Her breasts and nipples were clearly visible in the faint light cast into the room by the moon and the stars. He had to be blind not to see her nakedness. She could certainly see his. There was only one word for Sam in the flesh: magnificent.

She could smell a distinctive combination of masculine scents on him, on herself, even on the bedding underneath their bodies: It was the aroma of clean soap, of musky male sweat, and of something indescribably and inexplicably Sam.

And of sex.

Lots of sex. Incredible sex. Great sex. Mind-blowing sex. Physical, spiritual, intimate, soul-touching-sky sex.

The taste of him lingered on her lips. The feel of him was imprinted on every inch of her body. He was addictive: She found she had to have his breath in her lungs, his taste in her mouth, his scent in her and on her, his presence permeating every part of her. She was empty of everything but him.

A small inner voice warned: *You're a fool*.

Sam had told her this might be a mistake, a big mistake, potentially a huge mistake. He'd given her an out and she had declined to take it. Instead, she had informed him that it didn't have to be a mistake if two consenting adults consented.

What had been her exact words earlier this evening? *"There's no reason we can't handle this like adults."*

That was it.

Well, the joke was on her, and it was both terrible and wonderful. She wanted the one man she shouldn't want. She'd had sex with the one man she should have had the sense to keep at arm's length. She was infatuated with a man who was all wrong for her. And yet, he felt so right.

Oh, dear God, please don't let me fall in love with him.

Sam was stretched out with one arm around her and the other propped up behind his head, totally unself-conscious and totally comfortable with his nudity. A slight frown creased his brow. "There's something different about my bedroom," he said at last.

The hair on his chest tickled Gillian's nose. She brushed it aside and rested her chin in the curve of his shoulder. "Sylvia and I used a painting technique on the walls that adds texture and color. We also hung new drapes, and added a few pieces of furniture."

"It looks great."

"I'm glad you like it."

Safe territory. Neutral territory. Impersonal territory. If redecorating a man's bedroom could be considered impersonal. It had felt very personal at the time, as she recalled.

Sam was still studying the transformation that had taken place in his absence. "Those look like the prints from my first apartment, but they're not, are they?"

"They're the same. In a way. Those are vintage Cinzano." She hesitated. "Do you like them?"

"Of course I like them. I always have. But they must have cost a pretty penny compared to the cheap reproductions I purchased a decade ago. I think I paid ten bucks apiece for them. Frames and all."

"The cost is unimportant." She meant it. "Consider the prints my gift to you."

"And here it's not even my birthday," he said, teasing her.

There was so much to learn about him, she thought. So much she didn't know, would never know. She swallowed hard and said in a deceptively light tone, "When is your birthday?"

"March fifteenth."

"The ides of March."

"Yup."

Beside him, she pushed herself up on one elbow. " 'Beware the ides of March.' "

"So I hear."

" '*Veni, vidi, vici.*' "

"Julius Caesar. 'I came. I saw. I con . . .' " Sam stopped himself from finishing the famous quote.

She arched one eyebrow. "By any chance, were you about to say 'conquered'?"

He shook his head and grinned. "I wouldn't dare use the word 'conquered.' It's considered politically incorrect these days. Especially with women."

"Conned, then?"

He gave her an injured expression. "How could you think that for a moment?"

"Conceded?"

"Never." He had a few suggestions of his own. "Let's see. I definitely came. I know I saw. How about I conjoined? I consorted? Convulsed?" He gave her a speculative look. "Consummated?"

She couldn't help herself; she laughed out loud. "I think all of the above, but I particularly like the sounds of that last one."

"Me, too." He rolled onto his side and gazed into her eyes. "Do you know what my favorite change is to this room?"

Her pulse leaped. "What?"

"Having you in my bed." He buried his face in her hair and nuzzled her neck. "I love the way you smell," he said close to her ear. His tongue tripped across her skin. "The way you taste."

"And I love the smell and the taste of you," she admitted, breathing in deeply.

"I love the way you feel on the inside and on the outside," he murmured, moving his hands, his lips, and finally his body over hers.

"I love to feel you on me, in me," she confessed to him in a whisper. "Make love to me again, Sam."

"I will," he promised.

He kissed and caressed her. There was a moan of arousal. It came from Sam, but it echoed deep inside her. He brought her to one climax after another until she cried his name out on a sob, begging for mercy, begging for more, then begging only for him.

By the time the pale dawn, streaked with autumnal colors, was stealing across the sky, they were satiated, tired, happy. Sam wrapped his arms around her, tucked her head under his chin, and pulled the sheet over them.

Gillian fell into a sleep without fear and without "dark dreams." For the first time in a very long time, hers was the sleep of utter peace and contentment.

It was Max lying beside her in the antique sleigh bed when she woke up later that morning. It was past nine and sunlight was visible through a slit in the raw silk drapes.

Hammering could be heard from somewhere below. She quickly pulled on a pair of jeans and a sweater before heading downstairs to investigate. She found Minerva Bagley tacking wire to the ceiling of the front porch.

She opened the screen door and stepped outside. "Good morning, Minerva."

"Good morning, Gillian."

She glanced at the box at her feet. "Witch balls?"

The woman looked down from her elevated perch on the step ladder. "Sam said it was okay."

"I'm sure it is." Then, "When did you speak to Sam?"

"About an hour ago as he was leaving the house. I believe he was headed home to shower and change for a ten o'clock court appearance." With a perfectly straight face, Minerva added, "I must say, Sam seemed to be in exceptionally good spirits this morning."

Gillian reached down to pat Max on the head. Then she cleared her throat and said, "Do you mind if I ask why you're hanging witch balls from the porch?"

Minerva moved her head; a bobby pin or two went flying. "I'm testing a new product. Would you please hand me the amethyst ball first?"

One by one, Gillian took them from the box and Minerva hung them from the thin bits of wire.

"I want to determine if I should sell this brand at my booth during Cornfusion," Minerva explained.

Gillian frowned. "Cornfusion?"

"And the Amazing Maize Maze. They're both part of our annual fall festival." Minerva handed her the hammer before climbing down from the ladder. "Local farmers cut their cornfields into elaborate mazes. Then they charge so much per head for people to wander around in them. Can't say I see the attraction myself. Anyway, it's usually five dollars for adults; less for kids, of course. Refreshment stands sell apple cider, elephant ears, cotton candy, and pig-on-a-stick. Every Friday night they hold a taffy pull. There are hay rides and jack-o'-lantern contests. Face painting and clowns. An old barn is turned into a haunted house. Booths are set up for vendors to hawk anything and everything from Halloween masks to candy corn to my herbal teas and witch balls. Anyway, I've ordered a new variety and I want to test them out."

Gillian decided she needed a cup of very hot, very black coffee. "Would you like a cup of coffee?"

Minerva made a production of looking at her watch.

"No time this morning, I'm afraid. I have a meeting on-line with my webmaster and PR specialist in a half hour."

"Another time, then?"

"I'd like that very much. By the way, Sam said he'd take care of the ladder when he gets home."

The woman was down the sidewalk and almost to the front gate when Gillian called after her, "Minerva?"

She turned. "Yes, Gillian?"

She raised a hand to shade her eyes. "Is that the real reason you're hanging witch balls from Sam's porch?"

Minerva Bagley stared at the ground for a moment, then raised her head. "I didn't want to tell you the real reason."

"Why not?"

She peered over her bifocals. "I was afraid you'd think I was balmy or senile or even a little crazy."

Gillian gave her an understanding smile. "I think most sane people are a little crazy."

Minerva moistened her lips and stared at the hammer clasped in her hand. "I had a feeling, you see."

"A feeling about what?"

Troubled brown eyes lifted to hers. "You." Minerva pushed hairpins back into the graying bird's nest on top of her head. "I can't explain it, but I sensed danger. I felt that you'd recently had a close call."

Gillian froze in place. "Have you heard any gossip to that effect?" Sam had promised the incident involving her pickup truck would stay behind the two of them.

"No. No gossip. Just a feeling. I decided it couldn't hurt to put up witch balls. Perhaps they'll protect you from whatever was . . . is . . . out there."

There was a sudden and unexpected chill in the air. Icy fingers seemed to slither down Gillian's spine one vertebra at a time. "Thank you, Minerva." She looked up at the row of colored glass spheres dangling above her head. "Either way, they're lovely."

Her neighbor seemed to have something more on her mind. "It is often the people who make the least noise who are the most treacherous."

"Watch out for the quiet ones, huh?"

Minerva sighed. "Exactly." Still, she stood there in the middle of the sidewalk and made no move to leave. "Remember, my dear, some men are dangerous."

"Then I'll be careful," Gillian said, wrapping her arms around herself and walking back into the house. Minerva was right. Well, half right. Men were dangerous.

All men.

Chapter
twenty-eight

"A man is pretty much damned if he does and damned if he doesn't when it comes to women. At least some women." Doodles's pencil flew across the sheet of paper-clipped to his easel. "Leastwise the woman I was married to."

Sam contemplated that briefly. "So, how's it going with Mary Kay?"

"Better." Davison Weaver's hand never faltered for an instant as a face began to take shape on the page. "We're dating."

After a short while, Sam said, "It must seem strange to date a woman you were married to for . . ."

"Twenty-five years," came the answer. "Not as strange as living without her after all that time." Doodles shook his head, sending his ponytail swinging back and forth. "I sure have been stupid, Sam."

Yeah, he knew exactly what Davison meant. He hadn't been so brilliant himself when it came to women. Well, when it came to one particular woman. "I know how you feel."

"How's it going with Gillian?"

"Great. Good. Okay." Sam shrugged his shoulders and admitted, "Cripes, I don't know."

Davison looked up from his easel. He didn't mince words. "Are you in love with her?"

That's the question Sam had been asking himself. It wasn't the only one, of course. There were plenty of others. He blew out his breath and said, "It's complicated."

Another gem of masculine wisdom was offered by Sweetheart's resident artist. "With women it always is."

In his case the whole affair was further complicated by their attorney-client relationship. He'd been hired and fired by Gillian so many times in the past couple of weeks that he'd lost count. It usually followed the pattern of being fired at night and rehired the next morning. It was supposed to soothe his conscience. He didn't think it was working. He felt guilty as hell.

Doodles eventually said, "Is she in love with you?"

As a matter of fact, that was the other question he'd been asking himself. "Who knows."

Davison took the completed sketch down from his easel and slipped it into the portfolio beside him. From the number of sketches he'd obviously been doing brisk business at his Cornfusion booth. He put up a blank sheet of paper, clipped it into place, blew on his hands to warm them, and started a new drawing. "You know what they say."

Muscles in the back of Sam's neck tightened. "What?"

" 'The fool wonders, the wise man asks.' " The artist's

pencil moved across the page in sure, even strokes. "I'm guessing you haven't asked her."

Hell, no, he hadn't asked her. What did he look like: a glutton for punishment?

Apparently Davison took his silence for agreement. "Sometimes with women you've got to take the bull by the horns," he said. "As dangerous as they are."

"Women or bulls?"

The other man chuckled. "Women, of course."

Sam inhaled deeply and then slowly exhaled. The night air had turned chilly; he could see his breath. "It's not women who are dangerous. It's *a* woman."

"Amen, brother."

Sam watched as the other man worked his magic. A familiar face was emerging on the easel in front of them. It was Gillian. Davison had captured her perfectly: from the sweep of her long, fine hair to her aristocratic little nose, from those incredible eyes to that mouth that drove him crazy.

Funny, but the portrait reminded him of someone else. Sam couldn't think who. It was like having a name on the tip of his tongue. Or catching a glimpse of something, someone, in his peripheral vision. There, but not quite there.

As he was putting the finishing touches on the sketch, Doodles paused and looked up. "Who are you supposed to be, anyway?"

Sam frowned. "Be?"

A gesture was made that encompassed him from head to toe. "You know, your costume for Cornfusion?"

"I decided to come as myself."

Expressive brows climbed. "Clever." Then he inquired, "What about Gillian?"

Sam made an inconclusive movement in the air with his

hand. "She originally intended to come as Little Bo Peep, but I understand Max nixed the idea."

"What's Max got to do with it?"

"She had him cast in the role of the sheep."

The other man's expression spoke volumes.

"Yeah, I know," said Sam. "Apparently Max made it clear he's a Belgian sheepdog. He doesn't 'play' sheep; he herds them. So in the end, Gillian gave up on the whole idea and they both came as themselves, too." He noticed the white bandage, complete with blood stain, wrapped around his friend's ear. "Who are you supposed to be?"

There was a soft snort followed by, "Van Gogh, of course."

Sam's mouth twitched. "Of course."

"It was Mary Kay's idea. She thought it would be good promotion for my artwork."

"I hear you two are in business together."

Davison nodded. "I draw to my heart's content. She handles sales and promotion. She's even framed and hung some of my sketches in her B and B. So far the arrangement is working pretty well."

Sam's brows knotted. "Isn't that mixing business and pleasure?"

"I like to think of it as having the best of both worlds." The portrait was finished. "Where is Gillian, anyway?"

Sam glanced in the direction of Minerva's booth. Then he straightened up and looked around in earnest. *Damn.* "The last time I saw her, she was getting her palm read by Minerva."

"I like her costume."

Sam's attention was focused elsewhere. He asked perfunctorily, "Whose?"

"Minerva's. She's dressed like a fortune-teller with beads and bangles and even a crystal ball. But then I've seen a little bit of everything tonight, including the Great Pumpkin, Cher without Sonny, Garfield, that Crocodile Hunter guy on TV, and the usual Headless Horseman. That story always scared the bejesus out of me when I was a kid."

"What story?" Sam said, pushing away from the booth and scanning the crowd. He shifted his stance. He was suddenly uneasy.

"*The Legend of Sleepy Hollow.* Washington Irving." Doodles only hesitated briefly before asking, "What's with you tonight? And what in the sam-hill are you looking for?"

"Not what, who. Gillian."

"And you don't know if you're in love with the woman or not?" Davison made a sound that was somewhere between amusement and sympathy. "You should see the expression on your face."

Sam brushed it aside. "I'd feel better if I knew where she was, that's all."

"You feel compelled to keep an eye on her."

"Something like that."

"Does this have anything to do with the back fender of her pickup truck?"

Sam turned to him sharply. "How do you know about the fender?"

"I get around." Doodles immediately went on to say, "Okay, I was at the body shop when she brought her vehicle in for repairs. I wasn't the only one who wondered how her rear bumper got damaged if she'd swerved to miss a deer. Not unless the poor critter managed to collide with her from behind."

Sam was antsy. "I can't explain right now, Davison. But will you do me a favor?"

"Anytime, Sam."

"Keep an eye out tonight."

"For?"

"Anything that doesn't seem kosher. Anyone acting strangely. Anything suspicious. Use your artist's eye for faces and movement and body language."

"I'd be glad to."

"Thanks." He'd taken a couple of steps away and turned back. "I'd like to buy that sketch you made of Gillian."

"It's already sold. In fact, it was a commission."

Sam was curious. "Who bought it?"

"Miss Rogozinski." Davison nodded in the direction of the heated tent where most of the adults had congregated for hot cider or a beer and brats. "I can make another one for you."

"I'd appreciate it." Sam crossed the straw-strewn field and approached Minerva's booth. "I thought you were telling Gillian's fortune," he said without preamble.

"I was. I did," Minerva answered. Her arms were layered with jangling bracelets. Her fingers were adorned with rings of every size and shape. Somewhere on her person, bells seemed to tinkle every time she moved. There was a beaded shawl draped around her shoulders and an ostrich feather was stuck into her hairdo. She went on to tell him, "I'm in complete agreement, by the way, with the old woman she met at the base of the Pyrenees."

This was not the conversation he wanted to be having. "What old woman?"

"The one who read Gillian's palm. The one who told her she was going to find her true love at an unexpected time and in an unexpected place. Well, I agree."

"Right now I'd be happy to find her in an expected place. I thought she was with you."

"She was. Then a group of children—I suppose they were nearly old enough to be teenagers—asked her to go through the maze with them. They took off a few minutes ago, along with Max." Minerva was nobody's fool. "You seem disturbed."

"I am." His mouth tightened. "I don't like labyrinths, mazes, whatever they're called."

Brown eyes peered at him over wire-rimmed spectacles. "Actually the difference between a labyrinth and a maze has to do with intent. A labyrinth is traditionally structured and made up of semicircles; it's meant to lead one to a spiritual and physical center. A maze is designed as a puzzle, meant to confuse and frustrate."

"Maybe that's why I dislike them." God knows, he had enough confusion and frustration in his life without deliberately seeking out more, Sam thought.

"Understandably some people find them disturbing. After all, a maze could be viewed as an allegory for life."

He knew Minerva was going to explain that statement whether he asked her to or not. "In what way?"

"A maze could represent fear of the future, fear of surprise, fear of not knowing what's around the next corner."

"Fear of not knowing where you're going," he said, running a hand through his hair and exhaling deeply.

"Exactly." Minerva watched him for a moment or two. "But tonight I believe you have the same fear as I do, Sam."

He straightened. "What fear is that?"

She made a gesture and tiny hidden bells tinkled. "Something isn't quite right. I sense . . . danger."

He was immediately on red alert. "To Gillian?"

She nodded. "I've had the strongest feeling about her for the past several weeks. As if she's had a close call. I said as much to her the morning I was hanging the witch balls on your front porch."

"I wish you'd told me sooner."

She fixed him with a shrewd gaze. "I think you've been

fully aware of the incidents that have happened since she came to town, Samuel Law."

"Yes, I have." They exchanged meaning-filled glances. "If you see Gillian, please tell her to stay put until I come back."

"Where are you going?"

His features hardened to stone. "Hunting."

Chapter
twenty-nine

Where had everybody gone?

"Hello? Is anyone there? Max?"

One minute half a dozen excited, shrieking twelve-year-olds had been wending their way through the maze just ahead of her; the next they'd vanished into thin air, taking Max with them.

It was strange.

It was dark.

It was downright creepy.

This section of the Amazing Maize Maze appeared deserted except for a bale of hay with a jack-o'-lantern perched on top of it, and a scarecrow peering out from between towering stalks of corn. Now she understood why something as benign as a cornfield could be dangerous. It was easy to get lost.

And difficult to be found.

Gillian blew out her breath. The night air had a definite chill to it, making her grateful for the warm jacket Sam had suggested she wear this evening. At least she wouldn't freeze to death.

Where was she?

Directly in front of her were two seemingly identical pathways, except they headed in opposite directions. There was no sign which way Max and her young companions had gone. She tossed a mental coin and took the path that veered to the right.

It was the wrong choice.

Less than a minute later she ran into a dead end, with another bale of hay, another carved pumpkin grinning grotesquely at her out of the dark, and another scarecrow. The makeshift figure was draped in an old sheet and was apparently meant to be a ghost.

Gillian put her shoulders back and raised her chin a fraction of an inch. She wasn't lost. She'd merely lost her bearings; she was momentarily disoriented. Fortunately, the solution to the problem was clear enough. She'd simply retrace her steps. After all, this was the way she'd come. *That* must be the way back to the entrance of the maze.

She did an about-face.

It was soon obvious that *this* was not the way back to anywhere. In fact, it was another dead end leading to yet another dead end. She was no closer to finding her way out of the rabbit warren of pathways, bales of hay, carved pumpkins, macabre scarecrows, and towering cornfields than she'd been a quarter of an hour ago.

She went perfectly still.

Had she heard something? Someone? Were those footsteps approaching?

Gillian almost called out, but at the last instant something stopped her. Some sixth sense? Some niggling suspicion? Some doubt? Perhaps some basic survival instinct? Better to err on the side of caution, she thought, scarcely daring to breathe.

There it was again.

It was the sound of footfalls coming straight toward her. They were too plodding to be those of a child, or a twelve-year-old, or even a gang of preteens. It was an adult wearing some sort of boots. It was definitely not someone light on their feet.

"Miss Charles," came a muffled voice, indistinguishable as male or female, "where are you?"

Gillian opened her mouth and then closed it again without making a sound.

A raspy croak inquired, "Are you lost, Miss Charles? Do you need help finding your way?"

Gillian didn't move a muscle.

"Come out, come out, wherever you are, Miss Charles," came the singsong suggestion of whoever was approaching her location.

She didn't like this, not one bit. She wasn't about to cower in a corner like a frightened child, but as The Bard himself had written several centuries ago and more: Discretion was the better part of valor. This might be a very good time to be discreet.

Gillian held her breath.

Heavy footsteps came closer.

She had to do something. And fast. She sized up the scarecrow positioned behind the bale of hay to her right. She moved quickly and ducked down behind the straw figure just as a dark voluminous form appeared on the pathway some twenty feet from her.

It was her nightmare alive and in the flesh.

She broke out in a sweat. Dear God, had she been seen?

The creature paused, came two steps nearer, then several more steps, then stopped in the middle of the path. It was someone cloaked in black from head to toe. Well, to be perfectly accurate from *neck* to toe: there was no head to the costume.

It was the Headless Horseman.

"There is no escape, Miss Charles. I'll hunt you down sooner or later." This claim was followed by a peculiar laugh that was neither male nor female. "This is my game and we'll play by my rules," came the strange disembodied voice.

Gillian's blood ran cold.

The ominous presence stood and listened.

She was dead quiet.

Far quieter than the field mice scurrying underfoot through the corn. Far quieter than the nighttime breeze rustling through the dried corn crop that would be harvested immediately after the fall festival. Far quieter than she had ever been before in her life.

At last there was a click of boot heel against boot heel, and the Headless Horseman took off down a path leading away from where she was concealed.

She still didn't breathe.

She still didn't move.

She waited.

Then her cell phone began to vibrate. She carefully retrieved it from the pocket of her jacket and glanced at the readout.

"Sam," she whispered, cupping her hand around the mouthpiece to muffle her voice.

"Where in the blue blazes are you?" he demanded to know, his tone conveying his exasperation and his concern.

"Maze," she said succinctly.

"I can barely hear you. Why are you whispering?"

"Danger."

"Are you in danger?"

"Yes."

"From what? From who?" he said as if the words were stuck in his throat.

"Someone is following me."

"Who's following you?"

"Headless Horseman."

There was anger: no, not merely anger; this went far beyond the garden-variety anger she'd heard a few times in Sam's voice in the past. This was outrage. "Someone in a Headless Horseman costume is after you?"

She thought that was a fair and accurate assessment of her situation. "Hm-hm."

"Are you hiding?"

"Behind a scarecrow."

"Stay put until you see the whites of my eyes. I will find you whatever it takes."

She believed him. "Okay."

"Wait a minute . . ." Something was happening on his end.

"Sam?"

"The Headless Horseman is coming out of the maze right now. I'm going to have a chat with our friend, whoever he is."

"Be careful," she whispered.

She heard Sam bark an order. "Stop right there, mister." Then he demanded, "Who in the hell do you think you are frightening a helpless woman?"

A helpless woman?

He couldn't mean her. She wasn't helpless. In fact, she was perfectly capable of taking care of herself. She'd done it for years. On the streets of New York. And in Rome. And in Madrid. And bloody hell, even in Sweetheart, Indiana!

Then why are you hiding behind a scarecrow in the middle of a corn maze, Gillian?

"Take off the headpiece of your costume," she heard Sam command. "I want to see your face."

Silence.

A muttered and indistinguishable word or two. Then a surprised exclamation, "Esther!"

Gillian straightened. Esther? Esther Preston? She couldn't have heard right. It didn't make any sense.

"I can explain, Mr. Law," came the familiar voice of Anna Rogozinski's housekeeper.

"I sure as hell hope you can. And the explanation better be a good one," Sam said, sounding lethal.

"I was trying to warn her. But I couldn't find her. She wasn't with the children and Max when they came out of the maze. I'm afraid he may try to harm her." Esther was babbling. "He knew, you see. He knew about my lady. He got it all messed up in his head, of course. Sometimes he can't help himself. It's the liquor. It was no good for his daddy. It's no good for him. You gotta stop him, Mr. Law, before he does something bad. Before he hurts her."

"You mean Miss Charles?"

"Yes, sir. Miss Charles."

Suddenly Gillian caught a movement out of the corner of her eye. She turned. It was the creature in the long, billowing black robes. It was the Headless Horseman.

He was back.

"Sam," he heard Gillian urgently whisper on the other end of the connection, "you've got the wrong one."

He dropped his hold on Esther Preston and said, "What?"

"The Headless Horseman is still in the maze. I can see him. I think he's got a pretty good idea of where I am, too."

She added in a very low, but determined tone, "I'm going to have to make a run for it."

Sam's blood ran ice cold in his veins. But no colder than his fury. "Don't hang up, honey. I'm on my way. We'll find you." He whistled sharply for Max, who came trotting up to him, tail wagging. "Find Gillian," he said, hoping Max's breed could track half as well as they could herd sheep. He pointed. "Gillian."

Max gave a gruff bark, turned, and sprinted into the maze. Sam followed at a full-out run.

Hell, he'd been hunting in all the wrong places. Now he was as scared as he'd ever been in his whole goddamned life, Sam realized as he chased along behind his dog. Not scared for himself. He was never really afraid on his own account. But if anything happened to Gillian, he would never forgive himself.

And that was the least of it.

What would he do without her?

His gut clenched into knots. No time to think about that now. He needed to stay cool, calm, and collected for both their sakes. He needed his wits about him. He needed every ounce of his mental and physical strength. He needed to find her and find her fast.

Max was barking to beat the band.

Sam sped around the next corner and tried to slam on the brakes; he collided with a bale of hay. There was Gillian, putting up a valiant fight: feet flying, arms flailing, nails scratching. And there was the Headless Horseman struggling to get his hands around her throat.

The thought briefly crossed Sam's mind that maybe she wasn't such a helpless woman, after all.

Then it happened very quickly.

Gillian kicked out at the black-robed figure. Lord, she was wearing those Italian designer boots tonight; the ones

with the extremely high heels and pointy toes, the ones
Sam had teased her about earlier, saying they looked like
lethal weapons to him.

Thank God she'd ignored him.

The rapier toe of her boot connected with the man's
shinbone. There was a startled yelp of pain. Max barked
louder and louder and circled the pair, adding to the noise
and confusion.

In the midst of the madness and mayhem, the Headless
Horseman glanced up and spotted Sam bearing down on
him like a bat out of hell. The villain tried to get away from
Gillian, who was pounding his chest with her fists. He gave
her a shove that sent her reeling, and kicked out at Max. He
was poised to break free.

"No way, buddy."

Sam grabbed the first thing at hand. It was the smaller of
two pumpkins sitting on the top of the bale of hay. He sure
as hell hoped he hadn't lost his throwing arm. He gripped
the pumpkin in his right hand, measured the weight in his
palm, brought it back over his shoulder, and then, with all
the latent instincts and experience of the star quarterback
he'd once been, let it fly.

The jack-o'-lantern sailed through the air and hit the
Headless Horseman dead center between the eyes. Or at
least where Sam judged his eyes to be beneath the shape-
less costume.

There was a loud grunt.

Legs flew out from under the robed figure. He landed on
the hard ground with a tremendous thud. Max began to circle
him, taking little nips at his arms and ankles with each turn.
The man seemed stunned, as if the breath had been knocked
clean out of him. He lay there in the dirt without moving.

A group of local people had followed Sam and Max into
the maze. They stood and watched as events unfolded.

Sam approached the prone figure, reached down, and ripped off the black hood. "Warren Preston." He shook his head with disgust. "I should have guessed."

Warren sat up, glared in Gillian's direction, and began to whine, "Why should you get it all? You're just a Johnny-come-lately. You didn't do anything. You don't deserve it. Why couldn't you just leave town? I tried to make you leave."

Sam said, "You're a good shot, aren't you, Warren? You like shooting birds. Barn owls. Crows. And dumping them on other people's front porches."

Warren smiled smugly. "I'm a crack shot. Maybe the best in the county. My daddy gave me my first rifle when I was seven years old. It was a birthday present." Esther Preston stepped out of the crowd and stood staring down at her son, her eyes filled with unshed tears. "Then my daddy died. She poisoned him." He pointed to his mother. "So I tried to poison her." His hate-filled gaze found Gillian. "Never drank the damned tea, did you?"

Gillian frowned. "Tea?"

"I found it in your kitchen. It was called Sweet Dreams. I added a little something extra to it."

"I spilled the tea." Her eyes found Sam's. They both remembered the night. "I swept it out the back door."

It was Truman Hart who came forward and informed Warren, "Your mother didn't poison your father. Everybody in Sweetheart knows the doctors gave her medicine to put in his liquor. It was a last-ditch effort to help him finally quit drinking, to save his life. But it was too late. He'd already ruined his health beyond repair. He'd developed cirrhosis. Your father drank himself to death."

Warren looked up at his mother, "I know other secrets, Momma. I know all about your fine lady. What's hers should be yours one day and then mine in the end." He glared at Gillian. "She's got no right. She shouldn't get any of it."

Esther quickly dried her tears. There was no sympathy in her voice when she said, "You don't know any secrets about anybody, so you keep your crazy ideas to yourself, Warren. Don't you say one word about my lady. Not one word."

He opened his mouth and closed it again.

Sam stepped forward. "The sheriff is ready to take him away now, Esther. I think the authorities will recommend that Warren be detained at the county mental health facility for testing and evaluation. He needs professional help."

Minerva Bagley came up and put a comforting arm around Esther's shoulders. "Come on, my dear, I'll take you home."

"Thank you, Mr. Law," the housekeeper said as she turned and walked out of the maze.

Warren Preston was still muttering under his breath as he was escorted to the sheriff's waiting vehicle. "It's all her fault. It should have been mine. It was supposed to be mine."

Chapter
thirty

"I don't understand why Warren Preston considered me a threat," Gillian said to Anna the following afternoon. They were sitting in the front room
of the legendary pianist's home, not far from her beloved
Steinway, sipping cups of Earl Grey tea and nibbling on
poppyseed cakes baked by Minerva Bagley.

"Apparently Warren got the idea in his head that I
was planning to leave my jewelry, my belongings, even my
house—in fact, my entire estate—to his mother. He believed
one day it would all be his."

"He felt he was entitled to it."

"Yes, he did." Anna shook her head in dismay. "Although for the life of me, I can't imagine why. Esther Preston would never have entertained such a notion. She's an unassuming, hardworking woman, and a faithful friend and loyal companion to me."

"Poor Esther. She seemed as stunned as the rest of us by Warren's behavior."

"It only occurred to her yesterday that something might be amiss. She couldn't comprehend why her son insisted on wearing an identical costume to her own. Apparently he'd never shown any interest in attending Cornfusion in the past."

"Why now? Why dress up as the Headless Horseman?"

"Exactly." Anna seemed to give the matter some thought, and then said, "In his own aberrated way, Warren Preston is a pretty shrewd customer. Whatever he intended to have happen to you last night, there was a very good chance the blame would be placed on his mother instead of on him."

"Not exactly my idea of familial loyalty. But I still don't see what it has to do with me," Gillian said, taking a bite of cake. "He certainly had nothing to fear from my presence in Sweetheart."

Anna cleared her throat, put her teacup down on the table, and reached for Gillian's hand. "Actually, that isn't entirely true, my dear. Warren did have a legitimate reason for concern, from his viewpoint." Tension clung to the usually serene features. "I'm not sure how he found out. Perhaps I'd left something out on my desk, and he came across a photograph or a letter or one of my scrapbooks when his mother asked him to move some furniture for me last spring."

Gillian frowned and admitted, "I don't understand."

"My private keepsakes." The older woman wouldn't let go of her hand. "Would you please come with me? There's something I want to show you. Something I need to show you."

"Of course." Gillian offered Anna an arm to lean on. They made their way toward the rear of the house, into what was a charming sitting room. It was filled with treasures from piano concerts and command performances and worldwide travels.

Against one wall was a beautiful oriental chest with an ornate brass lock on the front.

"The key is in the upper-right-hand desk drawer toward the back. It's on a gold chain. Would you mind pulling up a chair for me before you unlock the chest?"

Gillian was happy to oblige. She got her friend comfortably settled before she inserted the key, managed to deal with the ornate lock, and raised the lid. Inside were dozens of photograph albums, stacks of letters neatly tied with colored ribbon, and folder after folder with the year clearly marked on the front. At Anna's behest, Gillian removed the album nearest to her and opened it to the first page. A recent photograph of herself stared back at her.

"I hope you can understand what I'm about to tell you, Gillian. I hope you can forgive me . . . forgive all of us for not telling you sooner." Anna's voice and hands were trembling. "It was your father's intention to give you the details when you were a little older. Then he and Elise were tragically killed in that car accident, and your grandparents did what they thought was best." She was forced to stop, take several deep breaths, and regain her composure. "I don't believe Jacob and Emily could bear the thought of upsetting you emotionally or causing you any more pain. You'd been through so much at such a young age. I had to abide by their wishes, naturally. That was part of our agreement."

Gillian reached for a stack of letters that were neatly tied with blue ribbon. The return address was that of the family's Manhattan brownstone; the handwriting on the front of the envelope was her grandmother's familiar and elegant penmanship.

Anna clasped her hands in her lap and went on. "Emily wrote to me faithfully for years: letters filled with stories and anecdotes, day-to-day occurrences. What Edward was studying in school. What sport he was playing. How his piano lessons were progressing. All the little details that make up our lives. Eventually she did the same for you."

Gillian felt the hair on the back of her neck stand straight up on end. An idea was beginning to form. She just wasn't ready to put it into words yet.

"Last winter when Jacob knew his health was suffering, he realized it was possible you would soon be left all alone. I was alone, as well. I have friends, but no family. He thought the two of us should have the chance, the opportunity, to get to know one another."

Gillian's heart began to pick up speed. "He purposely left it up to you."

"Yes, he did." Eyes glistened with tears. "I think it was because I met your father once. It was Emily's idea. Her intentions were good—Emily's always were—but it was a disaster."

"Why?"

"Edward was nearly thirty and engaged to be married to a lovely young woman named Elise. He came to my hotel—I was staying at the Waldorf Astoria for a few days before leaving for an extended tour of the continent—and we had afternoon tea together.

"Edward was polite, charming, but distant. We chatted about music and art and the weather, the way strangers do. We shook hands when he left an hour later." There was no mistaking the emotion in Anna's voice. "I never saw him again."

"Never?"

Her head moved. "He wasn't interested in any more meetings. Emily sent notes and photographs, of course. But I never tried to make contact with Edward again. That was part of the original agreement made between the three of us back during the war."

"I'm beginning to understand," Gillian said. "You and my grandfather had an affair and . . ."

"And from that affair there was a baby. A boy. I was unmarried and pregnant. Emily discovered she couldn't have any children of her own. So, with the legal help and discretion of Bert Bagley, Jacob and Emily were able to quietly adopt your father. And I returned to my music and my quest for a career."

"You're my grandmother."

"I'm your biological grandmother. I would never presume to think I could take Emily's place in your heart. I was simply hoping we could be friends."

Gillian blinked away sudden tears; her voice was thick with emotion. She took the thin, aging hand in hers and gave it an affectionate squeeze. "We're already friends, Anna."

He had a date for dinner.

He had two dates, actually. He was escorting Anna and Gillian to McGinty's Pub tonight for a lovely repast of corned beef on rye and afterward some of Hilda's famous pumpkin pie, topped with homemade whipped cream.

As he climbed the front steps, Sam could hear music—exquisite, soul-stirring music—coming from inside Anna's house. Gillian must have been playing for her. He didn't think Anna could manage anymore. Not with her severe arthritis.

He paused on the porch and looked in the window. The

two women were seated side by side at the piano. There was something about their hands: strikingly similar and yet completely different, of course, since one was old and one was young.

He studied their profiles. He wasn't imagining the resemblance. It was clearly apparent between the beautiful woman of eighty and the beautiful woman of thirty.

So, that's what had struck him about the sketch Doodles had drawn of Gillian last night. It had reminded him of Anna. Especially photographs he'd seen of Anna as a young woman.

"Now I know what you were up to, Jacob. Maybe you weren't such a crazy old SOB after all," Sam muttered under his breath. "I always said there was a method to your madness."

He stood there in the cool autumn night and listened.

So this was the reason Gillian had been sent to Sweetheart. This was the last gift from her grandfather: family.

Chapter
thirty-one

Sam found her exactly where he figured she'd be: out on the moon-watching platform in his backyard, sitting in one of her fancy lawn chairs, feet curled up under her, arms wrapped around her for warmth, Max beside her. She was staring up at the sky.

"It's a clear night and there's the Little Dipper just as you predicted," she said.

"Was there ever any doubt in your mind?" he replied, still standing; not sitting.

Gillian looked up at him. "Nope." She went on. "By the way, you got a postcard from your parents today. It was sent from Oshkosh, Wisconsin. They'll be home in time for Thanksgiving."

Sam put his head back and let out a loud guffaw.

Her brows rose in a questioning arch. "What, pray tell, is so humorous?"

"You. Specifically, you reading my mail. You know what that means, don't you?"

"No, I don't," she admitted.

"You have been good and truly Sweetheart-ized, Miss Charles. You're now one of us."

She sniffed. "That's what Goldie said as we were leaving Mike's tonight. She informed me that should any of those horrid paparazzi come snooping around, she will personally see to it that they leave town without a single shred of gossip to show for their efforts."

"Sweet of her."

"Yes, it was." She gave him a veiled glance. "I've also received an anonymous apology for the anonymous letter."

"What anonymous letter?"

"The one we found in the front door of our house that first night."

"Ah, that anonymous letter." He rubbed his chin. "My money's on Lynn Harrison. The note was too literate for Warren Preston."

"I agree. Besides, Lynn has a new boyfriend. So you're pretty much out of the picture now. His name is Clark Kent and he's a—"

"Newspaper reporter?"

She laughed lightly. "Clark's a dentist."

Sam paced back and forth. "By the way, I drew up the legal papers you requested. I doubt if anyone in town will object to buying back their properties for the price you're asking." He shook his head. "You're sure you want to sell for a buck apiece?"

"Absolutely. I want to give this town back to itself." She fell silent for a moment. "Somehow I think my grandfather would agree with my decision."

"I think Jacob would." Sam finally sat down and faced her. "We need to talk."

"I thought that's what we were doing."

"Not that kind of talk. Not business. Not frivolous stuff. Not gossipy stuff. We need to have a serious talk."

She hesitated and then said, "All right."

"I'll go first." Sam blew out his breath. His heart was racing and his palms were sweaty. Anyone would think this was his first date. "I've been thinking for weeks—months, really—about something you said to me that night on the telephone."

"What night?"

"The night you spilled the tea. Thank God." He made himself continue. "When I said to you that opposites attract each other, you quoted something about a bird and a fish may love, but where will they live? Do you remember?"

"Yes."

"Well, I think I have the answer."

She sat up straighter and uncurled her legs from under her. "Which is . . . ?"

"Some fish fly and some birds swim." He took a deep breath. "At least some of the time."

"What are you trying to say, Sam?"

"I don't want us to be like water from the moon. I don't want us to the one thing the other can never have."

"Neither do I," she said softly.

"So I've made up my mind," he said to her. "I'm moving back to New York."

Her eyes widened. "I thought you hated New York. I thought Sweetheart was the perfect—well, nearly—place for you."

"Not anymore. Not without you."

"Well, I've made up my mind, too. I've decided to stay on in Sweetheart for a while."

It was a minute or two before he could even think to say, "Why?"

Gillian gave him one of those Mona Lisa smiles that women were so good at and men never understood. "Because I want to give you ample time to come up with three good reasons why I should marry you."

He grinned. "How many?"

She held up three fingers. "Three. Count them, Mr. Law."

He reached out, took her hand in his, and pulled her into the circle of his arms. He kissed her completely, thoroughly, breathlessly, with everything he had to give to her. Then he said, "Marry me for the great sex."

Gillian put her head back and gazed up into his eyes. "That's one good reason."

He became serious for a moment. "Marry me because I love you and you love me. Because I can't imagine a life without you now. You've found your way into my heart, my mind, my body, my soul."

"I can't live without you. I never want to try," she said, pressing her hand and then her lips to his heart.

"That's two good—two excellent—reasons."

"Yes, it is." She waited.

Sam glanced down at his feet for a moment and then snapped his fingers and announced, "I've got it. I know the third reason you should marry me."

"What is it?"

He grinned. "Marry me for my dog."

As if on cue, Max jumped to his feet and began to dance around the pair of them, tail swishing wildly.

Gillian looked down at the sheepdog nuzzling her hand, laughed, and said, "Definitely."

Author's Note

To paraphrase the classic John Mellencamp song—I, too, was born and raised in a small town. Several, actually. And in the metropolitan area of New York City. And upstate New York. New Jersey. New Mexico. Pennsylvania. Ohio. Wisconsin. Iowa. Indiana. You name it.

One town was smack dab in the middle of rich farm country and had a population of one hundred, including "dogs, cats, and rats." One was Fort Lee, New Jersey, where the George Washington Bridge hits the Jersey side coming from Manhattan. Another was a picturesque and idyllic college town tucked into the Catskill Mountains.

Some I loved. Some I didn't. But they all became my "hometown." That's why I wanted to write the story of Sweetheart, Indiana: to celebrate the idea and the ideal of hometown America.

This book is also in loving memory of Dr. Harold E. Simmons (1922–1979), who was one of those brave young men of the 106th Infantry who fought through the fog and snow and enemy lines of the Ardennes forest. He survived the Battle of the Bulge, but he carried the wounds of war for the rest of his life.

Requiescat in pace.

Additional Author's Note

For those interested in knowing exactly what pieces of classical piano music Gillian plays, or Anna and Gillian play together, in this story, or other popular music referred to throughout the book (all my personal favorites), they are listed below, classical composers before their music; popular performers, when specifically mentioned, after the song title:

CHAPTER 8:

Mozart's "Sonata in C," KV 545, Allegro movement

Rachmaninoff's "Prelude in C-Sharp Minor," Op. 3, No. 2

CHAPTER 11:

"It's Only Make Believe," Conway Twitty

"Freeway of Love," Aretha Franklin

CHAPTER 16:

"Blame It on the Bossa Nova"

"Goodnight, Sweetheart"

CHAPTER 21:

Franz Liszt's "Liebestraume"

Mozart's "Sonata in C," KV 545, Andante movement

CHAPTER 22:

"Two Different Worlds"

CHAPTER 24:

"Angry All the Time," Tim McGraw and Martina McBride

"Handy Man," James Taylor

CHAPTER 30:

Franz Liszt's "Hungarian Rhapsody No. 2"

Turn the page for a special preview of
Suzanne Simmons's next novel

Goodnight, Sweetheart

Coming soon from Berkley Sensation!

A friend in need was a pain in the ass, even when that friend was his best friend and older brother.

However, at the moment, the greater pain was in Eric Law's head: an intense throbbing behind his eyes that competed with the big brass drum playing timpani on the back of his skull.

" 'Anything that can go wrong, will go wrong,' " he groused as he opened the glove compartment and reached for the bottle of Bayer. *At least according to Murphy's Law.* He tapped two tablets into the palm of his hand, threw the pills into the back of his throat, and washed them down with the last few drops of tepid water left in the bottle he had found underneath his car seat.

He wasn't a patient man, but Eric knew better than to

fight a headache. Part of his winning strategy in life—sometimes as the result of an intelligent and well-though-out decision on his part; sometimes by following his gut instincts; and at times, to be perfectly honest, through sheer dumb luck—had been knowing when to fight and when to forego that pleasure.

He leaned back against the leather headrest and closed his eyes, trying to give the aspirin time to work its medicinal magic. A few minutes later he opened his eyes, sat up straight, and demanded of himself, "Okay, what the hell did you do with it?"

He patted down the front of his tuxedo shirt. There weren't any pockets, just formal pleats sewn into vertical rows on either side of the pearlized buttons.

He tried his black dress pants next. The right front pocket contained an eighteen-carat-gold money clip engraved with his initials, E.A.L. The *A* didn't stand for Alan or Andrew or even Anthony as everyone assumed. It was for Anscomb, a name his mother, a dyed-in-the-wool romantic, had once read in a book.

His father, always the pragmatist of the family, had warned her that their youngest offspring would pay a price for having such a distinctive name. Devoted teacher and Anglophile that she was, Judith Law had insisted that Anscomb was an honorable name, a proud name, a noble name that meant "an unusual man who dwells in a special place."

In the end she'd gotten her way (his mother usually did) and he had been christened Eric Anscomb Law. But his father had been right, too. Growing up he had been taunted with a variety of nicknames, including everything from "ants-come" to "ass-comb."

"Sticks and stones may hurt my bones, but names will never harm me."

Whoever had coined that piece of traditional folk wisdom obviously didn't have a degree in modern psychology or a clue about kids. Kids could be cruel. Vicious. Merciless. In the first dozen or so years of his life he'd fought *and* won more than one bloody battle over his unusual middle name.

On the other hand, Eric reflected as he dug deeper into his pants' pocket, maybe a certain amount of adversity in childhood was a good thing. Maybe it had helped to prepare him for the adult world in which he lived and worked: the sometimes ruthless, always highly competitive world of corporate attorneys, ambitious politicians, and society's "movers and shakers."

He rummaged around and found a package of Listerine mint breath strips, a handful of loose change, and a small Swiss Army knife with a miniature corkscrew.

Never know when you might need to open a miniature bottle of wine, he thought wryly.

In his left front pocket was a ring box in Tiffany & Company's signature blue color. It was empty. He had already fulfilled one of his primary duties as best man: He had handed over the custom-designed wedding ring at the appropriate moment during the ceremony so Sam could slip it onto his bride's finger. As a matter of fact, his brother now wore a matching gold band.

Eric tossed the empty Tiffany's box onto the passenger seat and kept looking.

In his back right pocket was his billfold. Fashioned from the finest Italian leather, the tri-fold wallet was as soft and smooth as a baby's bottom. He usually kept his driver's license, some cash, and his credit cards inside his suit jacket to foil pickpockets, but, according to the signs posted at the outskirts of town, this was SWEET-HEART, INDIANA, WHERE EVERYONE IS YOUR FRIEND, POPU-LATION: 11, 238 (give or take), not Boston or New York.

Besides, he understood that pickpockets and petty criminals were pretty much nonexistent around here thanks to his cousin, Ben. Benjamin Law was a breed apart. He was also smart, tough-as-nails, and determined to do his job to the letter of the law. Most criminals, petty or otherwise, quickly learned that it was better not to have a run-in with the newly elected sheriff of Sweetheart County.

Eric continued with his search. His back left pocket contained a folded linen handkerchief. Clean. Pressed. Monogrammed. Ready in any emergency. As a matter of fact, he had everything on him but the one thing he needed.

No phone.

A thorough inspection of his car was the next order of business. He rummaged through the glove compartment. He checked the space between the bucket seats. He dug down into all the creases and crevices. Nothing. Nada. Zip.

That's when it hit him. "Brilliant. Just brilliant, Law. You left your cell phone in the jacket of your tuxedo. And where is your jacket? Back in town, of course."

Which was where he was supposed to be.

Murphy's Corollary: "Left to themselves, things tend to go from bad to worse."

It had all started less than an hour ago with a small favor, an innocuous favor: Leave the celebration just long enough to drive out to The Flying Pig, retrieve a briefcase containing his brother's passport and the airline tickets for his honeymoon, and bring it back to the wedding reception. Not too much to ask.

Eric had climbed into his Porsche 911 and inserted the key in the ignition. He had listened with satisfaction as the powerful engine sprang to life. Then he'd shifted into gear and driven off down the street, heading west out of town.

One touch of a button on the center console and the side windows had descended, the hood had opened and the roof over his head had folded into the back compartment. The whole process had taken a total of twenty seconds. Tops.

The drive out to The Flying Pig had gone quickly and smoothly. With no one else in sight he had pushed the pedal to the floor. Even going ninety, the Porsche hadn't broken a sweat.

The briefcase had been precisely where Sam had told him it would be: dead center on the kitchen table of the farmhouse, right next to a basket of plastic purple plums.

Eric had retrieved the forgotten leather case and headed back toward Sweetheart. He had been humming along at a good clip when the car's engine suddenly started to make never-before-heard noises. He'd pulled over to the side of the road just as the engine sputtered twice and quit on him.

Another goddamned Murphy's Corollary: "If there is a worse time for something to go wrong, it will happen then."

"Eighty thousand dollars worth of powerful,

precision-engineered sports car and you conk out on me now, Red," he said aloud to his customized tomato-red Carrera Cabriolet.

Eric got out of the sports car, slammed the door shut behind him—the sound rattled his teeth—and gave the front tire a jab with the toe of his dress shoe.

"Sonofabitch," he swore under his breath, reaching up to tug the formal bow tie from around his neck; he pitched it onto the passenger seat beside the empty ring box.

Without a car or a cell phone, he was pretty much up shit creek without a paddle.

The sun was a blazing yellow ball high in a bright blue sky. There was only the merest suggestion of a cloud here and there on the horizon. The afternoon temperatures had soared well into the eighties: warm for mid-June in Indiana.

He took off his dark-tinted sunglasses for a moment and mopped his forehead with the monogrammed handkerchief. His dress shirt was already damp and clinging to his back. He undid the top button or two. His shirt-sleeves were next; he rolled them up to his elbows.

Well, this was a fine how-do-you-do. Here he was playing the Good Samaritan, trying to help his brother out of a jam, and now he was the one in a jam. A pickle. A hell of a fix.

Eric told himself to relax and breathe, just breathe. He inhaled deeply, filling his lungs and his nostrils with the scent of country air: a mixture of dark, dank Earth, thick green vegetation, and sweet clover that grew wild alongside the road. Then he slowly exhaled.

Actually it was the first time today he'd felt like he could take a deep breath. That wasn't quite true, he realized. It was the first time since he'd driven into Sweetheart three days ago.

The problem was weddings.

He hated weddings.

They were right up there at the top of his list with root canals, traffic jams, and paying exorbitant taxes. Ironically there had been a virtual epidemic in the past eighteen months since his divorce was final. He'd personally been a member of no less than four wedding parties in the last year alone.

"It must be something in the air, or the water, or maybe it's the result of global warming," he said cynically, turning and leaning against the car door. The metal was hot at his back. He pushed his sunglasses up his nose and stared off into the distance.

Let's be honest, Eric. It isn't just weddings that make you uncomfortable. It's Sweetheart, Indiana. You definitely have a love-hate relationship with your hometown.

Little wonder. Growing up he'd been wild, undisciplined, incorrigible, the black sheep of the family, the bad apple in the bunch, the kind of boy mothers warned their daughters about. Teachers, ministers, neighbors, even law enforcement officials—including his own father, who had been the sheriff of Sweetheart County at the time—had thrown up their hands in frustration when it came to the youngest of the Laws.

Stifled. Smothered. Suffocated. Bored. Restless. Misunderstood. Rebel without a cause. That's how he would have described himself at sixteen.

He'd been the exact opposite of Sam and his sisters. In fact, the differences between himself and his three older siblings had been like night and day. They had all been excellent students, star athletes, and model citizens.

In his senior year Sam had been captain of the football team and had earned a full athletic scholarship to Purdue. A year later Allie had been the editor of the school newspaper, on the honor roll, and headed to the University of Chicago, while Serena, her twin, had been the president of the student body and voted most likely to succeed, which she did at Stanford. Two years later, he'd had the dubious distinction of being voted the *numero uno* "party animal" of his senior class.

At the time Eric knew his family had been disappointed in him. Hell, he'd been disappointed in himself.

The turning point had come the summer after graduation. He'd taken a job in a local factory. The pay had been excellent at eighteen dollars an hour, plus overtime and incentives, but he had found himself slaving away twelve hours a day, six days a week, on an assembly line building truck transmissions.

The worst part wasn't the physically demanding labor, although on a typical summer afternoon, even with huge fans blowing the air around, the temperature had soared above the one-hundred-degree mark inside the outdated manufacturing plant. No, the worst part had been the mind-numbing monotony. It had driven him crazy.

Eric realized that he'd reached that proverbial fork in the road. There had to be a better way and a brighter future for him. The very next week he'd applied to military school and been accepted on probation for the fall semester. For the first time in his life he'd worked hard at his studies, become a disciplined student, and earned straight As. A year later he had the grades to transfer to

Purdue University. Three years after that he'd graduated summa cum laude in pre-law. Then, following in his brother's footsteps, it had been on to Harvard Law School.

Funny how everybody had always wanted him to be like Sam, Eric thought, and now in many ways he was. He'd succeeded beyond his wildest dreams or anyone else's. In fact, to the outside world he appeared to be more successful than his older brother.

After graduating at the top of his class at Harvard, he had been inundated with job offers on both coasts. In legal circles from San Francisco to Washington, D.C., he'd been reputed to be worth his weight not in gold, but platinum. In the end, he had accepted an invitation to join one of Boston's most prestigious law firms.

His rise within the legal field had been meteoric. He had been on the winning side of one high-profile court case after another. He'd been written up in the *ABA Journal*, *The Young Lawyer*, and the *Boston Globe*. He had even been featured in a regional publication as one of New England's "fifty most beautiful people," a take-off on the *People* magazine list.

And the crowning glory: He'd become the youngest partner in the history of Barrett, Barrett & Hartmann, with offices overlooking the city and the harbor.

Eric knew what was said about him behind his back: He wasn't just good at his profession, he was brilliant, gifted, fearless, and utterly ruthless.

Within the hallowed mahogany halls of Barrett, Barrett & Hartmann, he was referred to as "Eric the Red," not for the color of his Porsche, but for his killer instincts. There weren't many in *or* out of the courtroom who had the guts to take a shot at the hotshot of BB&H.

Murphy's Military Law (learned firsthand during the year he'd attended military school): "There is nothing more satisfying than having someone take a shot at you, and miss."

Anyway, once his career was on track, he had set similar goals for his personal life. He'd married one of the senior partner's daughters: an educated, accomplished and socially prominent young woman. Soon after they had moved into a million-dollar home in an exclusive Beacon Hill neighborhood. He'd bought an expensive sports car. He had been making an obscene amount of money. By anyone's standards he had finally been doing everything right.

Then two years ago it had all started to unravel . . . beginning with his marriage.

Don't go there, buddy. It's water under the bridge. Dead and buried. Nobody can change their past.

Eric suddenly realized his headache was fighting back against the aspirin. He opened the car door on the driver's side, reached across to the glove compartment, and took out the Bayer again. The water bottle he had found underneath the seat was empty, so he tossed two more pills into his mouth and chewed them up dry. The bitter taste suited his mood perfectly.

So why was he in Sweetheart?

Because Sam had called him up on the telephone last November and asked him to come, that's why.

"I'm getting married next summer," his older brother had announced without preamble. "I want you to be the first to know."

Eric had leaned back in his sleek European-designed office chair and swiveled around to gaze at the spectacular view he had of Boston Harbor. He couldn't resist teasing Sam a little. "I hope I'm not the very first to know. You have informed the bride-to-be, haven't you?"

Sam's laughter had echoed in his ear. He sounded happier than Eric could ever remember. "Okay, you're the second to know, although I think Mom has her suspicions."

"Then I assume the lucky lady is Gillian Charles."

"How'd you guess?"

He had snickered softly into the telephone. "You're kidding, right? There aren't any secrets in Sweetheart. There certainly aren't any secrets in our family."

He could almost imagine Sam smacking himself on the forehead with the flat of his hand. "What was I thinking, little brother?" They had both chuckled at that since Eric was the taller of the two by several inches; he'd sprinted past his "big" brother sometime during their college years. Then Sam had turned serious. "I've waited a long time for this."

Eric had responded in kind, his voice soft, emotion-charged. "I know you have."

"I'd like you to be my best man."

A funny lump had formed for a moment in his throat. "I'd be honored, Sam."

It was true. Only for Sam would he agree to be the best man. Only for Sam would he return to Sweetheart. Not just return for the wedding, but agree to take some long-overdue vacation time and stay for a few weeks, maybe for the rest of the summer, and keep an eye on things while the bride and groom went on an extended honeymoon to Tuscany.

"Yeah, well, Sam won't be going to Tuscany, or anywhere else for that matter, if you don't get back to town pronto with his plane tickets and passport," Eric said, pushing off from his car and doing a three-hundred-and-sixty-degree turn.

Behind him there was a cornfield not quite "knee high by the Fourth of July," but then it was only June sixteenth. There was another field across the asphalt road, and row upon row of corn or soybeans as far as the eye could see.

Overhead, a flock of black birds swooped in formation and then silently lighted on a wire cable strung between two utility poles; they were lined up like some kind of macabre scene out of an Alfred Hitchcock movie. The only sound was the distant caw of a single crow.

There hadn't been a car or a truck or even a tractor drive by since his Porsche had stalled. That was going on thirty minutes now. Apparently his chances of being rescued anytime soon were somewhere between slim and none.

Murphy's Last Word on the Subject: "You never run out of things that can go wrong."

Eric folded his arms across his chest and stood there at the side of the deserted road. "I'm beginning to think Murphy was an optimist," he muttered under his breath.

BERKLEY SENSATION
COMING IN SEPTEMBER 2004

Beloved Imposter
by Patricia Potter
Rory Maclean has been away at sea, but now he returns to end a feud between his own family and the Campbells—and risks everything by letting the enemy into his heart.

0-425-19801-4

A Hint of Seduction
by Amelia Grey
Everyone thinks Catherine is in London to find a husband. The truth is she's looking for the father she never knew. But when she meets a handsome stranger, it could be love—or he could be her half-brother.

0-425-19802-2

Snap Shot
by Meg Chittendon
Diana Gordon thinks she is safe from her past. But a killer is watching her every move.

0-425-19803-0

The Painted Rose
by Donna Birdsell
Reclusive Lady Sarah hides behind her veils. But the sad eyes of her handsome tutor Lucien burn through layers of fabric right into her frozen heart.

0-425-19804-9